Table of Contents

Angel Guardian

Blue Phantom Book Two

Vijaya Schartz

Print ISBNs
Amazon print 9780228628033
Ingram Spark 9780228628040
BWL Print 9780228628057

Copyright 2023 by Vijaya Schartz
Cover art by Pandora Designs

Dedication

To all the friends who keep me sane while
I'm writing... thank you.

Chapter One

Laxxar – frozen planet – salt mining facility

A444 adjusted the hard hat over his wool cap and blew off the fine salt from his nostrils. At least, the frigid temperatures lessened the stench of recycled air and unwashed bodies. White powder covered his clothes. His gloved fingers cramped, and his numb feet weighed him like chunks of ice despite the worn-out boots.

The lights flickered in the mine, flashing rainbows on the glassy walls and square pillars. Then darkness. The whine of the laser harvester attacking the cave wall ceased, so did the purr of the air scrubbers. The emergency lighting turned on, offering a dim glow.

A444 and the other nine workers in his team stood immobile, listening. The two guards in warm fleece and sherpa boots glanced at each other through the clear visor of their heated helmets. The mine grew quiet, the kind of quiet only found several klicks deep into ice and frozen ground.

Holy Mandala! A444 willed his heartbeat to slow. Without power, the elevators couldn't operate. They would be stuck down here. No food, no water, not even rodents or bugs to eat. The salt kept them away. The oxygen level would drop. How long would it take for them to suffocate, kill each other for food, or turn into salt mummies? Then again, for most of them death would come as a reprieve.

The whine of excavation and the purr of the air-scrubbers resumed. A444 let out a sigh of relief. Just a minor power glitch. He must escape, soon, before the mine killed him. He couldn't die before fulfilling his destiny, his mission, whatever he was meant to do.

Pulleys and chains rattled as he cranked the tripod mechanism then loaded the suspended square block onto a dolly. He carted the large cube, wheels creaking, toward the conveyor in the main cavern. Where was an antigrav pallet when you needed one? But forced labor, chains and metal carts came cheap... cheaper than decent industrial equipment.

"Hey, Angel!" Tiny, the biggest worker in his team, called in a brisk whisper.

"Don't call me that." It was bad enough that other prisoners looked up to him for help and advice, without starting some kind of cult. "My number is A444. I have no other name... as far as I remember."

"No offense, pal, but you meditate all the time, and you never have a harsh word. Besides, there are worse nicknames than Angel." Tiny's breath feathered in front of his short beard. "Our memories were wiped, too, but we like our funny names. They show we are still people, not just numbers."

"I know." A444 had no idea what he'd done to end up drudging in this frozen hell, but good people didn't get mixed up with big gangsters like Lord Zethar, the crime lord who owned the mine. So, before being a numbered slave, he must have been some worthless riff-raff who needed to redeem himself. "Sorry for offending you, my friend."

"No sweat... not that we ever sweat here." Tiny chuckled at his own joke then shrugged bulky shoulders.

A444 didn't want to upset his friend. "You see... angels are special. They aren't regular people, and I don't deserve to be likened to one."

Tiny guffawed. "You speak of angels as if they were real!"

"They do exist." The affirmation startled A444. How did he know that? "The guards fear them. They tell stories about angels guarding the universe against evil... Somehow, I want the stories to be true." A strange thing to believe in such a hopeless place.

"Enough talk!" A guard in bulky fleece and comfy sherpa boots glared through the clear visor of his heated helmet and cracked the whip as a warning.

A444 turned away and quietly unloaded his square block onto the conveyor. He strained under the load, his muscles screaming in protest. Laxxar wasn't for weaklings. No wonder the workers died so fast.

One of his team ten feet away wobbled under his load. A444 rushed to him and stabilized the heavy block for him. Then he helped the exhausted man sit. He opened his coat and offered him his water flask, lukewarm from his body heat.

The worker drank. "Thank you. You truly are an angel of mercy."

"Get back to your own tasks!" the guard yelled. "If he's too weak to work, I can fix that." The guard aimed his blaster at the two men, gloved finger caressing the trigger. The next infraction would draw blood... or worse. "Move it!"

The exhausted worker slowly rose to his feet.

A444 turned his empty dolly around, and wheeled it back into the fresh tunnel, raising his scarf to cover mouth and nose. Salt not only dehydrated skin and eyes, but the dust also damaged the lungs. Many had died coughing blood since he'd arrived, months ago.

After the guard walked away, A444 saw Tiny catching up to him and lumbering at his side.

Tiny caught his breath as he pulled his empty cart. "The others say you must be an angel because you're still alive after all this time, and you look as fresh as if you'd arrived yesterday."

"Well, I've been here the longest." Few survived more than a few weeks on Laxxar. A444 glanced right and left. No guard in sight, and no surveillance recorders in the newly excavated area. "Why did you flag me back there?"

"You know, how you say you have a plan to get out of this place, and all you need now is access to the main hangar?" Tiny smiled, his big eyes full of hope, a rare thing in the mine. "Big Brain figured out how to get the code."

A444 caught his breath. His heart beat faster. "Access to the ships?"

Tiny nodded.

The last piece of the puzzle just fell into place, as if a higher power wanted him to escape and fulfill his higher purpose. Since no life could survive the frigid temperatures on the surface, the only way out of this miserable planet was to steal a ship and fly away.

Tiny pinched his lips now buried in his beard. "You're certain your medic friend can disable our tracking devices?" He slowly shook his big head. "It would be a shame to escape just to explode like a meat bomb, or be tracked down and recaptured in no time."

"Don't worry. Medic hates Lord Zethar. He will help." A444 firmly believe that.

Tiny frowned. "Still, he's not a prisoner like us. He has a lot to lose."

"But Zethar assigned him here against his will and refuses to let him go." Medic had also sworn an oath to save lives, and this place only killed people.

Tiny scratched his head. "He's taking a big risk to save the refuse of society. We are already dead to the universe. He is not."

"Medic is motivated. He will locate and remove our transponders." A444 knew he could trust the man. "But in exchange, we'll have to take him with us. Otherwise, they'll vaporize him, or worse, throw him outside, or down a mineshaft."

"To turn into a popsicle, or a dried-up salt mummy." Tiny's wide frame shuddered, shaking salt off his shoulders. "The frozen hells of Laxxar, they call this place. It's no joke, man."

A444 nodded. He had no idea what hell might look like, but this horrible place qualified.

* * *

Infirmary was a fancy name for the small surgical room full of outdated equipment and reeking of disinfectant. It looked even smaller, crowded with his ten-men team.

On the metallic table, a prisoner lay face down. With the wool cap off, his shaved head looked like an egg. They'd all gone through the monthly sanitary shave the day before. But the skin on the man's exposed back showed nasty old scars and goose bumps from shivering.

"Be very still." The man in a dirty white coat with *Medic* on the breast pocket, squinted through the magnifying glass under the only bright light. The laser scalpel seared through the patient's skin, high between the shoulder blades.

"Holy Mandala." A444 rolled his shoulders in empathy, feeling the fresh sting of his own laser cut. "This one is dangerously close to the spine."

"Yes. Most of them are. They do it on purpose." Medic selected a pair of tweezers from the metal tray. "And without deactivating the mechanism first, any rudimentary tool would trigger an explosion." The tweezers reached inside the smoking cut.

"What is a mandala?" Tiny frowned.

"I don't know. It's just something I say." As he watched the medic dig into his crew, A444 held his breath, as he had done for all his teammates.

In two swift pulls and a shake, Medic retrieved the chip the size of a grain of rice and held it to the light. Trough the magnifying glass, it looked like a bug with legs and antennas.

Medic dropped the chip in a metal tray with a flourish. "The last of the transponders."

A444 released a slow breath. "We can never thank you enough for all you did for us. You took a great risk opening our cell block and bringing us here. And now this procedure will save our lives."

Medic chuckled. "Oh, I'm doing it in large part for myself. I have to get out of this place before I blurt something they don't like, and they kick me down to the mine to work with you guys." He sprayed a layer of liquid skin over the small incision. "I'm not built for that kind of work."

"No one is." Tiny smiled. "Except Angel."

Medic straightened and lifted his magnifying glasses. He looked haggard, as if he hadn't slept in days. "All done."

A444 wondered how much time they had before the security office detected the deactivation. Then again, the guards should be asleep.

As the last patient sat up, screwed on his wool cap, and pulled up his rags over skinny shoulders, A444 considered the men in the infirmary... his entire team, plus Medic, and Cook. Despite their fear of getting caught, the light in their eyes brimmed with hope.

"I can't wait to leave this place." Tiny buzzed with excitement. He lifted one foot. "I put socks over my boots to walk quiet-like."

Others nodded and displayed their socked shoes as well.

"We should hurry." A444 took a deep breath. "Most of the guards are asleep, thanks to the drug Cook slipped in their hot toddy."

Cook, with a reddish face, seemed plump next to the workers. He nodded vigorously. "They won't wake up until morning. I guarantee it."

"Good. There are four guards on duty inside the hangar. They may still be awake if they didn't drink, but they are not expecting us." A444 turned to a short, skinny man. "Big Brain, you have the codes?"

"I've got the codes." Big Brain grinned and held up a security badge. "And I know how to disable the other ships to avoid any pursuit."

"Good." A444 trusted the universe would help them. "Weapons?"

Hobble, a man with a limp, raised two blasters. "Got these from the two guards passed out in the corridor. We can get more from the other sleeping guards."

A444 hoped they wouldn't have to use deadly force, but it would be unrealistic not to carry weapons. "I guess, we are ready. This is our chance at freedom. Let's do this!"

Whatever these men had done in a past they couldn't remember, they weren't the same louts anymore. They had suffered and learned compassion. They deserved a blank slate and a decent future, not this horrible death by forced labor.

The group crept in silence, along white corridors of solid salt, then up carved stairwells, avoiding the security cameras. They only met two guards, both asleep on the job. Keeping to the utility and maintenance areas, they bypassed the residential underground palace and sprawling quarters of Lord Zethar.

"Do you think the big boss is here on Laxxar?" Tiny asked in a whisper.

"Shush!" Cook glared at Tiny.

A444 hoped the rich crime lord was off planet. "Even if he's here, by the time our escape is discovered, we will be long gone."

When they reached the arched steel door marked *Main Hangar*, Big Brain scanned his guard badge then pulled a severed hand out of his pocket and used the dead fingers to punch a sequence of codes on the pad. The door opened with a woosh. The escapees with blasters entered first.

A444 followed. He couldn't bring himself to kill the guards unless there was no other choice. A blast of cold air stiffened the scarf on his mouth. On the hangar floor, several ships were parked. Mainly cargo barges and shuttles, and three raptors.

He pointed to the largest raptor. It looked in excellent condition. "This is the one we need. Disable the other two. The barges and shuttles are too slow to catch us."

He and Medic rushed toward the largest raptor, while Big Brain and Tiny, armed with blasters, boarded the other two. A444 stepped on the lower belly ramp and walked into a cargo hold.

"Stairs. Let's go up!" A444 rushed up the spiral stairs, past the living quarters, toward the top deck.

Medic followed him up. "How do you know the command deck is up top?"

"Just a lucky guess." He emerged into the command deck. Once in the pilot seat, A444 scanned the controls.

"Let me disable the ship's tracker." Medic pushed a few keys. The control monitors came alive.

A444 stared as the man's hands flew over the keys and several screens flashed on and off. Somehow it felt like a lot of hand operations. He focused his mind and spoke. "Computer, disable ship tracker."

A beep, then a feminine voice. "Tracker disabled, Captain."

Medic narrowed his eyes at A444. "Are you sure you don't remember your past? Seems to me you have a lot of useful skills, and you know a lot more than you think."

A444 also had that feeling, but had no recollection. He sensed he had something important to do... if only he knew what. "Start engines, prepare for take-off."

The onboard computer chimed. "Aye, aye, Captain."

Blaster shots exploded outside the raptor. Three other escapees rushed into the command deck from below.

"Where are Tiny and Big Brain?" A444 wouldn't leave them behind.

"Fighting for their lives." Cook ran down below.

"Then let's help them. Who has a blaster?" A444 scanned the small space and pointed to a weapons rack. "There!"

Medic snatched a weapon from the rack, then thought better of it and handed it to Wobbly.

Wobbly grabbed it and rushed below deck.

More blaster shots exploded.

"Computer, open the hangar doors." A444 hoped the order would be obeyed.

"Aye, Captain. Connecting with main computer. Hangar doors opening."

A444 released a slow breath. "Warm the drives, Prepare for takeoff."

"Aye, Captain." The computer flashed and beeped.

"Hurry, get onboard!" Cook below shouted to his comrades.

A444 called behind him. "Are they onboard?"

"Almost. Here they come." Cook called. "Everyone's inside."

Good. A444 leaned back in the pilot seat. "Computer, retract the belly ramp, seal the hatches and take off."

"Aye, aye, Captain," said the feminine computer voice.

Then the ship whined and shot out of the hangar like a fiery dragon out of a frozen cave.

And for the first time, as long as he could remember, A444 felt warmth inside his body. Holy Mandala, that felt good.

* * *

Zethar tapped his temple to switch his visual scanner. Then he turned away from the hologram of Dominara Azfet, in the sheer red gown that accentuated her curves. Ostentatious jewels decorated her headdress and barely covered her naked breasts. White marble pillars with gold and Nile-blue hieroglyphics framed her like a goddess of antiquity.

He didn't trust her reddish aura and inviting smile. She made him uneasy with the snakes curling around her arms. Surprisingly, he couldn't read her thoughts despite the gold and silver stripes of hardware striating his shaved head like a printed circuit board.

"Zethar... if you join my ranks, I'll make it worth your while..." Her caressing voice sounded full of promises. As she sat in her chaise, the enormous ruby between her breasts flared.

Zethar had long ago learned to resist seductive women. "You are wasting your charms on me, Highness."

Dominara Azfet chuckled and reclined in a languorous pose. "I can give you more riches than you can imagine, Zethar... and immense power over lesser minds... without all that hardware in your head."

Zethar caressed his smooth skull. He rather liked his robotic looks. But as much as he craved wealth and natural psychic powers, he wouldn't be seduced. He refused to relinquish control. "The problem is, Highness, I've risen from the lowest depths of poverty to this seat of power on my own. I've always considered myself a rebel and I'm allergic to following orders."

"Too bad. Just think about it." The Dominara smiled coyly with a tilt of the head. A snake head on her headdress hissed. "By the way, I like your new bodyguard."

The hologram vanished.

Zethar turned to Spartacus, the large feline draped over the back of the couch. The violet stone on the cat's black collar glowed. He'd recently retired the fighting beast from the gladiator games, to be his bodyguard. Cats could be trusted... people could not.

Spartacus growled, wrinkling his nose, baring his cracked fangs. The long scars on his red pelt rippled, and his powerful claws spread menacingly.

"Spartacus not like Highness," the cat's gravelly voice said in his mind.

Zethar understood. "Neither do I, my boy. Neither do I. But the more dangerous an enemy is, the closer you want to keep it."

Spartacus shook his head and emitted a snort of disgust.

The door chimed.

Zethar checked his reflection in the polished gold of the door. He straightened his black fur-lined coat cinched at the waist. Being so thin and wearing heels on his boots made him look even taller. Good. A sharp appearance gave a man more influence over weaker minds. "Come in."

The door slid open on a sturdy guard carrying a blaster. The man looked haggard, stomping his sherpa boots on the plush rug. Snow dripped from his hood and puffy coat in puddles.

The guard opened his clear visor. "My lord, we have a security breach in the main hangar and blaster fire. One raptor took off without authorization. Also, several prisoners are missing from sector A."

"Sector A?" Zethar shuddered. *Not that prisoner.* "What am I paying you for? Where are the other guards?"

"Asleep, my lord. Possibly drugged." The man stared at the blue rug.

Zethar's anger roiled like a cauldron of lava ready to erupt. "Send a raptor after the fugitives. What are you waiting for?"

At the angry tone of voice, Spartacus growled and bared his fangs.

The guard noticed the cat and took a step back. "We can't, my lord. They disabled the drives on the other raptors."

"Track them, then. Where are they?" Zethar struggled to remain calm.

"We don't know where they went, my lord. We can't track them either. They must have removed their individual transponders and disconnected the tracking signal on their stolen ship."

"Really? How is that possible?" This confirmed Zethar's suspicions. They had help from the inside. "I am surrounded by a bunch of farking morons." Zethar struck his fist against his open palm, to vent his rage.

Spartacus roared menacingly as if in empathy.

Zethar still hoped his fears were unfounded. Azfet wouldn't take kindly to the loss of her prized prisoner. "How many escaped?"

"Ten, maybe more..." The guard was guilty of negligence, and he knew it.

"No slave escapes Laxxar. When sent here as forced labor, you work and die on Laxxar. Loose security is bad for business." It would also tarnish Zethar's reputation as a shrewd crime lord. These puny escapees made him look like a fool, or worse incompetent.

"How did the prisoners disable their individual transponders without getting killed? How did they even know where the trackers were located in their body?" This reeked of treason.

"We don't know, Boss. But the security feed of the infirmary only shows static." The guard stared at his furry boots.

"Arrest the medic and detain him. I'll shoot him myself!" Zethar should never have recruited a civilian medic. They tended to have a conscience.

"Sorry, Boss. The medic can't be found. He may have gone with them…" The guard's voice grew weaker.

"Of course, he did." Zethar hated traitors and lazy guards. "Who are the missing prisoners?"

The man wobbled from foot to foot. "Seems it's A444 and his entire team. Boss."

"Of course, it is." Zethar's blood rushed through his veins. He should never have accepted such a risky charge, but Dominara Azfet had paid handsomely for his keep and would be outraged if Zethar lost him.

"What are your orders, Boss?" The guard's voice shook a little.

"Never mind. I'll find them myself." Zethar glared at the man. "They didn't access my ship, or did they?"

The guard hesitated. "No, Boss. Your raptor is secure in its private hangar."

"Good." Zethar drew his small laser gun, aimed at the guard, and shot him between the eyes.

The man dropped like a sack of salt, a tiny red dot on his forehead. Small consolation. Zethar hated worthless guards.

He holstered his weapon and mumbled. "If you want something done right, you have to do it yourself."

He winked at his cat. "Come, Spartacus. We are going on a hunt."

"Spartacus like hunt." The large feline slowly unfolded from the couch and stepped down to the rug, rolling his muscular shoulders in a deliberate stride.

The violet gem on the cat's collar caught the light. The scowl on the feline's face and the long, deep scars on his bulging muscles, attested to his violent past in the arena. He exuded dangerous vibes, and Zethar liked that about his bodyguard. Besides, unlike people, well fed animals never betrayed their masters.

Chapter Two

A444 eased off the throttle and the engines quieted. He relaxed in the pilot seat. A wave of pure relief flooded his entire being. "Holy Mandala, we are officially in free galactic space!"

The men on deck cheered. "An-gel, An-gel, An-gel..."

"I asked you not to call me that!" But he couldn't get mad at them. He shared their elation. "So, where do you want to go?"

His team mates glanced at each other and shrugged.

Tiny stepped forward. "With no memories, we don't have a home, a planet, or a family to get back to."

"True." A444 turned to Medic and Cook. "How about you two? You were hired staff. Your memories weren't wiped like ours."

Medic shook his head. "I don't want to return home. I want a new life not controlled by crime lords or riddled with corruption."

Cook pursed his fat lips. "Truth be told, I came to Laxxar with only my cooking talent. My memories were also erased. So Laxxar's frozen hell is the only home I remember."

"Computer, find a warm, easygoing planet, with relaxed security." A444 had heard the guards, after a few drinks, mention such planets as ideal places to retire.

"Yes, warm. I vote for warm." Tiny emitted a deep belly laugh that made his short beard tremble. "With pretty girls on the beach."

A444 smiled but didn't share Tiny's tastes. Girls weren't his concern. He must fulfill his destiny, whatever that was.

The computer beeped. "Closest summer planet located. Displaying coordinates."

"Good." A444 would drop off his friends there, then he would strive to regain his memories, figure out what he was meant to do. His mission was more important than a vacation life.

Alarms chirped and blinking lights lit up consoles and viewers.

"Converging vessels detected," the female computer voice went on without missing a beat. "Their weapons are locked on this raptor. Attack imminent."

What now? A444 couldn't lose everything now. His team deserved freedom. He needed to escape. They must survive. "Shields up!"

The side viewers acknowledged his order.

The forward viewer displayed a group of vessels, speeding toward the raptor. Pursuers or pirates? Upon magnification, the diversity of the ships and their gaudy colors indicated pirates.

The computer chimed. "Shields at one hundred percent."

A loud salvo burst on the shield, shaking the raptor.

"Shields at eighty percent."

"Retaliate. All guns, fire on the pirate ships!"

The computer executed the order. Then the pirates responded. Another salvo sent the raptor on a spin. The men standing on deck rolled to one side.

The computer chimed. "Shields at seventy percent."

"Everyone, hold on to something! Evasive maneuvers, and counterattack." A444 banked the raptor, wondering where he'd learned to do that.

Bringing the raptor about, A444 fired all its weapons on the pirate ships then banked again and turned, but the pirate ships on the viewer kept getting closer. Another salvo from the pirates sent the raptor reeling.

"Holy Mandala!" A444 struggled with the manual commands to stabilize the ship.

"Shields at ten percent. Five percent. Sorry, Captain, shields are disabled," the computer said in a calm female voice. "The enemy is upon us. We are surrounded. Prepare to be boarded."

Visions of captivity and slavery flashed in his mind. A444 couldn't stand the idea of his men killed or caught and sold again. Strangely, his own fate didn't seem to matter to him, as if it had been determined eons ago.

He had no fear... as if he were immortal, or already dead, with nothing to lose. The universe would protect him, so he could fulfill his mission. Really?

A444 checked the state of the escape pods on a side viewer. Perfect. He'd chosen the right ship. "Everyone to the escape pods!" He palmed a few knobs, struck a few keys and swiped a few screens. "Computer, program the escape pods with the coordinates of the summer planet."

"Aye, Captain."

A444 motioned for the men to clear the deck. "Hurry to the pods. Good luck to all of you."

A444 didn't mention he might see them there later... he knew he wouldn't.

The men behind A444 stampeded as they rushed out of the command deck and down below. He hoped they would survive and get a fair chance to lead productive lives.

"Coordinates implemented. Escape pods' course laid in, Captain." Still no urgency in the feminine voice.

A444 thought of escaping as well and setting the raptor to self-destruct, but it wouldn't work. If he did, the escape pods would be easy to spot and become targets. He must keep the pirates focused on the raptor, to give his friends time to vanish from radars and scanners. Besides, his fate called him elsewhere.

On the viewers, the hull cameras transmitted images of a pirate ship attached to the raptor and breaking the seal.

Tiny still stood there and laid a strong hand on his shoulder. "What about you, Angel?"

A444 smiled, unwilling to correct the name. "I'll keep the pirates busy until the pods are out of scanner range. You should go."

Tiny's forehead wrinkled with concern. "I better stay with you, or these thugs will eat you alive."

"No, they won't. Don't worry about me, Tiny. I always have a plan. Besides, something tells me the universe wants me to survive." He slapped his friend's shoulder. "Go now, hurry. I hear them drilling through the hull."

"Are you sure?" Tiny's voice cracked.

"Go, now. I'll be fine. I can escape any situation." A444 hoped he would. He didn't promise to meet Tiny in their tropical paradise. He didn't want to lie. That would be wrong.

"Your call. But don't tell me you are not an angel of compassion." Tiny shook his head. "Good luck, Angel!" He ducked under the hatch and disappeared.

"Be safe," A444 whispered after him.

He noticed that he remained perfectly calm, no fear, no apprehension. Why? Shouldn't he be scared? His plan was to fight as long as possible, to give his friends time to escape.

A444 needed weapons. He plucked a few blasters from the rack, then rummaged through the storage compartments of the command deck. He pulled a deep bottom drawer and found grenades, and an assortment of military knives.

As he explored the back of the drawer, his fingers touched cold metal. A long sword in its scabbard. He grabbed it, unsheathed the blade and tested its balance. Perfect. Who in this universe still used a sword? But the weapon called to him.

He also found snow-camo uniforms, dropped his rags to don a fresh shirt, still puzzled at the strange tattoo on his arm. He also slipped on pants, and a utility belt. Without the beanie, his shaved head in the reflective bulkhead shone, reminding him of his captivity. He smiled at his newfound freedom, and his blue eyes lit up with a new spark. For the first time in memory, he felt truly alive.

Then he hung the weapons around his waist and tried on the boots. Perfect size. As he hooked the scabbard to his belt and sheathed the blade, the ritual seemed strangely familiar.

The loud banging from the other side of the locked hatch called him back to reality. It wouldn't take long for the pirates to get through. He straightened and stood, facing the hatch, blasters at the ready.

He'd been reluctant to kill the guards on Laxxar, because he knew them. They only did their jobs in a harsh environment, and many of them had families to feed, and no other job opportunities. But he had no qualms ridding the galaxy of the disgusting pirate scum. They killed, maimed, and raped for pleasure. Such evil didn't deserve to live.

He wondered where he got that notion, but as hard as he tried to remember, his past remained blank. It bothered him to have all these thoughts and opinions, not knowing where he'd learned to think that way.

The hatch exploded in a fiery blast.

A444 crouched behind a bank of consoles. Shredded hot metal flew overhead showering the deck. Smoke filled the command area. Wild men and women in dirty yellow and orange garb emerged from the smoke. They didn't seem to care about being seen. Stealth wasn't their strategy.

A444 threw a grenade. It exploded, sending pirates flying. Good.

Kneeling behind the consoles, he rested his blasters on the flat surface, then aimed and fired in rapid succession. Several pirates fell with a hole the size of a fist in their chest. A444 kept firing through the smoke, but there were too many, coming too fast.

When one blaster died and the other exploded, A444 drew his blade. The pirates surrounded him but kept a safe distance. They could have killed him easily with blasters. He wondered why they didn't.

The reason became clear when a big man stepped forward in fine leather boots. Flowing red silk covered his armor. An assortment of guns and blades hung from his hips and clinked as he walked. Not stealthy at all. His kind liked to instill fear in their victims.

The other pirates bowed to the newcomer. "He's all yours, Captain."

"Search the ship. Find the others." The pirate captain cast A444 a side glance. "You are the one I want." His brow rose as he noticed the sword. "Are you any good with that blade?"

A444 had no idea whether he was good or not, but he needed to keep the pirates occupied, so they wouldn't realize his companions had escaped. Their pods were still in radar and weapons range.

He slashed the air with a flourish then effected a small bow. "Would you like to test my skills?"

The pirate captain grinned with a mouthful of shiny metal and diamonds on his teeth. He drew a curved blade in a wide arc. "Don't mind if I do. I'm getting the fat reward whether you are dead or alive, and worthy opponents are hard to come by."

Dear or alive? Why would Zethar put such a high bounty on his head? He could buy new slaves for a lot less. The remaining pirates widened the circle around them, and A444 saw credit sticks changing hands. They were betting on the outcome of the fight.

The big pirate took a wide fighting stance. "May I have your name, sir, so I can add it to my list after I properly skewer your body? The bounty calls you A444, but surely, you must have a name."

"Sorry to disappoint, Captain, but I have no name to offer you." A444 stepped sideways, circling his opponent. The long handle of the two-handed sword felt familiar and reassuring.

"How mysterious of you." The pirate circled, facing him, eyes narrowed in concentration. "Are you a fencing champion? Should I be worried?"

"I can't tell you that either." And that was the truth. A444 never lied, not even to his enemy. Another silly notion.

The pirate captain attacked sideways.

A444 barely evaded the blade then stabbed, but his sword only tore through red silk. The man's metal armor seemed impenetrable. As he fought, A444's leg muscles flexed and sprang with astonishing agility, his arms slashed with surprising strength. His muscles remembered what he didn't. Images of other fights flashed upon his mind. He was good at this. How odd.

His powerful overhead strike chipped the pirate's shoulder plate.

The pirate captain stepped back in surprise and scowled. Then he motioned with his chin to one of his men in the wide circle. Not a good omen. Pirates weren't known to fight fair.

A444 wondered how far the escape pods were by now. Hopefully far enough, because his opponent would sooner have him slaughtered than be defeated in front of his crew.

A blade whistled in the air behind him. A knife was flying at his back. A444 side-stepped. Not fast enough. The impact of the knife, burying itself below his right shoulder bone, knocked him down. He willed the pain away and pulled himself up, but his long sword slipped from his grip.

Then his opponent's curved sword sliced through the muscles of his upper arm. Holy Mandala.

As A444 struggled to breathe, the smell of blood overwhelmed him. He tasted metal. Blood dripped noisily to the deck. All the sounds seemed enhanced. The frantic beat of his heart was deafening. Was he going to die? Strangely, it mattered to him. He hadn't accomplished his mission... What mission?

When his legs gave out, he collapsed. The deck pressed on his face from the weight of a leather boot on his head. Infernal laughter and cheers erupted all around. Then he fell into a bottomless pit, and all went black and silent.

* * *

Weak and thirsty, A444 let his head loll. Where was he? He vaguely remembered being stabbed in the back, but he could hardly feel it. The sword cut on his upper arm had bled all over his shirt and crusted over. He took a small, painful breath and almost retched at the stench of wild beasts, like in a menagerie. The muffled sobs, laments, cries, and animal growls, unsettled him.

He made an effort to raise his head and hold it up, then he opened his eyes upon a vast cargo space, packed with large cages, most of them occupied... and he sat in one of them. He should be dead. Did the universe have other plans for him?

In the cage next to his, lay a very large cat, white as snow. A rare albino beast... with deadly fangs and claws. The cat opened striking blue eyes.

A444 shuddered. "Hi, there."

The white cat blinked and stared at him.

He sensed the beast's loneliness and reached to caress the wide paw through the bars. "What could you possibly have done in your short lifespan to deserve ending up here? Whatever this place is..."

The white feline purred, displaying no sign of aggression. Her grace and the smaller size of her head marked her as a young female.

Focusing on his location, A444 realized he no longer was on a spaceship. Wrong configuration, and no engine whine. But he recognized the sound of air scrubbers... not very good ones, as they didn't clear the stench. The lighter artificial gravity said he was still in space. If not on a ship, probably on a space station.

Then he read the signs lining the top of the bulkhead. Divided sections, with names of owners. One of them was Lord Zethar, who owned Laxxar and the salt mines. So, the pirates had collected their bounty. Conversations he'd overheard amongst the guards surfaced in his mind. Lord Zethar ruled a space station named Pandemonium. Maybe that was it.

The guards on Laxxar also mentioned the games. Gladiator games, where they bet on who would live and who would die. Large beasts against warriors, cats against other cats, gladiator against gladiator. They also held public executions by wild felines, and the spectators could bet on how long it would take for the poor sob to die or be devoured.

Would that be his fate? He should be scared, but his mind was at peace. Somehow, against all logic, he believed the universe would provide.

A444 petted the big cat's paw through the bars. "I guess you may have to kill me later, or even eat me alive," he said softly. "I wish there was more kindness in this universe."

The cat head-bumped his hand. *"Panthera call for help,"* a young female voice said in his mind. *"Stay alive, Angel Kal..."*

Did the cat talk to him? "Did you call me Angel? That's what my team-mates called me in the mine. And who is Kal?"

A444 must be hallucinating as death drew near. He was speaking with a wild feline. A very young female cat named Panthera.

Exhausted and weak from blood loss, he closed his eyes and passed into oblivion.

Chapter Three

"Angel Kal hurt... Angel Kal dying... Please help!"

The urgency in the female mind voice pulled Indra out of her meditation trance. She opened her eyes and lowered her levitating body to the blue crystalline bench, keeping her legs crossed in front of her. "Who is this? Who is Angel Kal. Where are you?"

"Pandemonium. Hurry. Angel Kal dying."

Indra shuddered. Pandemonium was a retched place. Still, angels didn't die easily, so this was serious. Indra focused on her interlocutor and realized the mind-speaker wasn't a person. "What's your name?"

"Panthera. Hurry. Help Angel Kal."

Ah! A telepathic feline. That explained it. "Don't despair, Panthera. I'll alert the captain."

Indra severed the communication, dematerialized from her quarters, then rematerialized above deck, in the clear observation dome, with black space all around, and the occasional shimmer of the *Blue Phantom* shields.

Indra alighted to the deck, folded her wings, and bowed to the tall female angel with short blond hair, standing in the middle with an AI angel. "Captain, I received a distress call."

Graziella the Merciful nodded. "Show me."

The AI angel stepped away from the captain and bowed.

Indra stared into her captain's piercing blue eyes and recalled the communication received from Panthera.

Captain Graziella narrowed her gaze. "I see..."

"I've never heard of Angel Kal." Of course, Indra hadn't been an angel very long.

"Neither have I." The captain turned to the AI angel. "Iaco? How about you?"

The AI shook his head. "No such angel name comes up in my memory banks, Captain."

Indra wouldn't give up. "But if Panthera recognized him as an angel, he must be one. Cats are exceptional judges of character."

"Excellent point." Graziella smiled. "Let's go to Pandemonium."

Graziella the Merciful closed her eyes and Indra sensed her intense focus on the *Blue Phantom.*

Slight prickles rained on Indra's skin as the entire ship dematerialized, then rematerialized. She could now see, through the clear observation dome, the large, clandestine, space station only a few klicks away. Surrounded by docks and towers, the amalgam of cubes and domes bristled with

EMP cannons and an impressive battery of giant laser guns.

Dozens of heavy freighters floated around the imposing structure, while smaller vessels and shuttles navigated between them. Many raptors dotted the docking ring like barnacles, most of them exhibiting pirate markings.

Captain Graziella opened her luminous blue eyes. "We'll remain here, in stealth mode. Fortunately, the *Blue Phantom* never needs to dock. Indra, you will rescue Angel Kal yourself."

"My first solo mission? Yes, Captain." Indra's heart beat faster. In the three cycles she'd been an angel, she had never performed a mission on her own, but she'd intercepted the distress call. When called upon to save the worthy, an angel must always answer in person.

Iaco, the AI angel, glowed and nodded to Indra. "You must hurry, Indra. Pandemonium never remains at the same coordinates for long. Its powerful engines can propel it through space at great speed."

"Call if you need help." Graziella the Merciful smiled. "I trust you will perform beautifully. Good luck."

"Thanks, Captain. I'm on it." Indra wanted to excel, and show her captain she could do this job, despite her lack of experience.

Then Indra visualized the inside of Pandemonium and willed herself there.

She remained invisible as her feet touched the deck of the main fare, a wide avenue crowded with people of all species. She took care not to bump into anyone. That would be awkward.

On each side of the wide concourse, trade shops advertised sex slaves for sale, as well as illegal drugs and weapons. The tumult of loud voices matched the gaudy ads and garish colors on the screens. The smell of cooking fires and meat, mixed with filth and perfumes, assaulted her senses. She almost retched but resisted the urge.

Now she had to find the angel in distress in this obnoxious mess.

Indra cringed under the assault of the surrounding evil thoughts. Gamblers, thieves, murderers, criminals from all over the galaxy. She gagged at the sight of disgusting gladiator games displayed in bloody colors upon large screens, to encourage visitors to bet on the outcome.

She wished she could stop that evil... but whether she liked it or not, evil had its place in the universe. It challenged and tested everyone. It allowed people to grow and evolve. Without it, civilizations would stagnate. The balance of good and evil must be maintained at all times. Only when evil threatened to overcome and prevail, did angels go to war to restore the balance.

But Angels were also sworn to protect the innocent. Indra must concentrate on her mission.

She could fly over the crowd, of course, but wings created wind and sound, and she didn't want to attract attention. Remembering her training, she focused on the 3D blueprint of the station. Then she listened to the homing beacon of Panthera's lifeforce. *"Where are you, Panthera? This is Indra. I am on station, coming to you."*

"Hurry, Angel Indra. Angel Kal hurt." The young feline's mind voice grew desperate.

Focusing on Panthera's lifeforce, Indra pinpointed the specific area on the 3D map in her mind. There! Near the arena. A guarded cargo hold, with heavy security. All doors required DNA bio-codes. Only guards could enter.

Fortunately, Indra didn't need to open any doors. She focused on the holding area, dematerialized, then rematerialized inside.

She almost choked at the animal stench. Then she looked around the dimly lit area. Rows and rows of large cages, half of them occupied by animals and people. She wished she could free them all, but she mustn't intervene on that scale. She must stick to the mission. *"Panthera, where are you?"*

"Here. Hurry."

Sensing the direction of the call, Indra ran along the narrow aisle between the cages, then she stopped as she recognized Panthera's lifeforce. She was a beautiful white feline, a young female with keen abilities.

The cat rose at her approach.

"Can you see me?" Indra was still in invisible mode.

"Panthera see." The cat's blue eyes staring straight at her had an angelic quality. The feline nuzzled the hand of a man in the next cage. *"Angel Kal need help."*

The man didn't seem alive, slumped over, no visible breathing. His head had been shaved but showed dark stubble. He wore standard military white, like an angel, and dark blood stains marred his arm and back. Had he been wounded in the games? He'd lost a lot of blood.

Indra dematerialized then rematerialized inside Kal's cage and made herself visible. She knelt beside him and straightened his torso to lean his back against the bars. He moaned. At least, he was still alive, but his eyes remained closed.

He was tall and muscular, with a strong jaw, straight nose, and symmetrical features... like a genetically enhanced soldier... or more likely, an Avenging Angel. She touched his cheek... warm and stubbly. She opened one of his eyes... blue like an angel's eye, but he didn't seem to see.

"This man needs intensive care. I can't heal him here." She turned to Panthera. "Let me hold your paw, and I will transport you both to the *Blue Phantom.*"

"Panthera go with angel?" The cat's blue eyes widened.

"Yes, Panthera. Your beautiful soul doesn't belong in this horrible place." She hoped there was no rule preventing her from rescuing the animal.

The cat purred and offered her paw. *"Panthera like Indra."*

Grabbing a hold of Kal's muscular arm with one hand, Indra reached through the metal bars and latched on Panthera's paw. Then she focused on the *Blue Phantom* and dematerialized the three of them.

* * *

A444 peered through lowered eyelashes, not daring to stir. Where was he? In a warm, comfortable bed with clean linens. Was this a dream? The room seemed bathed in an eerie blue glow. Something in the air sang... like crystal chimes in a summer breeze. But the artificial gravity resembled that of a large ship. Not a dream.

He sensed activity around his bed. People. Who were they? He needed more information before dealing with them. Did the universe intervene in his favor?

Still, some old habit, deep inside, told him not to trust anyone. Training? Or fear? No, not fear. Fear was an illusion created by evil to manipulate people. Only the mission mattered. What mission? It was important... but he couldn't remember it.

Then the sword fight with the cheating pirate came back to him. The knife flying through the air and planting itself in his back, the pirate sword slashing his arm. Strangely, he didn't feel any pain. Then he remembered the cage, and the white feline in the menagerie of the arena.

The fragrance of cherry blossoms spread around him... he remembered that from the cage as well... along with a musical feminine voice.

"Angel Kal, are you awake?" That same fresh feminine voice.

Who was this Angel Kal people kept calling? But he couldn't resist the angelic voice and opened his eyes. "Sorry to disappoint, but I am not an angel, and I have no name."

"Really? My name is Indra." The lovely creature standing by his bed had cascading black hair, blue eyes, and honey skin under the white military attire.

He looked around the caerulean glowing room. What an unusual ship. The arched ceiling reminded him of ancient cathedrals in historical records.

Indra frowned. "Why can't I read your mind?"

Strange question. Was it a joke? "Maybe it's because my mind is empty. My memories were erased."

"Why?" The inquisitive tone remained charming.

"If I knew that, I would also know who I am, wouldn't I?" He'd rather not tell her he escaped from the frozen hells of Laxxar. Only hardened criminals went there, and somehow, he wanted to make a good impression. Omitting wasn't lying. One was allowed to keep secrets.

"What about your most recent memories? Of Pandemonium, of the holding cage? I can't access them either." The tone turned accusatory, as if he'd done something wrong. "Are you shielding your thoughts from us?"

"I don't know what you mean." He sat up, realizing he was bare to the waist, wondering why he wasn't in pain from his injuries. "Are you a sneaky mind reader into the habit of reading people's minds?"

Her face softened. "Sorry. I'm not very good at this angel business. Sometimes, I go overboard."

"Angel? Like the Guardian Angels of the Universe?" He scoffed. "You are joking, right?"

"Absolutely not." Indra sounded offended.

A444 checked himself. He touched his upper arm. The skin was smooth. It had completely healed. He wondered again at the strange tattoo on his arm. His back felt normal. No sign of his brush with death. Was he dreaming? Was he dying and hallucinating? Or worse?

"Am I dead?" If he were, he didn't mind at all.

Indra chuckled like a babbling brook. "No, silly. Don't you remember being rescued? I came to you on Pandemonium and brought you here to be healed."

"Healed how?" A444 remembered the white cat and the cage. He'd been close to death.

She smiled mysteriously. "We have special healing ways."

He wondered how long he'd been there but didn't ask. "I guess, I should be thanking you for saving my hide."

"Thanks are not necessary." Her smile illuminated the entire room. "We'll talk about remuneration later."

"Remuneration?" Strange notion. Nothing was free in this universe. Everyone wanted to profit... even angels, apparently.

The lovely girl stepped closer and laid a hand on his. Her touch tingled and woke him up more than he wanted. A surge of longing warmed his blood. What was this? Sexual sorcery? Heat crept up his throat. This was not permitted. He pulled back his hand.

"What is this place?" He perused his surroundings. Strange ship. The caerulean, crystalline bulkhead seemed to pulse as it emitted a soft glow.

Indra smiled. "You are on the *Blue Phantom*."

"The legendary angel ship?" The very one the guards mentioned with dread in their fantastic stories. "So, the *Blue Phantom* is real?"

"Of course, it is, and you are inside it." No sign of deceit, only compassion in Indra's blue eyes.

The elusive ship was said to glow in dark space, appear and disappear, and never register on scanners. "So, you are a real angel?"

"Yes, like everyone onboard." She sounded sincere.

"Except me." A444 felt very small.

"Possibly, maybe... but not for long." She smiled mysteriously then deployed beautiful white wings. "Now, you need to rest, Angel Kal."

"I'm not an angel." Repeating it was tiresome.

But she'd already vanished into thin air, leaving behind the sweet scent of cherry blossoms.

"Holy Mandala!" He always wanted to believe in angels, but this surpassed all his expectations. And what did she mean by remuneration? or not for long?

As he struggled to focus, a sudden urge to close his eyes invited him to lean back on the silky pillows and surrender to oblivion.

* * *

In the control room of Pandemonium, Zethar fumed as he stared at the clear media wall. The security recording from the menagerie a few hours earlier showed a brief blur, then the image turned grainy. Through the static fog, a winged female manifested inside the prisoner's cage then vanished with A444 and the white feline.

"Her intrusion should have triggered the alarms. Why didn't it?" Zethar would find out how the angel woman circumvented his security. He hated powerful beings who made him look like a fool.

The large cat at his side growled. *"Spartacus not like menagerie."*

"That's understandable." Spartacus had come from that depressing place. "Well, you have the perfect life now, big boy. No more starving, no more cracking whips or bloody fights."

"Spartacus happy..." The big cat purred. *"Spartacus miss Panthera."*

"Panthera? The albino feline stolen by the angel with my prisoner?" Why did Spartacus care?

The genetically enhanced feline licked his enormous paw beans, extending deadly claws to facilitate the job. *"Panthera okay with angels."*

"I don't like angels interfering in my affairs. How dare they steal my property?" And what he wouldn't give to have their incredible abilities. Although he drew the line at becoming Azfet's minion. Her offer was fraught with malevolent entanglements.

He caressed the gold and silver circuits imbedded in his smooth skull. All the hardware and software in the galaxy couldn't match what these angels did with one simple thought.

"And why did they take A444?" That prisoner must have more value than Zethar realized. Azfet hid the truth from him. "The Dominara will be peeved."

"Spartacus not like Highness." The violet gem on the cat's collar flared.

The main viewer chimed and Dominara Azfet's voluptuous figure appeared in a long red gown, slitted on one side. Ostentatious gold jewelry with a ruby the size of a fist didn't quite cover her bare breasts.

How dare she hack his secure feed and appear on his viewer unannounced? Her call was no coincidence. She must know what happened, but how? Zethar hated her keen insight.

On the viewer, Dominara Azfet stood against a hieroglyph-covered pillar. Then she walked to a gold Sphynx statue and molded her body to the curves of the beast in a sexy pose, giving a peek of a long, flawless leg. "Did you miss me, Zethar? I understand you have distressing news."

"Yes, Highness..." How did she know? Zethar kept his head high. He refused to bow... to anyone. "It seems A444 escaped again... this time with angel help."

"I had high hopes for you, Zethar. I paid you handsomely to keep that prisoner contained, and you made me an unbreakable promise. You disappoint me." The low, sexy voice carried a definite threat, then the live snake on her headdress hissed. "I do not like being disappointed."

Zethar wouldn't be intimidated. "I apologize, Highness, but he won't go far. I will recapture him soon. I promise."

"You better succeed… or else." Her menacing stare would intimidate a lesser man.

"I will succeed." Zethar wondered why this prisoner was so important to the psychopath lady. Of course, A444 had defied all odds and survived Laxxar beyond the human threshold. Was he not human? "Maybe you should tell me why this fugitive is so important to you, Highness. Why not kill him outright if you don't want him around? Life is cheap. A large bounty would start a galactic man hunt."

"A444 as you call him is not that easy to kill, Zethar." Dominara Azfet sighed contentedly, as if relishing the challenge. "He is smart, resourceful, and too dangerous to roam free. Besides, I might need him later as a bargaining chip."

Zethar wondered who the other bargaining party might be. "A444 must have very special skills beyond what you just said. I still don't understand how he survived that long on Laxxar, or managed to escape. Before him, all who tried died horribly in the process."

"Don't you worry, Zethar. I have the utmost confidence in you." Dominara Azfet played with the large red gem dangling between her exquisitely displayed breasts and winked at him. "Would it help if I told you where he is hiding?"

"You know where he is?" Zethar took a calming breath. He hated being manipulated. "Of course, it would help."

The Dominara chuckled. "Your fugitive is aboard the *Blue Phantom* as we speak."

"The legendary angel ship?" That was the worst news for Zethar. "And how am I supposed to find that ship? It's invisible and our scanners are blind to it. It can't be detected or tracked."

"Are you certain of that?" Dominara Azfet smiled mysteriously. "Ask Spartacus! He knows where the *Blue Phantom* is. Right, big boy?"

Spartacus growled. The violet gem on his collar flared then returned to normal.

The Dominara had vanished from the viewer, leaving the golden Sphynx sculpture to fill the screen before it went dark.

Zethar frowned and stared at his feline bodyguard. "Spartacus, are you keeping secrets from me? Do you know where my prisoner is?"

The scary beast flashed his damaged fangs and growled a warning. *"Spartacus know. Spartacus not tell."*

Flabbergasted at the revelation, Zethar reconsidered his lenient approach toward the cat. Maybe he should adopt the whip method used in the arena... but Spartacus was tough and stubborn... and extremely dangerous to his enemies. Better remain his friend than provoke his wrath.

Zethar patted the big cat's rump then caressed the violet gem on his studded collar. What a strange stone for a killing beast. And it seemed to flare each time the Dominara called. "This is a very expensive collar... rather unusual for a fighting feline."

Spartacus purred. *"Trophy... for good fight. Spartacus always win."*

"Do you know who provided such a gift?" Evidently someone of great means.

"Secret admirer. Spartacus champion. Many secret admirer." The big cat closed his eyes, as if reliving his past glory in the arena.

"Secret?" That word again. The Dominara's friendly attitude toward the cat indicated she might be that secret admirer. Could the collar be a spying device? Or did she possess extraordinary mind-reading abilities, even at a great distance? In any case, she knew more than she shared.

Zethar played with the clasp under the cat's chin. "Would you let me remove your collar, just to examine it?"

"No." Spartacus hissed and his lips pulled back, baring his fangs. *"Trophy mine."*

Zethar pulled his hands away from the razor-sharp teeth. "Sorry I asked."

"Spartacus champion. Keep trophy."

"I respect that. You fought hard to earn it." Zethar knew better than to confront the cat. He might have to drug the beast, make it sleep. "Why won't you tell me where the *Blue Phantom* is?"

"*Spartacus not tell.*" The sharp tone in the gravelly mind voice carried a warning.

"But why? I thought we were friends. Is there an important reason?" Very intriguing.

The cat turned his back to Zethar and licked his paw. *"Panthera safe with angels."*

"Panthera? The albino female, again?" Why did the rugged beast protect another cat? Did animals care more for each other than people?

Spartacus shook his pelt in a mighty tremor, then strode toward his sleeping bunk under the console panel, indicating he'd say no more.

Then Zethar remembered Dominara Azfet had been the first one to suggest he adopt Spartacus as his bodyguard. Clearly, she had been manipulating him for a while, and Zethar didn't like the feeling, not one bit, but he would discover the hidden truth.

Chapter Four

Indra basked in the serenity of being one with the positive energy of the cosmos, weightless, fulfilled, her mind empty of selfish concerns. "Please, O Formless One, allow me to contribute my mind, to facilitate your work for the greater good of this universe."

Time stopped as she melted with the collective angel minds, floating among billions of stars, filled with the vibrations and the pulse of the origins of life.

Something knocked her out of her meditative trance, and she fell down to the crystal deck, pinned under the pouncing paws of a large white feline, who now licked her face with a raspy tongue.

"Panthera!" Indra couldn't help but chuckle. "We have to talk about boundaries."

"Panthera take bath. Panthera hungry... Panthera want meat. Panthera hunt prey."

"There is no prey on the *Blue Phantom*. Also, we do not kill... and we certainly don't eat other animals." Indra found the notion revolting... although not so long ago, she was still eating meat.

"No meat?" The look of surprise widening the cat's deep blue eyes turned to disappointment. *"Fish?"*

"No fish either, but don't worry. You might just love our food. Don't knock it before you try it." Indra mussed Panthera's head, kissed her nose, then rose and brushed imaginary hair from her uniform.

"Panthera very hungry." The cat yawned, showing sharp teeth.

"I ordered special meals of reconstituted proteins from our galley. Come with me."

Panthera huffed, seemingly unconvinced, and followed Indra across her small quarters. The living area included a white couch, and crystal cubes serving as side tables or seats. A counter and an empty ice box lined one side. The sleeping area seen through the open hatch had double bunks with comfy mattresses, the lowest showing Panthera's lounging imprint.

Indra opened the main hatch and Panthera followed her out, and along crystalline corridors. "So, what do you think about sharing my quarters?"

"Panthera like big sand box, and crate castle, and comfy bed... and toys... and Angel Indra." The large feline trotted, tail up, like a happy kitten.

"Glad to hear it." Indra shuddered at the memory of the dirty cage on Pandemonium, where she'd found the cat. "If you need anything else, just let me know."

"Panthera not like bath." The beast shook her pelt as if still wet. *"Panthera clean with lick."*

"But now you smell so good and you look so pretty. Don't tell me you miss the dirt and the bugs..." She scratched the big cat's head as they walked side by side. "I saw Angel Kal this morning. He's healed and doing fine. All he needs now is rest."

"Panthera like Angel Kal... Angel Kal very sad."

"Kal is sad? Did he tell you that?" Strange that he didn't share that with her. "When I spoke to him, he didn't seem to remember his own name, or that he is an angel." She turned to the cat. "How do you know he's an angel?"

"Panthera know. Angel Kal from faraway stars. Angel Kal hunted like prey, ambushed... crystal stolen... not remember mission." Panthera's mind voice sounded sad.

Could the cat read Kal's mind while Indra could not? Angels never lied and never kept secrets from each other. And sometimes, while away on long missions, they carried a crystal to preserve their angelic abilities. "What mission?"

"Panthera not know... Angel Kal too hard to kill... sent to Laxxar to die. Angel Kal escape. Lord Zethar hunt Angel Kal... want him dead."

"Wow! Kal is a fugitive from Laxxar?" A horrifying thought. No one ever escaped from that forced labor facility. But it would explain his shaved head and the memory wipe. Indra remembered the name Zethar from the station records. The rich gangster ruled Pandemonium... and owned the Laxxar mines. "How do you know all that?"

"Panthera read many mind..."

Indra wondered whose minds. The cat must have gleaned that information on Pandemonium. Animals did not lie, although they sometimes misunderstood, or kept secrets for self-preservation.

"How far? Panthera hungry."

"Here we are." Indra stepped into the dining hall, lined with long tables and benches of the same luminous blue as the bulkhead and cathedral ceiling. At one time, when the *Blue Phantom* was a military destroyer, it must have been the officers' mess.

It wasn't meal time, so the tables stood empty. Indra went to the bare buffet line beyond which a male angel stood and smiled. "I ordered food for Panthera, our feline guest."

Panthera rose on her hind legs and rested her front paws on the counter, in violation of every sanitary rule. *"Panthera hungry."*

"Of course." The angel on the other side smiled at Panthera and slid a large tray with a huge mound of what looked like raw hamburger meat. "Hope you like it. If not, we can adjust the formula."

"Panthera like hamburger." The cat salivated, then she jumped on the counter and started gulping the synthetic meat like a wild beast.

Indra and the other angel laughed.

"No, no, no." Indra took one of Panthera's round ears and pulled her down from the counter. "If you want to live on this ship, you must learn some manners."

Panthera mewed a sheepish agreement then shook her head out of Indra's grip.

"Follow me." Indra took the tray and led the big cat to a corner of the room then set the tray on the floor. "Here. This is a good place where you can eat in peace, without being disturbed, or disturbing anyone else."

While Panthera wolfed down the reconstituted protein, Indra went to get her a large bowl of water. By the time she set it on the floor, the cat had already swallowed the entire mound of food.

"Panthera like hamburger. Panthera hungry. Panthera want more."

"More? Did they not feed you on Pandemonium? You don't look skinny to me." But apparently, the poor beast must have been ravenous. Probably kept hungry to savagely feed on her victims in the arena. Indra shuddered at the thought. "All right. I'll get you more... hamburger."

* * *

Kal relished the hot shower flowing on his shaved head and bare skin, a luxury he didn't remember enjoying... ever. On Laxxar, only waterless sonic showers, taken fully clothed and in groups, were available.

He flexed his biceps. His wounded arm didn't even show a scar from the pirate's blade, below the strange tattoo he didn't remember getting and couldn't explain. It was a dark circle, and inside it, two white wings and a pink sword. The runic symbol under it was foreign to him as well.

His back was no longer stiff when he stretched, and he couldn't feel a scar from the throwing dagger either. His Laxxar friend, Medic, would be amazed at this healing feat. No trace remained of his injuries. Even the most advanced technology couldn't accomplish such a miracle in one day.

Kal also felt better than ever before, as if the angels had given him superior health.

He now referred to himself as Kal, since the angels insisted on giving him that name. For some reason it seemed to fit... although it probably wasn't his true name.

He stepped out of the shower and let the hot wind dry him. Then he grabbed and donned the fresh clothes waiting on a shelf. White, military style pants and Tee... he liked it. Then he walked into the spacious quarters, with caerulean glowing bulkhead, a comfortable bunk and all the amenities. It baffled him how kind the angels were to him.

They provided healthy fresh food and gave him this luxurious abode on their ship.

It made him feel like a fraud. What had he done to deserve this kind of royal treatment?

Then again, he'd thought the same thing about being enslaved on Laxxar. Maybe life was ruled by pure chance and had nothing to do with what people deserved. He found the thought upsetting.

He also had that nagging feeling that he should be doing something important... but what? If only he could remember who or what he was before his memory wipe... but as hard as he tried, he couldn't.

The hatch chimed. A visitor? He hoped it was Indra. "Come in."

The beautiful Indra with long, flowing black hair walked in, a big smile lighting her blue eyes, strikingly bright in her tan face. "How are you adapting to your new quarters?"

He shouldn't be looking at her, but he couldn't resist and smiled back. "Life aboard the *Blue Phantom* certainly is different from the menagerie where you found me."

Indra's eyes sparkled. "I can only imagine. I'm glad we found you in time."

"I never thanked you properly." Kal must have been a mess. "I don't remember much about the menagerie, but I was so delirious, at one point I thought the white feline was talking to me in my mind. How pathetic, right?"

"Oh, you didn't imagine that." Indra pushed back a strand of glossy black hair. "In truth, Panthera is a natural telepath. She is the one who called me and asked us to rescue you."

"What? So, I didn't dream it..." How strange... but also familiar. "Then I should thank her, too."

"She would like that." Angel Indra's bright blue eyes narrowed. "Don't you remember anything of your former life?"

"Nothing at all." He pointed to the tattoo peeking below his short sleeve. "I don't know where or why I got this, or what it represents."

"It looks like an esoteric symbol, but I've never seen it before." She stepped closer and touched his skin.

Kal pulled back his arm. This was forbidden. Her direct contact was too intense. Their eyes met. She looked confused. She must be exuding pheromones. How inappropriate.

"So, what do angels do around here to fill the day?" He struggled to sound casual.

She turned away as if scanning his quarters. "We meditate a lot. We also see to the maintenance of the ship, but as a guest, you do not have any assigned chores."

"So, meditation... not prayer." He couldn't help the sarcastic tone. Did she tell him what he wanted to hear? For what purpose? "Is this some kind of religious cult?"

She chuckled. "Not at all. There is no worship here. All of us are from different planets, different cultures, different religions. On this ship, we meditate to stay in tune with the energy of the universe. We are tasked with preserving the balance of good and evil."

He whistled. Was she joking? "That sounds like an ambitious job."

"Yes, it is." She looked dead serious. "Good and evil are opposite sides of the same coin, and both are essential to the evolution of the self-aware races... but evil has a way of always craving more control. We are here to prevent evil from taking over this galaxy."

Despite the angel legends, Kal wasn't sure he believed everything she said. "I hope you have a grand army for that kind of task."

"Our numbers are small, but we have the means to handle evil." She deployed a magnificent set of wings and levitated in front of him. "We can also vanish and reappear somewhere else at will. We are trained fighters, and we have these." When she drew the blue sword at her belt, it glowed.

Kal stepped back and inhaled deeply. "Impressive."

"Angels have other abilities, like the power to read minds." She narrowed her eyes at him. "But for some reason, I can't read yours."

He was glad she couldn't. "I'm sorry. As I said before, my mind was wiped."

"I know that, but I can't even read what you are thinking right now. It's disconcerting." She frowned prettily.

"Sorry, I don't know why that is." Kal thanked the powers that be for that small boon. He would be mortified if Indra knew what he was thinking. She was too lovely, too attractive to be an angel. She wreaked havoc on his self-control. This was wrong.

"I should be able to read you, unless you are consciously blocking me." That accusing tone again. "But for that you would have to possess superior abilities."

"Believe me, I am no angel and I have no special abilities whatsoever." Out of respect for her, he should tell her whatever little truth he knew. So much for making a good impression. She might leave him alone after that. "In fact, if my recent past is any indication, I must have been a low-life brigand to deserve a life of forced labor in the mines of Laxxar."

"Laxxar? That must have been horrible." Her eyes softened. "But it doesn't mean you deserved to be there."

"It was hell." Kal shook his head to chase away the gruesome memories. "And before Laxxar, I remember nothing."

"How did you escape from that frozen hell?" Her eyes widened.

"Somehow, I did. Lucky, I guess." He attempted a smile. "My friends and I made it out of there."

She still stared at him with these piercing blue eyes. "Were they recaptured with you?"

"I don't think so. I fought the pirates who came for the bounty, to give them time to escape." He remembered the sword fight. "As far as I know, they made it to freedom. I hope they did."

"That was very brave of you to sacrifice yourself for them." She laid a gentle hand on his shoulder.

Her contact sent heat rushing through his body. His heart beat a furious tempo. He shrank away from it and turned as casually as he could to regain his calm. "Sorry, my mind is agitated. I do not deserve to be here."

"That's not for you to decide." Her voice was so soft. "Meditation can help you find your inner peace."

"I tried that on Laxxar." But it didn't bring back his memories.

"Maybe you did it wrong." Her eyes took on a dreamy quality. "I sit quietly, let go of selfish concerns, and allow my mind to fly away and melt with the universe all around."

"It sounds wonderful." But in his experience, nothing was that easy.

"Try it. Once you get the hang of it, it will bring balance, harmony, and happiness to your life." She had a slow, kind smile.

"Happiness?" What a strange and foreign concept. "Definitely worth a try."

"Then I'll leave you to it." She deployed her wings then vanished, releasing the sweet scent of cherry blossoms.

Kal inhaled the fresh fragrance then exhaled a sigh of relief. How pathetic and humiliating, for an undeserving man with forbidden appetites, to be attracted to an unreachable angel of love and perfection, who understood happiness.

Duty, mission, sacrifice, Kal understood these words. But the very concept of happiness seemed foreign to him.

* * *

Later that day, in his residential quarters on Pandemonium, Zethar closely examined the collar removed from Spartacus, after a special reconstituted hamburger meal saturated with a sleeping agent. The large cat lay passed out on the sofa, belly exposed, four paws in the air, snoring like a drunken sailor. He wouldn't wake for hours.

At first glance, the black leather collar itself seemed quite simple in its composition, although it included metal spikes and other silvery decorations that made it sparkle. All that metal could easily hide small trackers.

Zethar raised the collar to the computerized scanner emerging from the bulkhead of his quarters. He let go of the collar and it levitated in midair. "Scan for any kind of electronic devices, ID chip, transmitter, transponder, radio signal, recorder, power source, or any other suspicious element."

A zillion narrow rays of green light hit the collar from all angles and danced all around it. The computer chimed. "Scanning... scanning... scanning..."

Zethar would find the information he needed and use it against his enemies... in this case, Dominara Azfet. She seemed to be involved in everything these days. Obviously, she was rich and powerful, but all that mystique around her may not be justified. If she used high-tech spying gadgets like Zethar did, she wasn't the mighty sorceress she portrayed to the outside world.

"Scanning complete." The computer chimed again. The ballet of dancing laser rays stopped. "All elements of the object are inert and have no unusual properties, chemical, technical, electronic, or otherwise."

How disappointing. But sometimes quartz could be used to store information and energy. "How about the gem itself?"

The computer chimed. "The gem is exotic and unique in color and composition. Never seen the likes of it before... but it shows no special, technical, or interesting features, no reaction to technology at all. Somewhat comparable to violet iolite crystal, it is not a spying device as it is completely inert."

"Then why does it flare every time Dominara Azfet appears on my viewer?"

"Unknown." The matter-of-fact computer voice annoyed Zethar.

"Any farfetched theory?" Zethar berated himself for asking a dumb computer to show imagination.

"The flaring could be a trick of the light." Even the computer tone indicated doubt.

Duh! Zethar didn't believe that. What he'd seen was no trick of the light. "Anything else unusual or unique about that stone? You said you've never seen anything like it before."

"Yes." The computer beeped. "Given its exotic composition including a few unknown minerals, that particular stone cannot have originated in this galaxy."

"Really?" Exotic indeed. "Can you extrapolate what part of the universe it might have come from?"

"Negative. With no information about the unknown minerals, the origin of the gem cannot be extrapolated."

Zethar snatched the collar from midair. "That will be all."

The computer scanner beeped, retracted itself into the bulkhead, then turned itself off.

Even though the scanner didn't detect anything suspicious, Zethar refused to eliminate the possibility of a spying device. Too many unknowns. Besides, he didn't believe in coincidences.

Tempted to get rid of the device to thwart the Dominara, he decided against it. It would tip the crazy woman about his doubts... and Spartacus might react aggressively. Instead, Zethar walked to the couch and carefully slid the collar under the beast's sleeping head, then he locked the clasp under the furry chin and patted the feline's head. "Good boy."

Spartacus harrumphed and snorted, then turned to his side and resumed his loud snoring.

Although disappointed, Zethar remained intrigued. Something smelled fishy and he wouldn't give up until he figured out the truth.

Chapter Five

Too upset to dematerialize, Indra marched along the glass-blue corridors to calm herself. Why couldn't she read Kal's mind? That was suspicious. Angels didn't keep secrets, nor did they shield their thoughts from other angels.

As for regular mortals, they did not have the ability to hide their thoughts at all... except for the Zephyrians... but they usually had peridot-green eyes. Kal's eyes were blue.

The hatch slid open and she walked into her personal quarters then stopped in utter shock. Her peaceful and orderly residence looked as if a tornado had hit the deck. The glass furniture lay on its side, the couch and its cushions exposed their white entrails, and shredded stuffing snowed all over the rug. The cold box lay wide open and reconstituted protein meals lay half eaten on the deck with wrappers everywhere.

What a mess! Indra searched around for the large feline and found her eating behind the dilapidated couch. "Panthera, why did you do this?"

The cat raised her head, ears straight up, and licked fake hamburger stuck to her lips. *"Panthera hungry."*

"Still? You could have called me… in your mind. I would have come and fed you." That animal had an insatiable appetite. She could eat all day. Was it normal? Indra had no experience with big cats and would have to learn from this one.

"Panthera bored."

"Bored? Maybe we should exercise together." Indra picked up a gutted cushion, held it to the blueish glow and frowned.

"Panthera sad. Miss Spartacus." The cat did sound sad.

"Who is Spartacus? Your former handler?" Indra never thought of asking about the cat's past.

Panthera harrumphed in derision. *"Not handler. Handsome beast, arena champion."*

"So, you have a crush on another cat from Pandemonium?" How cute, but Panthera seemed very depressed about it. "You miss him? I understand. I miss my family, my tribe."

"Spartacus magnificent, brave, strong, kill many." Much pride in Panthera's mind voice.

How disconcerting. Indra shuddered as images of the bloody games flashed in her mind. But Panthera seemed to know more about Kal than anyone else, including Kal himself. "Panthera, how do you know so much about Angel Kal?"

"Spartacus tell Panthera." The young voice in her mind sounded proud. *"Spartacus know... Friend with big boss."*

"Zethar? The rich gangster who rules Pandemonium?" That might be interesting.

The white cat blinked. *"Spartacus friend with Zethar."*

"Zethar knows where Kal came from?" Who better than Zethar to know Kal's planet of origin.

The cat shook her head. *"Zethar not know. Spartacus know."*

"All right." As an angel away from home, Kal should have carried a crystal, to help him retain his angelic abilities. "Did Spartacus tell you if Kal carried a blue gemstone when he was taken?"

Panthera shook her big head. *"No..."* The cat licked her flank once then turned her deep stare to Indra. *"Not blue."*

"But he carried a crystal, didn't he?" This could prove he was an angel.

Panthera harrumphed. *"Violet crystal."*

"Violet?" Indra's blood retreated from her extremities. Purple crystal had proven to be evil in the past. "Are you sure?"

"Spartacus not lie." The sharp mind tone indicated offense.

Although Indra didn't sense any evil in Kal, the violet crystal was an alarming detail. "Do you know where that crystal is now?"

Panthera licked her paw with obvious indifference. *"Panthera know."*

"Where is it?" Finally, Indra might get some answers.

"Panthera not tell."

"What?" Indra checked herself. Rushing Panthera would not work. The cat had been trained to react aggressively for the games. "Why won't you tell me?"

"Panthera protect." The cat's blue eyes did a slow, dreamy blink.

"Who are you protecting? Zethar? Spartacus? Kal?" Indra wondered why, and what did that say about Kal?

"Panthera not tell." The cat rose, turned around, and slinked toward her napping bed... on a very full stomach, low to the deck.

Indra didn't like what she'd just learned. The strange crystal made Angel Kal look like a possible agent of darkness, and she must tell her captain about the violet gem. She had no choice. Angels did not keep secrets, especially dangerous ones.

Yet, Indra was torn. She refused to believe Kal was evil, but what if the angels of the *Blue Phantom* decided he was? Would they harm him? Kill him? Worse, what if the *Blue Phantom* was sheltering a mortal enemy?

Indra must trust her captain. Graziella the Merciful would know what to do. Indra focused on Graziella. *"Captain, there is something I must tell you."*

"I know, Indra. Meet me and the council in the observation dome in a few minutes." The captain severed the connection.

"Wow!" Indra had never been privy to the council.

But she couldn't leave her quarters in such a mess. Closing her eyes, she visualized her quarters whole, neat, and tidy, as she left them this morning. Then she focused her mind on the energy of the universe. The scattered debris floated back together and mended themselves, until the place was back in its pristine state.

Having angel abilities helped in many ways... even to perform the most tedious tasks, like cleaning and repairs.

* * *

Indra steadied her heartbeat as she stood in the circle of angels inside the observation dome. For her first time attending the council, she felt inadequate. They all looked formidable and magnificent. A few of the angels present weren't even biologic entities. They were luminous and blue, but had silvery limbs, an artificial mind, and a crystal heart.

Outside the clear dome, star-studded black space extended to infinity.

Graziella the Merciful, captain of the *Blue Phantom*, stood at the center of the wide circle. "I summoned you to discuss a potential threat. As many of you already know, we rescued someone from Pandemonium, suspecting he was an angel."

"Yes, Angel Kal," Iaco, an android angel, said in a neutral voice.

Many angels nodded gravely.

The captain cleared her voice. "We since discovered that not only can he shield his thoughts from us, but his mind was wiped and he doesn't remember who he is."

"Are we certain of that?" Iaco seemed skeptical. "If he can hide his thoughts, he could be lying."

"We know his mind was wiped. The records from Pandemonium verified it." Graziella sighed. "But most alarming is the fact that he recently escaped Laxxar's labor fortress."

A cold breeze blew over Indra and some wing feathers in the circle ruffled. No regular being could have escaped Laxxar, but an angel might, even deprived of his memories or of his angelic powers. It also begged another important question.

One of the high-ranking angels, with five stars on his white collar, frowned. "Do we know what the charges against him were to deserve such a horrible and painful fate in the frozen salt mines?"

"We do not. These records are sealed." Captain Graziella sighed. "It's standard procedure after a memory wipe, so no trace of the crime remains."

Nothing out of the ordinary there. Still... Indra had shivers thinking about the possibilities.

"But..." Graziella hesitated. "We just learned that when he was first caught, before his incarceration, he carried a violet crystal."

"Violet? Are you certain?" The five-star angel frowned again.

"Unfortunately, yes." Captain Graziella sounded sad. "Our sources do not lie."

Several angels gasped at the news. Indra had reacted the same way when she'd learned that scary detail. Various crystals had different properties. Black, red, and purple gems had proven deadly to angels in the past.

"Where is that crystal now?" Iaco, the android angel, asked.

"We do not know," the captain kept her voice slightly above a whisper.

"Who was his accuser?" The general sounded resolute. "Who sent him to Laxxar? Do we know that? They would know what his crime was."

"Yes." Captain Graziella summoned a 3D image from her mind of a beautiful woman in a slitted red gown and gaudy jewelry adorning her bare breasts. She also wore a gold headdress like a crown. "She's a little-known noblewoman from a far-flung world... Dominara Azfet. She insists on being called *Highness* and remains in regular contact with Lord Zethar."

Indra wondered why that gorgeous woman had Kal arrested. She was too sexy and beautiful, with a conniving smile, and the wicked spark in her eyes could not be trusted.

"So, this Dominara Azfet could tell us what the initial charges were." The five-star general sounded relieved. "To be sent to Laxxar, it has to be a major crime against nature, against life itself."

"In ordinary circumstances, yes." Graziella sighed. "Unfortunately, the lady is immensely rich, and Zethar is not above taking bribes. Nor are small planet officials innocent of falsifying records."

Iaco, the android angel, glowed brighter. "We must seek advice from the high council of Azura."

"No." Captain Graziella's strong voice silenced the entire dome. "Although we are angels like them, the *Blue Phantom* does not recognize Azuran sovereignty. We are separate, independent. We make our own decisions. If, as we learn more, our suspicions of evil at work are confirmed, we shall warn Azura, as a courtesy, but we do not seek their counsel."

Indra shuddered. Despite her kind and merciful heart, Captain Graziella, a former Amazon warrior from Skeera, could be shrewd.

"Captain." Iaco's voice sounded neither male nor female. "Permission to consult the Formless One directly."

"That is an excellent suggestion." Captain Graziella nodded. "Let's all help by emptying our minds and focusing on the Formless One."

Wow! Indra had never seen the androids exercise that function. They could channel the Formless One directly, without emotion or mind filters of any kind. On Azura, they served as a direct channel to the Formless One. Apparently, they filled that role on the *Blue Phantom* as well.

The three android angels present rose in the air and gathered several feet above the captain's head, under the high dome of the observation room. The vibrations inside the clear dome intensified. Pleasant musical resonances filled the air.

Indra closed her eyes, emptied her mind, and a joyful sense of wellbeing flooded her.

"O Formless One," Graziella's commanding voice rose among the humming harmonies. "We seek information and advice about a certain Angel Kal, who carried a violet crystal, and is impervious to our mind probes. Is he the bringer of evil forces to come? Should he be stopped? Or is he a victim we should protect?"

Indra held her breath. She wasn't supposed to take sides, but she fervently wished Kal wasn't evil.

"Angels of the *Blue Phantom*..." The booming voice echoed inside the large dome. "The violet iolite stone is more powerful than your blue crystal. Neither evil nor good, it can be programmed by any master of the mystic arts for a specific purpose. You must discover its purpose to know whether it is charged with good or evil intent."

"What about Kal?" Indra bit her lips, regretting her outburst, expecting a rebuke.

Silence followed, then the voice of the Formless One, channeled by the AI angels rose.

"Once an Angel Guardian in his own world, Kal comes from another universe, stranger than you can imagine. His secret mission could change this universe forever. Although he lost his angelic abilities, along with his crystal and his memories, his mind remains shielded and he keeps dangerous secrets. Evil came with him to your galaxy, so, you should prepare to face it."

"How? How do we destroy that evil before it becomes unstoppable?" Captain Graziella sounded worried. "Is Angel Kal our friend or our enemy?"

Indra held her breath. That was the true question for her.

"Good and evil are both part of a balanced universe. Friends and enemies switch sides in the blink of an eye. Good in one universe can be evil in another and vice versa. Only when the balance of good and evil is threatened, angels must restore it. At this time, I see no unbalance. The scales have not tipped." Always true to its lofty nature, the Formless One never took sides.

"So, what must we do, O Formless One?"

"Figure it out yourselves, angels. The Formless One never gets involved." The last words trailed as if the presence was pulling away from the dome.

The highly charged vibrations abated. The harmonies weakened. Indra realized her wings were deployed, and she'd been floating above the deck. She lowered herself, found her footing, and folded her wings. All the angels in the circle did the same.

The light in the three android angels hovering above the captain faded. They floated away from each other and regained their place in the circle as well.

Indra held her breath. Despite the incredible experience, the Formless One was no help at all. The wise words raised more ominous questions about dangers to come... and about Angel Kal.

Captain Graziella took a deep breath. "Although the Formless One does not participate in our struggles, we learned a lot from this contact. The danger is real and we should not ignore it. But we must solve this mystery ourselves."

"What are your orders, Captain?" The five-star angel stood at the ready.

The captain nodded. "We should find out more about Angel Kal. Only he knows all the details of the danger threatening our world."

Iaco the AI stepped forward. "I suggest we ask Angel Kal's consent to perform a mind opening ceremony."

"Excellent idea." The captain scanned the circle, as if waiting for an objection. None came.

Indra shuddered. She'd heard of these ceremonies, when the angels used their collective powers to open someone's closed memories and discover their secrets. Usually it was an evil sorcerer, and it could be very painful. In some instances, people had died under the strain.

The Formless One confirmed Kal was an angel in his own world, but remained vague about whether he was good or evil, according to Indra's definition. She liked Kal and didn't believe he was a bad angel. She didn't want him to suffer, or worse...

* * *

As Kal walked along the crystalline corridors of the *Blue Phantom*, escorted by sturdy angels on all sides, he hoped this ritual of theirs would finally free his memories. Despite the dangers they mentioned, he wanted to know who he was, where he was from, and why he came. Now more than ever, he believed he had a mission of the highest importance.

As he stepped inside the glowing temple at the heart of the *Blue Phantom*, Kal marveled at the vibrations affecting his entire body. The caerulean glow, the incense, the musical harmonies, all made him feel light, uplifted, despite the trials to come.

He was gently guided to the center of the crystal cathedral. Many angels stood all around him in a wide circle. A few looked like androids made of silver and artificial fibers. They glowed from the inside.

Kal recognized Indra, standing to the side, with Panthera sitting at her feet. The lovely woman glanced at him with worry etching her face. She seemed to care about him. She shouldn't. Emotions made one weak and could muddle a mission.

The captain, a tall female angel with short blond hair, cleared her voice. "Angel Kal, you kindly agreed to go through the dangerous process of recovering your memories with our collective help. I assume you must have questions."

"My question is, what do you hope to accomplish, and how can my memories help you in any way?" Kal sensed he had a mission, but was he an angel as they believed? He possessed none of their extraordinary powers.

The captain took a slow breath. "We learned from a higher consciousness that a great evil accompanied you from a faraway universe to this one, placing ours in jeopardy."

"I come from another universe?" Kal swallowed hard. Angels did not lie. This could get complicated... and if evil came with him, deadly.

Captain Graziella cleared her throat. "It is our duty to protect this universe from evil.

We hope the information locked in your mind can help us fight that evil before it overcomes us."

Kal wanted to be on the side of good, but above all he wanted to know. "Like you I value the truth, and I very much want to remember who I am and why I came. Now, at this time, I want to help you. But when my memories are restored, if I prove to be your enemy, what will you do to me, then?"

"We are a humane culture." Captain Graziella smiled. "We do not kill individuals we can easily contain... like you."

"Good to know." Kal sighed. "Although sometimes, imprisonment can be worse than death." The frozen hells of Laxxar came to mind.

"Not here." Graziella's face softened. "We hope to discover who you work for, what your mission is, and whether or not you are a danger to us... You could be an ally, or an enemy, or possibly a timebomb rigged to explode and destroy this entire galaxy."

Holy Mandala! That was heavy. But Kal understood. "I hope I can help you. I hope to find the truth. I agree to all the risks you mentioned to me before."

"I appreciate your willingness to help us, Angel Kal." Graziella's deep blue stare pierced him to the core. "Even if you are found to be our enemy, we promise to exercise mercy."

"Thank you." Kal wanted to know the truth, whatever it may be. If he ended up being an agent of evil, he might never see Indra again. Although he could never have her, that would be a dreadful shame. He took a calming breath then nodded to the captain. "Let's get on with it."

Captain Graziella blinked. "It might help if you try to remember your past, while we join our minds to break your mental shields."

"All right." Kal closed his eyes and immediately felt his feet leaving the deck.

He was floating in midair, a curiously comfortable sensation. All around him, he heard strange vibrations, like soft music penetrating his entire body and making it vibrate. He focused on recent memories, then worked his way farther and farther into his past... like he had done many times before. But beyond his arrival on Laxxar, all he could see was blank, not even a familiar smell or sound to help him remember.

Soon, the high vibrations shook all the molecules in his body. Could it scramble his brain? He wanted to scream, but angels never screamed from pain. Only in combat, to scare their enemies. How did he know that? Had he seen combat? The captain said he was a Guardian. He'd shown unusual skills with that sword against the pirate.

The vibrations grew to an intolerable level, but Kal didn't want to stop the process. He'd accepted the risks. So, he focused as hard as he could on remembering his past, grinding his teeth not to scream.

Then complete silence. All stopped, and Kal floated, disembodied, in a state of weightlessness, amidst rainbow colors emanating from a luminous violet stone calling to him. He recognized the stone, his affinity with it. The stone was the answer. Only the violet gem could restore his memories and his angel abilities. Reunited with the stone, he would be powerful, unstoppable... Angel Guardian Kal again. But what was he guarding? Was he protecting good? Or evil forces?

He opened his eyes and the angels around him looked stunned. They glanced at him sideways, as if suspicious of him.

"Sorry, Kal." The captain bit her lips. "The angel ritual failed. Which says your mind is stronger than any we've ever met. We learned the violet stone is the answer to recovering your memories, but it will also restore your full powers, and if you are an agent of evil, it could spell annihilation for our universe."

"I understand." Kal couldn't blame them for not trusting him. "I still could be a timebomb sent to destroy your world."

"We need the information in your head to assess the threat against our universe." Captain Graziella turned to make eye contact with the angels assembled. "It's risky, but I suggest we search for the violet stone, and take precautions."

The angels murmured their assent.

Captain Graziella turned to Kal. "We should keep you in a safe place until you can be reunited with the source of your power in a neutral environment, where we can ensure the safety of this crew."

Great, another prison. Would Kal ever stop being a prisoner? Deep inside, he wanted to be free to fulfill his mission. "You mean to keep me in the brig?"

"Yes." The captain smiled sadly. "We can make it comfortable for you and allow visitors."

"I understand and I agree to help... in the name of the truth." Kal still wanted to know what he was and why he had come. No matter what. "I shall remain in your custody until my name is cleared. It's the logical course of action."

But a prison, any prison, would challenge his need for freedom. No one ever accomplished an important mission while locked up in a cell... and his mission was paramount.

Chapter Six

As she walked with Panthera loping at her side, Indra still couldn't believe Captain Graziella ordered Kal locked up in the brig. No one could read his thoughts, so they didn't trust him. What a degrading insult for an angel.

The white cat coughed. *"Panthera like Angel Kal."*

"I know you do. So do I." Fortunately, Indra was allowed to visit, without bars or glass between them, and her heart sang at the prospect of talking to him. Kal reminded her of a time when she dreamed of love and a family.

Although Kal had no memories, she found him fascinating, strong and determined, but so sexy despite his amnesia. Deep inside, she knew Kal must be good. Even without angelic powers, his true nature shone through.

Panthera rubbed her head on Indra's arm.

Indra scratched the big head then grabbed both furry cheeks. "Don't be alarmed, but in Kal's cell, we will not be able to mind speak."

"Why?" The cat's big eyes rounded.

"The cell is designed to dampen all supernatural powers... telepathic and otherwise... to prevent a gifted prisoner from escaping by using special abilities."

The cat harrumphed. *"Panthera understand."*

As they approached the brig, Indra smiled at the angel guarding the hatch. He was newer than her and took his role very seriously.

The angel nodded and opened the hatch, letting Indra and Panthera through. Then the hatch closed and locked behind them.

The inside of this cell wasn't made of crystal like the rest of the ship. The white substance lining the bulkhead emphasized the old architectural details of metal beams and bolts. Probably from the time the ship was a military destroyer in the GTA fleet.

It also radiated some strange vibrations with total lack of harmony. No one could meditate here. Indra felt heavy, like on a dense planet. The air smelled like metal. She could feel her heart working harder to pump her blood, and the ceiling seemed low, like a heavy lid. No way could she deploy her wings, dematerialize, levitate, or fly here.

Kal was doing pushups on the deck, looking so good in relaxed angel whites. He rose when he saw her. He seemed comfortable enough in his new accommodations. Rather basic, nothing like his previous quarters on the *Blue Phantom.*

Indra stepped closer, trying not to stare at the pectoral muscles bulging through his tee-shirt, his muscled arms, or the strange tattoo peeking under the short sleeve. "I assume the power-dampening aspect of this cell doesn't affect you at all... since you don't have any of your angelic abilities without your violet crystal."

"Right... assuming I ever had such abilities." He turned away to grab a towel then dried the sweat from his brow and smiled. "This unexpected visit is quite a surprise. After the memory retrieval failed, I feared everyone on this ship would want to avoid me."

Indra's heart fell. Did he think so little of her? "I would never abandon you. I know you don't deserve to be locked up like this."

"That's kind of you to say. It seems everyone else in this universe wants me in prison." He stepped up to her. "But how can you possibly know what I deserve? I don't even know what kind of man or angel I may or may not be."

She couldn't answer, entranced by his close proximity. She reached to touch his arm, but he shrank back and turned away. How frustrating.

Panthera raised her front paws and laid them on Kal's shoulders, then licked his face. Kal laughed and mussed the short fur between the cat's ears.

Panthera purred. It seemed strange not to hear her mind comments.

Indra brushed back a strand of hair that had escaped from her bun. "Is there a place to sit?"

Kal indicated the bunk. "It's the only sitting surface. Not even a bench here."

Indra sat, Kal sat next to her, and Panthera spread on the deck at their feet.

"I would offer you refreshments..." He chuckled. "But I only get food and drink at meal time." He turned away slightly, as if embarrassed by her proximity.

Indra gently turned his chin with one finger to peer into his eyes. "I'm ashamed at the captain's decision."

He bit his lips. "I agreed to it. I understand her reasons. Even I don't know if I'm good or evil."

"I know." She wanted to lose herself in his blue gaze. "Some intrinsic qualities do not lie."

"Like what?" His stare drilled through her, but he remained distant.

"I do not judge people on hearsay, but on how they behave." Indra felt so much strength in him. Why didn't he trust himself? "So far, you behaved honorably, humble and grateful, like a kind and generous person."

"Thank you for saying that." His expression softened. "Coming from you, it touches me deeply."

"Really?" Indra struggled not to hug him for fear he would shrink from her touch again. She valued his opinion so much. She wanted him to like her... and more...

As if sensing her need to touch him, Kal rose and stepped away from the bunk. "So, what do you think of my new living quarters?" His hand-wave encompassed the entire space. "I understand even the strongest angels have no powers here."

"True." Indra chuckled. "No flying, no invisibility, no dematerializing or rematerializing in or out, no reading or influencing minds, no powers of any kind, and absolutely no possible communication through the shielded bulkhead."

Kal nodded, as if assimilating the information... like a spy or a soldier would. "Does it mean this cell is not monitored... and whatever we say or do here remains our secret?"

Indra felt heat creeping up her neck. What she wanted to say and do to Kal wasn't exactly forbidden on the *Blue Phantom*, but other angels might frown upon it. "As long as we remain here, our thoughts and actions remain private. But when I leave, if anyone asks, I am bound to tell the truth."

"Bummer." He narrowed his eyes at her. "Do angels often ask personal questions?"

"Not usually, no." Indra smiled. "We respect others' privacy and never read each other's thoughts without consent. It's considered bad manners. That's how we keep harmony among the crew."

"Yet, you tried to read my thoughts without asking first..." His light teasing tone accused her.

Indra felt herself blush. "I'm sorry. I'm impulsive and I was curious."

"That's quite all right. I do understand." He nodded. "How about security devices... cameras, recorders of any kind?"

Was he fishing for information? She didn't care. "Angels don't need such low-tech devices, since they can focus and see and hear and instantly know anything they need to know..."

"Well, except what happens in this cell." A slight blush flared on Kal's cheeks.

"Yes. Nothing said here leaves this cell." She flashed a devilish smile. "But primitive recording devices don't work on the *Blue Phantom* anyway. The crystal disables them by draining their power packs."

"Yet, you have android angels." He paced the cell. "They must have a personal power source, and a compatible technology. How do they function?"

Indra hesitated. This was secret angel knowledge. Why was he asking so many questions? Then she remembered when she first came aboard the *Blue Phantom*. She, too, had lots of questions. "The androids have crystal brains and hearts."

"Really?" He turned his face to her with intense interest.

"The crystal gives them life and provides an unlimited power source." Indra swallowed hard. She hoped she wasn't leaking secrets to the enemy. "They are also in constant communication with the

Formless One, which makes them incorruptible."

Kal whistled. "Impressive. Anything else I should know about the angels of this universe?"

"Angels are quasi-immortal… they never grow old." Indra liked that part. "They are also difficult to kill, as their resilient bodies heal fast."

"What about weaknesses? Do they have any?" No apparent malice in the question, only curiosity.

Indra should not be so suspicious. "Yes. Away from the crystal, we lose our abilities and gradually return to a regular, mortal, biologic state."

"What do you mean?" He frowned. "The crystal is what gives you powers? Weren't you born an angel?"

"No one was ever born an angel. Prolonged exposure to the crystal makes the angels sterile. And a pregnant woman would likely die giving birth on this ship." Indra shuddered at the thought.

"Holy Mandala! Until now, I barely noticed it, but I saw no children on this ship." He gazed into her eyes. "No loving families, no pets, only tough angels."

The thought made Indra sad. "This used to be a military vessel and still functions like one."

He shook his head. "Yet, somehow, you do not strike me as a soldier."

"I am not." Indra couldn't believe she was telling him that. "I never was."

He snorted. "So, if none of you were born angels, where do angels come from?"

She took his hand and held on to it when he tried to pull it back. "We all come from different walks of life. Exposure to the crystal made us angels."

"Holy Mandala!" His eyes rounded in amazement.

"And you probably became an angel the same way." She let that sink in.

He paused and his eyes blinked a few times. "So, anyone exposed to the crystal eventually becomes an angel? No exceptions?"

"Right. Each of us, at one point, faced a life-changing choice. We dedicated ourselves to maintaining the balance of good and evil in the universe." Indra wasn't certain she'd make the same decision today. She missed her friends, her family. She longed for a loving partner, children of her own.

"So, you believe it might be the same with me and the violet crystal." Kal rubbed his smooth chin. "If I had angel powers once, when separated from the crystal, I would have lost those powers."

"Exactly." She watched the understanding washing over his face. "And if you were an angel, even an evil one, your crystal probably made you sterile as well... as long as you were exposed."

"Me, sterile? That would explain a lot." His blue eyes widened. "What happens when angels are no longer exposed? Do the reproductive functions resume as the angelic abilities fade away?"

"That's what I've been told." Indra wanted to tell him so much more, but hesitated. "Listen. I know the captain promised to show mercy if you turn up to be evil... and she will. She is Graziella the Merciful."

"But?" His eyes narrowed. "I feel a *but* coming."

"She may not have a choice." Indra felt guilty about betraying her kind, but Kal didn't deserve to die. "The androids among the crew are ruthless. They have no empathy and show no mercy when it comes to evil. They might kill you against the captain's orders if they deem it necessary."

"Thanks for the warning..." He bit his lips, deep in thought. "Although, at this point, I'm not sure I can use it."

"Kal, I care about you." Why did she tell him her deepest secret? Did he have power over her? Even in this cell? "I don't want you to die."

"I know. I don't want to lose you either..." He froze as if he'd said too much. "But I no longer have a choice. I let myself be locked up for the greater good. I am now a prisoner, powerless over my destiny."

"Not necessarily." Indra couldn't believe what she was about to propose, but she always followed her gut... and her heart. "What if I gave you another option?"

"What option?" Kal glanced all around as if expecting guards to burst through the hatch. "I'm listening."

"What if you renounced your memories? Forget about your past, renounce your lost angel powers, forget the violet crystal. You and I could escape this ship together and make a life for ourselves, far from here... I happen to know a hospitable planet, that of the Anvad, my own people. The Land of Many Waters."

"Are you a rebellious angel? This is wrong! What you propose is forbidden, and shameful." Kal frowned. "I thought all angels were of the same mind. Why would you defect? Why defy your captain?"

"Maybe I care too much about you." Indra felt heat on her cheeks. "Or maybe, I do not deserve to be an angel."

"Don't say that." He shook his head and walked away. "You are the embodiment of good."

"Yet, I never felt like a true angel." Indra sighed. "Often, I think I'd rather live a short, ordinary life, with a loving mate... and start a family."

Panthera rubbed her head against Indra's knees, purring like a kitten. Although the white cat couldn't mind speak, she seemed to understand everything.

Indra held her breath. Did she dare to propose her half-baked scheme? "I know it sounds shocking, but I don't care what you were before. I just want you to be safe and happy. We could have a wonderful life together, away from all this turmoil."

Kal sighed. "I could never imagine myself as a family man."

Indra's heart dropped like a rock. "Why not?"

"I have a mission." Kal shook his head. "Would you be happy abandoning your duty? Knowing that you selfishly left your brethren in a time of danger? Would you let them fight to protect this universe while you fool yourself into thinking you are happy?"

"Maybe not. But I'm not much help here." Still, Indra felt guilty. "But I want you to live. I couldn't stand to see you die."

"Indra... you must understand that my mission comes first." Kal's eyes softened with so much compassion. "That's why I shall accept your offer to help. But although I care about you, I cannot run away with you. I must live and fight evil, and I can't do it from this cell."

"You care about me?" Indra's heart sang. She held on to the hope they might run away together. "I can get you out of here."

"But if I escape, I must go alone..." He stared deep into her eyes.

Indra wasn't sure how she felt about letting him leave without her. "Promise you will come back for me after all this is over."

"I promise." He softly kissed the top of her head. "Help me escape, alone, and when this crisis is over and I know who I am, I'll come back, and we shall discuss the future together."

"Yes!" Indra's heart beat faster. There was hope.

Panthera rubbed her head against Kal's knee.

Indra hugged Kal and kissed his cheeks, relishing the heat of his body burning through her. "Thank you. I shall help you escape."

He didn't resist the hug, but soon held her away from his body. "What about the consequences for you? You cannot keep secrets from the other angels. They'll know you broke me out of jail."

"Don't worry about me. I'll be fine." Indra hoped so. "Angels don't punish each other like regular people. I'll probably have to isolate myself and meditate all day for weeks, to re-align my energy with the Formless One."

"That's it? Are you sure?" Kal narrowed his eyes at her.

"Certain." Indra felt abandoned when he let go of her. She blew him a kiss. "Be ready tomorrow when I visit again. I have a plan, and all will be in place by then."

She couldn't resist rushing back to him. She hugged him again, briefly, finding new strength and hope in the wonderful feeling of being in his arms. For now, it would have to suffice.

"Come, Panthera. We have work to do."

The large feline rose on all fours and stretched, then followed her to the hatch.

Breaking the rules made her feel so alive... Indra nodded at the angel guard who opened then closed the hatch behind her, glad angels respected each other's private thoughts. She also hoped she wasn't being manipulated by an agent of evil.

* * *

Kal paced his cell, listening to any sound signaling Indra's visit. He hoped she didn't place herself in real danger. He wasn't familiar with the ship's rules, but he suspected acting against the captain's orders might carry a severe sentence. He wished he could take her with him, but it was too dangerous. Besides, she was too distracting and blurred the lines of propriety for him.

Since he'd learned about the violet crystal, Kal couldn't stop thinking about it. His release couldn't come fast enough. He would find his stolen gem, retrieve his memories, and fulfill his mission... whatever it may be. Some innate sense of duty pulled at his gut. He must resolve his important business as soon as possible. It felt as if the fate of the universe depended upon it.

When the hatch opened, Indra stepped into his cell brandishing a piece of pipe. "Come quick, hurry." Red-faced, wide-eyed, she sounded excited and out of breath. "The guard isn't going to stay down for long."

As if some former training took over his body, Kal rushed out through the hatch.

Panthera greeted him profusely. *"Panthera like Angel Kal."*

But there was no time to waste. Kal knelt and checked the guard's neck for a pulse, to ascertain he was still alive. Then he unhooked the guard's blue sword and tucked it into his own belt.

Indra stared at him. "Stealing from an angel?"

He patted the sword. "A good weapon is always handy."

Indra seized his arm and Panthera's neck. "Ready?"

Kal felt a familiar tingle as his scrambled molecules disintegrated then reconstituted in a different part of the *Blue Phantom*. "Holy Mandala!"

Indra reached to stabilize him. "Are you okay? Most people get a little sick."

"I'm fine." Kal kept perfect balance. He looked around in amazement. He stood in an enormous hangar bay where many luminescent ships stood in neat rows, clamped to the deck. "Are these combat flyers? I didn't realize the *Blue Phantom* was such an enormous vessel."

"It used to be a military destroyer with an entire fleet of stingers." She sounded proud.

"Do they still work?" They looked well maintained.

"Not only do they work, but they have been upgraded to use blue crystal as a power source. They have invisibility cloaks, crystal-powered weapons, and if need be, they can be remotely piloted from the command center."

Kal whistled. "Remind me not to piss off the angels of this universe... although it might already be too late."

"Don't worry. This way." She marched ahead toward the parked birds.

Kal followed Indra and Panthera along rows of small flyers, trying not to focus on her lovely figure. A larger triangular vessel stood up from the other ships, a luminous raptor of advanced design, with a battery of impressive weapons. The name on the side said *PRISM*.

The belly ramp was down. Indra pointed to it. "*Prism*. That's the one."

As she hugged him, he felt guilty for enjoying it. Her hair smelled of cherry blossoms. "Thank you for all you did for me."

She tilted her head to kiss him, but as much as he wanted to, he pulled away. Strange how she affected him.

She chuckled. "You better hurry."

"Right." Kal stepped onto the ramp then turned back to carve the picture of Indra in his memory. It was better that way. He might never see her again, and something told him he wouldn't be good at relationships anyway.

Still, she looked so lovely, standing there on the deck of the bay, holding Panthera by the neck. She didn't seem sad. Strange. She had soft, liquid blue eyes, and a smile to light up any spirit. As if sadness could never touch her.

The thought he might die on his mission and never see her again saddened him.

He hesitated. "How do you pilot that thing?"

She smiled. "The ship is intuitive. Talk to it, or visualize where you want to go, and it will take you there."

"Sounds easy enough." But flying away from Indra would not be. Kal steeled his resolve. The mission was everything. "I should be fine. I didn't have any problem piloting a raptor when I escaped from Laxxar."

Indra waved. "Go, now. Before the other angels find out you escaped your cell."

Kal waved back. "Farewell."

"We'll see each other again, soon." She blew him a kiss.

Then Indra and Panthera vanished from the bay.

Kal remembered the general layout of a raptor from his previous experience and took the spiral stairs up to the command deck. Time to be the Angel Guardian Indra believed him to be. "Close the ramp, open the bay doors, unclamp this raptor from the deck, and fly far from here, out of radar range."

"Aye, aye, Captain," the ship computer answered in a soft feminine voice.

Once in deep space, invisible to radar scans, Kal would decide where to search for his violet crystal. He hoped his affinity with it would guide him toward the rare gem. Or, maybe, there was a quicker way.

"Computer, search all the databases for the recent mention of a violet crystal in this quadrant."

"I am not exactly a dumb computer, but I can search." The feminine voice dripped with disdain.

Great. A computer with an attitude. "Whatever are you, then?"

"I am a highly evolved artificial intelligence. I am the soul of this ship. You may call me Prism."

"Prism? Like this ship?" Kal sighed. "All right. I'll try to remember that." Now he had to deal with a self-aware ship computer with a chip on its shoulder.

"Searching... searching... searching..."

* * *

Dominara Azfet caressed her red gem and relaxed on her chaise, enjoying the luxury of her private temple. Bas-reliefs depicted her heroic battles, tales of her incredible feats told in hieroglyphics on white pillars. Everything around her screamed divinity. She was a goddess, adored and worshipped. And soon this entire universe would be at her feet.

Azfet smiled as she focused on the vision. The red gem hanging between her breasts pulsed warmly, making her feel powerful. There... she could feel Kal but couldn't see him. He had escaped the angel ship and was searching for the violet crystal. Good.

His natural affinity with the stone should guide him back to Spartacus, and Zethar would be waiting for him. Before Kal could reach his prize, Zethar would capture him, enslave him, contain him.

Azfet wished she could kill the Guardian herself, but it would be too dangerous for her to be in his vicinity. Besides, all the bounty hunters she'd sicced upon him had failed. It seemed, in this universe Kal might be unkillable. So, she must rely on Zethar to hold him for her.

She focused on her unwilling partner. "Zethar, you should know that your infamous escapee ran away from the *Blue Phantom* and will soon find his way to you."

Zethar's hologram squinted at her. "Why would he do such a stupid thing?"

"You ask too many questions, Zethar. Just be warned, and be ready. I'm counting on you to catch him and keep him effectively contained this time."

"He already escaped from Laxxar and from Pandemonium. What makes you think he won't escape again?" Zethar paced his office, caressing the shiny metal plates on his skull. The man didn't like to lose. "How can

I contain him when angels want to steal him?”

“I know how to make a cell impervious to angelic powers and interference…” Azfet let her voice trail for dramatic effect. “I could share that technology with you.”

“Really?” Zethar’s eyes remained doubtful. “That would be handy against meddling angels.”

“Wouldn’t it be?” Azfet rejoiced. He was taking the bribe. “Think about it… no more angels thwarting your lucrative business…”

Zethar’s calculating eyes blinked. “But why would I want to oblige you? You are a liar and a manipulator. You could be lying to me right now.”

“I’ll take that as a compliment.” She lay back on her chaise and batted her eyelashes for dramatic effect. “But since I want Kal contained, it’s also in my interest to share that secret with you. Besides, I’ll pay you a king’s ransom to do it.”

“Well, you are lucky I want that bastard captured for making me look like a fool.” Zethar grunted. “But it’s the last favor I do for you, Highness. You have too many secrets, and I suspect powers far beyond mine. Helping you further might eventually become detrimental to my health.”

“Oh, Zethar, I would never harm you. You are such a handsome man… and a useful ally.” She infused her voice with seductive wiles.

"Flattery won't work with me, Highness." Zethar scrutinized her. "Why don't you come in person and help me with this? You almost seem like a shadow. Are you even a real person, or the empty mask of a galactic corporation?"

"Of course, I am a real person. But you'll understand if I prefer not to be directly involved in suspiciously illegal business." Azfet smiled mysteriously. Zethar had no clue how dangerous Kal was to her and she wanted to keep it that way.

"I see." Zethar sighed. "All right. Send me the specifications for that special jail, and I'll take care of your dirty business for you."

"Much obliged." She let go of her blood stone, and the hologram of Zethar vanished.

She rose and walked along the aisle of golden Sphynxes to clear her mind. Zethar was a ruthless gangster and didn't need to know all the details. She also failed to mention the violet crystal on his beast's collar could be detrimental to her health. She'd gotten a little too close to it, once, and it burned her, badly. She caressed her shoulder in remembrance of the pain.

She hated that crystal. The rare stone came from her universe... also Kal's universe... the place that had condemned her to eternal hell. She shuddered at the memory.

But she had escaped that hell. Now, she was free in a new universe, where her abilities were unmatched, and she could play and rule, and wreak havoc unhindered.

She hoped Zethar was up to the task of containing Kal and his infernal violet stone, because she liked it here, and she refused to go back to hell.

Chapter Seven

Kal sighed with relief and relaxed in the pilot seat. Through the bay window of the command deck, he could see black space and billions of stars. He was free, on a fully armed and untraceable ship, in deep space, away from any prison. And although he didn't remember being an angel, evil or otherwise, logic dictated he must have been one, with an important mission to boot.

Some notion burned deep into his brain kept telling him to complete his mission. Then, maybe, he could retire from the fighting. If he survived... Indra came to his mind. What a lovely possibility, but not for him.

"Computer, any luck in locating the violet crystal?" Kal hoped the gem would restore his memories, as the angels believed.

"No mention of such a crystal so far, Captain." The feminine voice sounded upset. "And please, call me Prism."

"Sorry, Prism. I'll remember next time." When did ship computers get so sensitive? "Well, Prism... keep searching."

"Searching... searching..."

Something deep inside told Kal he must hurry. Only when reunited with the violet stone would he be whole again... be whatever he was supposed to be. Good or evil, or anything in between, it didn't matter. He needed to be himself again, but the road to his crystal might require fighting.

In order to be ready for a combat situation, he would need armor, blasters, and blades. Although the blue sword glowing at his side would be his favorite. Smart of him to snatch it from the guard in the brig of the *Blue Phantom.* Although Indra did not approve of theft.

While Prism located his crystal, maybe Kal could practice his sword.

He could also ask the moody computer to take an inventory of his resources, but better not interrupt its search for the crystal. This was a large enough ship with sophisticated weaponry, many compartments to store supplies, weapons, and other things. So, he decided to explore.

Like the raptor in which he'd escaped Laxxar, the triangular ship had three decks. The top command deck offered a clear view of space, a pilot chair crew stations, and weapons control. Kal took the spiral stairs down. Ignoring the middle deck, with the crew quarters and the galley, he headed below, to the largest cargo hold on the bottom level.

Various metallic crates, stacked neatly and held by straps, showed side labels identifying the contents in galactic standard. A vague memory flashed in his mind, of being bent over galactic standard writings, deciphering them as an alien language. Had he been raised speaking another tongue? Most likely.

The side labels on the crates said clothing, food rations. He suspected angel rations would be plant based, but might taste better than the military kind. How did he know what military rations tasted like? Had he been a soldier? In what army? The strange tattoo on his arm could be military. Maybe later, he'd ask Prism to search for similar symbols in this universe.

None of the labels mentioned armor, gear, or weapons. What a disappointment. Did angels not use weapons? If they adapted a ship to work on crystal energy, why not blasters and explosives?

Maybe the weaponry was stored in another hold.

A subtle sound set his senses on alert, but he didn't freeze. Doing so would betray his awareness to an observing intruder. There shouldn't be anyone onboard. Did some robot or piece of machinery get activated by accident? Kal didn't believe in accidents... or coincidences. Everything happened for a reason. Did his training cause him to question everything?

Slowly, with measured movements, Kal inventoried the crates, reading the labels while listening for any sign of an intruder. Now, he felt the unmistakable pinpoint burning sensation on the back of his neck... someone was watching him.

His body went into infiltrator mode. Did he used to be an angel spy? He casually slipped behind a tower of crates, pulled out his glowing sword and peeked around the corner to see who was watching him. He saw no one.

But angels could make themselves invisible. And if some angel had boarded the raptor in the bay of the *Blue Phantom,* or manifested in flight, the intruder would have powers of invisibility. Did the angels discover Indra's scheme? Did they send someone to kill him?

Kal walked away from the hiding crates, brandishing his sword, facing the direction of the perceived intruder. "I know you are here. Show yourself, or forever be known as a coward."

Someone gasped. A faint trace of floral scent teased Kal's nostrils. Cherry blossoms?

Marching toward the sound, he thrust his sword forward. "Show yourself now!"

"All right, all right." A familiar feminine voice echoed against the bulkhead of the cargo hold.

"Indra?" His heart skipped a beat. He didn't want her in the path of danger.

Before his eyes, the beautiful woman took shape, and descended to the deck, folding her majestic white wings. Panthera appeared at her side.

Kal released a slow breath in an attempt to contain his frustration. "What are you doing here? It's unsafe. You shouldn't be here!"

"I know. I know." Her disarming smile melted his anger.

"You can't stay here." His attempt to sound stern failed. "You must go back to the *Blue Phantom*."

"I'm not going back." The lovely woman planted her hands on her hips. "I can't let you go alone into a dangerous situation. I want to fight evil, too. You need me and Panthera at your side. Let's face it. Without powers or memories, you are helpless as a babe."

"Helpless?" Kal felt many things, but helpless was never one of them.

"Panthera like Angel Kal. Panthera help." The calm feminine voice of the white feline surged in his mind. At least, he could trust the cat. Animals never lied.

Indra walked toward the crates he'd been inspecting. "What are you looking for?"

"Anything useful in a fight." He couldn't stop staring at her... and imagining her naked. He shook away the forbidden thoughts. Back to reality. Did she come as a friend? Or was she tasked to help him escape then kill him? "I was hoping for blasters, armor, explosives..."

"You won't find any of these here... but I can help." Indra was probably more qualified to find what he needed quickly.

Kal couldn't afford to trust her, but he could never harm her. "Don't angels use blasters? That would be handy."

"Blasters are for savages." She chuckled. "But I'll find something you can use."

Did she think of him as a savage? "I'm going back upstairs to search for my crystal. Let me know if you find anything useful."

"Aye, aye, Captain." Indra gave him a mock military salute... so cute... and possibly lethal.

He shrugged and forced himself to look away and walk toward the spiral stairs. What in the frozen hells of Laxxar would he do with her? He didn't want to kill her or face her as an enemy.

He didn't want her as a partner in a fight either. He'd worry about her getting hurt... and she was too distracting... especially when he imagined her without clothes. He shook himself and swept the image of her perfect skin away from his mind.

"*Panthera help Angel Kal.*" The feline loped toward him and followed him up the stairs.

Kal took the steps two at a time. "Prism? Any luck finding mentions of the violet crystal?"

"Not yet, Captain... still searching..."

Kal sat in the command chair, watching the search scrolling at a fast pace on several screens.

The big cat lay down under his feet. "*Panthera see violet crystal.*"

"You saw it? You know where it is?" Kal stared down at the big cat with renewed respect.

"Panthera know where, Panthera know who." The cat snorted.

"You know who has it?" How could Panthera know such a thing? But animals did not lie. Her information had always been reliable.

The big cat purred. *"Panthera feel Spartacus."*

"Spartacus?" Strange name. A gladiator? "Who is he? Where is he?"

"Pandemonium. With Lord Zethar." The big cat grunted in disgust. *"Panthera not like Lord Zethar."*

Who could blame her? "I don't like Zethar either."

The cat growled her assent.

"Prism? Find Pandemonium and set a new course."

"Aye, aye, Captain." Prism beeped then the screens indicated the new destination.

Kal settled in his chair. He didn't relish the thought of confronting Zethar, but he might have to. If this Spartacus was on Pandemonium with his crystal, Kal would soon know who he was before his mind wipe. Since there were no coincidences, the universe wanted him to complete his mission. He must remember what it was.

He just hoped he could keep Indra safe.

* * *

Indra wondered if she'd done the right thing. Helping Kal might have been a mistake. What if he were in league with evil, and turned against her when he retrieved his memories? She stepped onto the command deck holding an armful of blades, bows, and arrows.

She set the weapons on the console in front of Kal. "I wasn't sure what you can operate. Do you have any military training?"

"Probably, but I can't tell you for certain." Kal stared at the hoard. "That's all you found?"

Indra wouldn't let him mock the angels. "There are angel weapons, but you don't have the abilities required to wield them."

Kal patted the blue sword at his belt. "Judging from my previous skirmish with pirates, I'm sure I can use this quite effectively."

How overconfident of him. "The angel sword is used as a conduit to expand energy in battle... not to slash or stab, like a traditional blade. I don't think you have the ability to use it correctly."

Kal bit his lips as if she'd insulted him. "Don't worry. I'll be fine in a fight."

Indra chuckled. "Yes. Like the time I had to rescue you from a cage on Pandemonium... after the pirates left you for dead."

Kal cast her a sideways glance. "I may or may not have had training, but I know how to fight. What about you? Did you train to be a warrior since childhood?"

"No. I never was a fighter." She sighed. "But I had some training on the *Blue Phantom*. Every angel onboard needs to train for battle."

He narrowed his eyes. "So... where were you before? How and when did you get aboard the *Blue Phantom*?"

Indra sat next to him and turned her seat to face him. "Three cycles ago, I was an Anvad travelling on a freighter full of refugees. We were attacked by Marauders then rescued by the *Blue Phantom*. Its captain at the time demanded a price in lives. Five of us for saving the lives of five thousand."

Kal whistled. "Holy Mandala! So, that's what you meant when you talked about compensation for being saved? I thought that was strange. What's the price of my rescue?"

"I'm not the one to decide, but there is always a price." Indra hoped it would keep him close to her.

Kal frowned. "I can't afford to serve on the *Blue Phantom*. I have my own mission to complete... as soon as I remember what it is."

"If you don't know what it is, don't worry about it." She hoped he'd change his mind about that mission. "Things have a way of falling into place in harmony with the universe."

"Easy for you to say, but I know what you mean." Kal scratched the dark stubble on his head. A very handsome head. "So why were your people refugees?"

Indra felt nostalgic, remembering the Anvad, her family, her culture. "The totalitarian galactic regime took over our planet, slaughtered our aristocracy, and most of our people. The survivors were forced to flee."

He raised his brow. "People in this galaxy still let aristocracy rule?"

"In our case, the royal family carried the blood of our ancient goddess, Helsara." The memory of togetherness brought tears to her eyes.

His finger moved toward her face, as if to wipe her tear, but quickly withdrew. "By what miracle were you placed in my path?"

Indra swallowed her sadness. "It's no miracle. It's the blue crystal."

He squinted at her. "How so?"

"It carries the will and the power of the Formless One. It gives us the strength to fight evil. It guides us to do the right thing." Yet, Indra didn't feel worthy of being an angel... she'd just disobeyed her captain and broken many angel rules.

Kal shook his head. "Good thing I left the *Blue Phantom*. In order to complete my mission, I cannot be subject to an unknown influence like the blue crystal. I wouldn't be myself, and it would compromise my work."

Indra managed a sad smile. "I wish there were no conflicts, no battles, no evil. We could just run away together to the Land of Many Waters and be happy there together." She gazed into his blue eyes. "I hope we can go there, when your mission is finished."

Kal's expression hardened, and he turned away from her gaze. "Sorry. I can't make any promises. My mission comes first and should be my only concern."

She reached for his arm, enjoying the tingling contact. "But you would like to elope with me, wouldn't you?"

He pulled his arm away. "There is no point in dreaming of what can never be. I must remain focused. You should have stayed on the Blue *Phantom*. Your presence here is too much of a distraction."

Hiding her hurt at the rejection, Indra forced a smile. "If I'm such a distraction, it means that you care about me... a lot."

The computer beeped. "Getting closer to Pandemonium, Captain."

"Pandemonium? Why didn't you tell me?" Indra felt betrayed. "That's a horrible place. Why go there?"

"I didn't tell you because you snuck in as a stowaway." He scoffed. "Besides, it was Panthera's idea. Pandemonium is where my violet crystal is located. I need it to recover my memories."

"Your crystal is there?" So, Panthera had secrets, too. "It would be nice to be part of this team."

"I'm sorry. I didn't realize we were a team." He cast her a slanted glance. "Are you certain you want to be part of this? I don't even know if I'm an agent of good or evil. There is no telling what I'll do when I get my memories back."

"You should have more confidence in your goodness, Kal. I can't read your mind, but I believe you are a good person." She sighed. "You can't fake being a good person."

"Good for you to be sure, but I'm not." Kal shook his head.

"Whatever. I refuse to let that ruin my day." Despite the frustrating fact that she couldn't read Kal's mind, Indra trusted him. "Well, since I can't convince you to give up your mission, I might as well help you finish it, so we can enjoy the rest of our lives... together."

"What you propose is impossible." He turned away from her.

Indra sighed. She wanted to remain positive. And in the back of her mind, she hoped she wasn't aiding and abetting an agent of evil.

Chapter Eight

In her lavish temple, Azfet relaxed on the white chaise as she peered through her blood crystal pendant and rejoiced. Here. She could see the invisible ship, a stolen raptor carrying the fugitives. Her nemesis had two acolytes, a female angel and a white feline. Invisible to most, the *Prism* was speeding toward Pandemonium in full stealth mode... straight toward the violet crystal. Perfect.

She was well inspired to commission one of her minions to set the crystal into a collar for Spartacus. Manipulating Zethar to adopt the cat had been easy. The violet stone would never fail to attract her nemesis, and with her help, the crime lord could keep him contained.

If only she could have Kal terminated... but all previous attempts by mortals had failed. And she couldn't risk getting close to him... or to the violet crystal. Both, especially together, could possibly kill her. That would ruin everything.

She hadn't escaped hell and come all this way from another universe to die like a simple mortal. After ages and ages of suffering in hell, Azfet would have her happy forever after. A reward of immense power, unlimited pleasures, and license to kill whenever it pleased her. She would be the goddess of chaos… again.

But right now, she must set her trap to neutralize her nemesis. She laid the red crystal gently between her breasts and waved her hand, as she mentally navigated through the cyber security of Pandemonium, and breached their communication system.

An image of Zethar appeared in a 3D hologram. He was rather handsome despite all the hardware, but she didn't feel anything for such a lowly minion. He seemed startled by her intrusion and winced.

Azfet made her voice suggestive and spread on the charm. "Still looking for our fugitive, Zethar?"

The beast next to him roared and the stone on his harness flared. Azfet could tell Spartacus was developing supernatural abilities from the violet crystal. Good. It would make the feline powerful, invincible even to an angel. The perfect protector for such an important gem. No one should be allowed to wield it.

Zethar frowned his discontent.

Azfet chuckled. "What's the matter Zethar? Did Spartacus refuse to share his knowledge of your prisoner's whereabouts? Cats can be stubborn that way."

"Enough!" Zethar's clenched jaw and the intensity of his stare indicated he was ready to explode. "Are you going to tell me where my escapee is or not?"

"Oh, Zethar. I am not that bad." She caressed the bare skin of her exposed breasts but the man didn't even seem to notice. How annoying. "I'm on your side... and willing to share. I just told you he was on his way."

Zethar slammed his fist on his desk. "Then, where is he exactly? And don't speak in riddles."

"I won't." Azfet reclined on her white chaise, stretching one long leg through the high slit of her red gown, hiding her irritation under a seductive smile. "He is now aboard the *Prism*, an angel raptor speeding toward Pandemonium as we speak."

Zethar frowned. "Again, why would he come back here? An angel freed him from the menagerie as he was gravely wounded, and about to be thrown to the beasts in the arena. He was free and hidden by the *Blue Phantom*. Why risk getting caught again? It makes no sense at all."

"I'm telling the truth. Our escapee must have his reasons." But she wouldn't tell Zethar it was the violet stone. "The *Prism* is invisible to radars, as it hails from the *Blue Phantom*, but I can tell you how to detect it... and how to trap it."

Zethar narrowed his greedy eyes at her. "What's the catch?"

"No catch." She stretched her arms, languorously. "I can also tell you he has a female angel and a large cat onboard."

Spartacus growled. *"Panthera coming. Panthera close."*

"See?" Azfet winked. "I can tell you how to trap angels and hold them in a jail engineered to neutralize their supernatural abilities."

Zethar's cold eyes widened at the prospect. He was hooked. "But will you?"

"Of course, I will... You and I want that prisoner contained. We are a team." Azfet rose and paced the stone deck along the bas-reliefs depicting ancient battles. She swayed her hips for good measure.

But Zethar didn't seem to notice.

How frustrating. "I will also tell you that our fugitive is attracted to the female angel traveling with him, and that makes both of them vulnerable. I suggest you keep them together in captivity."

She didn't tell him Kal used to be an angel. The crime lord didn't need to know. No one in this universe should know how powerful Kal could be if reunited with the violet crystal.

Zethar clenched his jaw. "Are you the one who gifted Spartacus his collar?"

"Absolutely not. I do not value wild animals." She sighed. "I believe the collar came from an anonymous admirer." The man didn't need to know she had contracted that eccentric of many talents to act on her behalf.

"That's what I was told." Zethar didn't seem convinced. He cast her a sideway glance. "How do you know so much about neutralizing angels?"

"It's not my first encounter with their kind." She smiled seductively. The angels of this universe were meeker, kinder, and easier to fool than the shrewd, hard-core Angel Guardians of the place from which she came.

She shuddered at the recollection. Once an Angel Guardian, as she hid among them, she'd rebelled against the ridiculous rules. She was a happy maverick, a chaos junkie, sex junkie, everything junkie. She enjoyed life to the fullest.

But the Angel Guardians of her world had no tolerance for her shenanigans. They forced her into the very pit of despair, stripped away her powers, and made her suffer. She would never return to that hellish prison.

And she wouldn't let a single Angel Guardian get in the way of her new conquest. With her powers back tenfold, thanks to her new lover, in a weak universe with soft rules, she could now live the life she craved, powerful and worshipped. This universe would be hers... starting with this galaxy.

Zethar cleared his throat. "So, how do I trap this angel raptor, and how do I build a jail to neutralize angel powers?"

The question brought Azfet back to the task at hand. "Simple. All you have to do is..."

Aboard the *Prism*, Indra bit her tongue as she observed Kal, calm and collected in his pilot seat. He kept secrets from her. Why?

She leaned against the backrest. "Sounds dangerous to return to Pandemonium, after they put you in that cage. They would have fed you to the cats if I hadn't intervened."

"That's a risk I have to take." Kal's brow furrowed, making him look resolute. "I must retrieve my crystal. It's the key to my memories... I need them to fulfill my mission."

"Some mission. You don't even know what it is." Indra didn't like the risks. But despite his secrets, she didn't want to lose Kal. "What if they recapture you?"

"Easy." He offered a nervous smile. "I didn't plan on it, but since you joined me onboard, I'm bringing an angel to get me out of a tight spot."

Indra shook her head. "We are far away from the *Blue Phantom*. My abilities might fade."

He turned and frowned at her. "What do you mean, fade?"

"Yes." She sighed, wondering how much to tell him. After all, what if he were an agent of evil? "Away from the crystal core that powers the *Blue Phantom*, I may lose my abilities over time."

"How much time?" His blue eyes widened.

"I don't know." Indra couldn't lie, but she didn't want to say too much. "Since I boarded the *Blue Phantom*, I've never been away from it for a long time."

"But there is crystal on the *Prism*, too, isn't there?" Kal scanned the bulkhead. "Isn't it what makes it glow?"

"Yes." Indra took a deep breath. "There is a miniscule crystal core, and the bulkheads glow, but they only contain infinitesimal traces of crystal. It may not be strong enough to maintain my abilities."

The white cat head-bumped Indra's hand. *"Panthera protect."*

"Thank you, sweet girl." Indra scratched the cat between the ears.

Panthera purred under her ministrations.

Kal straightened in his seat, stared into nothingness, and his handsome face filled with awe. "I can feel it. I can sense it. My violet crystal is close. I feel stronger."

Indra chuckled. "Easy, big guy. You are not invincible. No angel is."

Panthera straightened her head and her round ears perked up. *"Panthera feel Spartacus."*

"Spartacus? The guy close to Zethar, who has my crystal?" Kal frowned. "Who is he?"

The big cat licked her paw. *"Panthera not tell. Panthera protect."*

Kal cast Indra a questioning gaze. "Do you know who she's talking about?"

"I do." Indra chuckled. "But I won't tell either. It's a secret between girls. Right, Panthera?"

The cat snorted in agreement.

"I thought angels never lied or kept secrets." Kal sounded frustrated.

"I'm not lying. There are just things girls do not share with boys." Indra enjoyed the reversal. Let him see what it felt like not to know what she thought.

The *Prism* bucked, jolting its occupants. Panthera planted her claws into the soft decking.

Indra braced herself in her seat, heart pounding. "What happened?"

"I have nothing on scanners, except Pandemonium a few klicks away, but they shouldn't be able to detect us." Kal stared at the screens. "I don't see anything amiss but we are stuck. Computer, report."

"I am not a computer. I am a sophisticated AI with more abilities than most biological entities!"

"Sorry, Prism. Why did we stop? Why aren't the controls responding?" Kal's voice sharpened. Was he scared?

The computer chimed. "It appears I have been taken over by an external force, Captain. Unable to shake the hold, unable to correct the problem. I shall follow hostile takeover procedures and sever myself from the main drive."

The lights flickered, died, then returned.

"Prism? What do you mean?" Kal's voice strangled.

No response. Indra shuddered. This couldn't be good. She also felt woozy.

"Great!" Kal shook his head. "I can't believe that stupid computer turns itself off at the first sign of a problem."

"I don't understand this either." Indra tried to make herself invisible but couldn't. "My abilities are gone... but I don't think it's natural. I feel something choking my powers."

"It seems we are moving again." Kal punched keys and swiped his console. "But I have no control. We are going straight for the Pandemonium space station."

Panic threatened to rob Indra of her usual calm. "Probably a tractor beam. But how did they spot us in stealth mode?"

"I don't know." Kal's jaw clenched. "I see no vessel in close proximity, but this is definitely a hostile takeover."

Indra couldn't shake the cold dread invading her. "There is a strong power at work. I feel like I'm sinking in molasses. I don't understand what's happening and I can't fight it."

Panthera growled. *"Highness very dangerous. Spartacus say Highness help Zethar."*

"Highness?" Kal's eyes narrowed as if the title startled him. "Who is that?"

"Panthera not know. Panthera weak. Not speak now." The cat's eyes rounded in surprise. She was losing her natural abilities.

So was Indra. Through the bay window, she watched with horror as the *Prism* approached the landing ring of Pandemonium. A large bay door opened, then the raptor slid into the open bay and landed smoothly. The dock clamps closed on the landing gear with a loud metallic clang.

Indra struggled not to panic. Without her abilities, she felt vulnerable. And none of her angel weapons would work if she lost her powers. "What do we do now?"

Kal checked his sword then rushed to the simple weapons Indra had selected for him. "Now, we fight for our lives. I suspect Zethar is behind this. Prepare yourself. We are about to be boarded."

Indra held her breath. How could she fight without her abilities? She selected a spear from Kal's pile. She hadn't trained with the bow, and she wasn't very skilled with her glowing sword. "Disarming an angel before a fight is a new trick to me."

Kal nodded as he selected a bow and several arrows, and tucked throwing knives in his belt. "Zethar is shrewd, but this is unexpected... even for him."

Indra took a calming breath. "Without crystal energy to expand, I'm not the best fighter. I hope my mediocre skills with spear and sword will suffice."

Kal steeled his resolve as loud banging indicated the hostiles had forced open the main hatch down below. Kneeling behind the row of consoles, he aimed his arrow toward the narrow entrance to the command deck.

He wished he had a blaster and a few grenades, but no such arsenal. "Ready?"

"Not really…" Indra, at his side, looked resolute, brandishing a spear. "But I'll give them a fight."

Kal sighed. "I feel like a primitive warrior who brought a knife to a gun fight."

"At least, you know how to fight. I never was a warrior." She scoffed. "And without my angel abilities, my favorite weapons are useless."

Panthera straightened, ears pivoting to listen, all senses in alert, ready to pounce. Good cat.

The hatch to the stairs exploded, enveloping the area in smoke and flames. Mercenaries in black military gear surged up from the stairs to the command deck. Zethar's private army.

Kal shot several arrows, hitting the mark each time. He wished he had more as he quickly ran out. But he knew how to wield a blade.

Indra, at his side, threw a spear and pinned her target to the bulkhead.

As the smoke dissipated, the mercenaries formed a semi-circle in front of the fugitives, aiming their blasters.

Indra glanced at him, her face screwed in determination, blade at the ready.

"I'm not dying without a fight." Kal drew his stolen angel sword and leapt over the consoles.

Panthera pounced and downed one man, ripping his throat.

Kal engaged the closest soldier and loped off the man's head. Like with the pirate, he did it with ease, his arms and legs flexing with strength and agility. His angel sword flew and pinned another soldier to the bulkhead. Kal rushed to free the sword then cut a blaster in two. Nice edge.

At his side, Indra fought valiantly. She was better with that sword than she believed. She was fast and agile. She ducked under arms, slicing the flank below the armor. She knew the weak points of armor and body.

Then some kind of silent explosion hit Kal's ear drums. He lost balance and fell to the deck. From the corner of his eye, he saw Indra and Panthera falling as well, as if in slow motion, in utter silence. Some kind of debilitating vibration rendered them powerless.

He could feel his strength draining, he wanted to fight but didn't have the strength to get to his feet. A black-clad soldier snatched his sword. Kal wanted to protest but couldn't move, not even his lips. His throat clenched. No words came out. How humiliating.

Indra and Panthera seemed to be in the same predicament. The mercenaries laughed like in a silent video clip and slapped each other's backs. Then they pulled out their ear plugs. The small devices had protected them from the soundless blast.

Then the mercenaries loaded him, and the slack bodies of Indra and Panthera on floating pallets and escorted them along the corridors of the Pandemonium space station. The three floating pallets and their armed escort came to a sophisticated prison complex, deep inside the station.

They passed heavily armed guards, security screens, security checkpoints, biological ID codes... and many hatches, like so many blast doors to the inside of a safe.

Kal couldn't believe he'd been taken so easily. He couldn't understand what happened.

They were deposited, like so much cargo, inside a white cell that reminded him of the power-dampening cell on the angel ship.

After the black-clad mercenaries left them and bolted the door, Kal struggled to get up. Not an easy feat. His legs had gone numb. He could barely move, still unable to speak.

Next to him lying on the deck, Indra seemed to have the same problem. So did Panthera.

Within a few minutes, Kal could move again but felt very weak.

"How did Zethar get a hold of angel tech?" Indra spoke slowly, as if she had difficulty articulating. She looked around, trying to get up, her balance precarious at best. "I can't believe it. This cell uses the same technology we use on the *Blue Phantom*."

"I noticed." Kal finally found his voice. He sat up and turned to the big cat. "Are you okay, girl?"

No answer came, although Panthera's eyes said she was trying to communicate.

Kal shook his head. "Panthera's natural abilities don't work here either, like on the *Blue Phantom*."

"I can't do anything. My angel gifts are gone." Indra closed her eyes. "I can't feel anything at all outside of this cell."

"We are stuck." Kal shook his head. He felt guilty. He'd led Indra into this trap. Then he chose to see the bright side. Not the worst company to be stuck with. But he must focus. At least, he was closer to the violet crystal.

Panthera managed to get up, went to Indra and bumped her hand.

Indra obliged her with a scratch between the ears.

Kal had an idea. "Panthera? Can you understand when we speak?"

The cat raised her head and nodded yes.

"Can you feel your friend Spartacus?" The fellow might be willing to help.

Panthera shook her head no.

"So much for that idea." Kal sat up on the deck and braced his knees. "I don't see a way out of this place, but it doesn't mean there isn't one. We'll just have to keep thinking."

Indra gazed up at him. "They'll have to open this door sooner or later. We should have a strategy."

Chapter Nine

Zethar sat at his desk on Pandemonium and swiped a few keys to initiate a call. He couldn't believe Azfet had told the truth and her technology actually neutralized angel powers. She must really want that prisoner contained. He wondered if that tech could contain Azfet herself...

She had many enemies, and capturing her might rake a fat reward. Of course, he'd keep the angel technology and the special power-dampening cell for further use. It might come in handy.

As if reading his mind, Azfet manifested as a hologram, wearing a tight red gown as usual. Her bare shoulders and bejeweled breasts revealed more tan skin than the situation required. "So, Zethar, I hope you have good news for me."

The gem on the big cat's collar flared again. Why?

Zethar shuddered. He didn't trust Azfet's languorous green eyes. "Yes, Highness. A444 is back on Pandemonium, in my custody, with the angel woman and the white cat, all contained in the special cell you designed."

Spartacus growled. *"Panthera here? Spartacus not feel Panthera."*

Azfet smiled at the big cat. "It's because your precious feline friend is in a shielded cell, big boy, but she is fine." Azfet pointed to a monitor and it lit up, showing the inside of a cell. "See? Here she is with her friends and nothing bad will happen to her. She is safe in the maximum-security sector."

"Spartacus hate cell... hate cage." The big cat shook himself and turned around, then exited Zethar's office, as if in protest.

The monitor went dark again.

Zethar cleared his throat. "What about the credits you promised, Highness?"

"They are being transferred as we speak." Azfet's hand caressed the giant ruby between her bare breasts. "But I can give you a lot more. How about a kingdom in my new empire? A large planet, perhaps? Something more lucrative than Laxxar?"

Zethar didn't trust her and didn't want to be beholden to her. "No, thank you, Highness. Credits will suffice."

"As you wish." Azfet waved her hand with nonchalance.

One side of Zethar's large screen showed the credits scrolling into his account.

Azfet's hologram vanished.

Zethar shuddered. He hoped he'd never have to deal with that psychopath again. He was in it for the credits, but the Dominara seemed a little too intense for his taste.

* * *

Finally, with Kal out of the way, Azfet could now set her plan in motion. She lay on the white chaise and caressed her red crystal. Then she held it up to the light and focused on an entity that would make any angel tremble... but not her.

"Nyxor, my love, come to me." The very name electrified her flesh.

Red smoke filled her luxurious temple, obscuring the bas-reliefs and the blue and gold hieroglyphs on the white columns. Out of the thick cloud emerged a splendid man with crimson skin and beautiful ram horns. Tall, naked, with shiny black eyes, he smiled with perfect white teeth.

Nyxor inclined his head. "You called, Beloved?"

"I missed you, Nyxor." Azfet stretched on the chaise invitingly, twirling a small snake around her finger. "Are your legions ready to attack? The angels of this universe are soft, and I know how to neutralize them. They won't stand a chance against our armies."

Nyxor glided to the chaise and lay against her, caressing the curve of her hip. "Once these angels are destroyed, nothing will stand between us and our dreams."

Azfet shivered under his caress. "We shall rule unchecked like the gods of old."

"We shall bathe in the blood of many sacrifices..." Nyxor chuckled. "We shall request virgin slaves for our temples then deflower them in sacred rituals."

"We shall have agapes and orgies, and beautiful music, punctuated by the screams of the chosen sacrifices pleading for mercy." Azfet thrilled at the very thought of absolute power over an entire galaxy, an entire universe.

"Together we shall rule without limitations." Nyxor's melodious voice made her want him even more.

She ran a light finger on his pectorals. "We shall spend eternity in luxury and unbound power."

No one would ever take anything from Azfet again. Especially not her freedom. She had suffered enough at the hands of strict Angel Guardians. No more. This was her time to rule her own universe, and be worshipped as a goddess. But first, she must destroy its puny angels.

* * *

"Boss, you have a visitor." The man in black security uniform bowed to Zethar.

Zethar straightened at the announcement. Why not use the com system? "Who is it?"

"It's not a who, Boss." The guard cleared his throat. "It's not an ordinary AI either. It has silvery wings, and it glows blue. It looks like one of those angel figurines in the souvenir shops."

What now? "Let him in."

Before the man could leave, the glowing AI stepped into the office with the grace of a jungle cat. "For your information, I am neither he nor she, but an android angel, with a crystal brain and abilities far beyond any biologic entity."

Zethar rose from his chair, fascinated by the marvel of engineering. "Do you have a name?"

"My name is Iaco... engineered to slay demons. I belong to the demon-slayer cast."

"Demon slayer?" What had this world become? "Welcome to Pandemonium. I've never seen the likes of you before. Impressive." But Zethar cringed inside. He tuned his brain software to read the AI's mind, with no success. This couldn't be good. "What's the purpose of your visit, Iaco?"

"I was sent from the *Blue Phantom*, looking for three fugitives." The voice, neither male nor female, remained chilly.

"Fugitives?" Zethar wondered how far the AI's abilities could reach. Could it read his mind? "Angels never asked permission to search these premises before. "Don't your abilities allow you to scan for these fugitives of yours?"

"Usually, yes... but in this case, we spotted their ship in this vicinity, then they vanished without a trace." No emotion, just cold facts.

"Wow!" So, Azfet's special cell not only neutralized their powers, but it made them indetectable by other angels as well. Good to know.

The AI stepped directly in front of Zethar, staring at him at eye level. Any lesser man would find it intimidating. Of course, most men only came to Zethar's shoulder... and he wore lifts in his boots.

The AI narrowed his luminous eyes. "We know you are holding our fugitives. I came to negotiate their release into our custody... for a price of your choice."

"Anything I want?" Zethar swallowed hard. "I wouldn't mind integrating some of your beautiful hardware into my cyborg body."

"It wouldn't be compatible with a biologic entity. We are not Cyborg." The formidable AI turned away. "Our parts only function with our special kind of energy. Our consciousness is pure energy in permanent contact with the Formless One."

"Okay..." Zethar hid his disappointment. He also didn't feel hardware should come with religious mumbo-jumbo. But the flat refusal was just as well. As much as Zethar would love to stick it to Highness Azfet, she might react negatively to his betrayal and decide to end him. "What makes you think I have your fugitives?"

"We have been in constant contact with the *Prism* since it left the *Blue Phantom*, and we followed it here, where it simply vanished." The accusing tone didn't bode well for Zethar. "Besides, I can read your mind."

"You caught me there." Zethar fumed inside. He hated supernatural beings, and magic beings of any kind. There was just no way to manipulate them or pull the wool over their eyes, even with the latest mind-reading software.

"Where did a simple crime lord acquire the technology to trap one of our ships and detain one of our angels?" Iaco's accusatory tone demanded an answer.

Zethar forced an easy smile. "Angels are not the only ones with great abilities, my friend. See, there is someone else interested in our escapees... and she pays very well."

"Who is she?" The AI loomed over Zethar and the luminous eyes flashed and narrowed.

"Dominara Azfet." Zethar hated to blab, but the AI angel could read his mind anyway. "She wants to be called Highness. She is some kind of sorceress, keenly interested in the male prisoner, and adamant on keeping him contained. She told me how to make a prison cell angel-proof."

The AI broke the stare and turned away, offering a view of his magnificent silvery wings. What Zethar wouldn't give for the gift of flight...

"Dominara Azfet..." As if reading Zethar's thoughts, Iaco the AI turned to face him. His entire body seemed to be digesting the information in Zethar's mind.

"Do you know her?" Zethar's voice squeaked. How embarrassing. "She's a piece of work. A psychopath of the first order."

"The Formless One warned us about a powerful supernatural being that could cause grave damage to this galaxy." Iaco buzzed, as if its circuits would overload. "This Dominara Azfet could be the great evil we are after."

Zethar took a calming breath and released it slowly. Religious talk always made him uncomfortable. "I wouldn't be surprised if she were that evil you speak of. She certainly is wicked... and that comes from me."

Iaco stared again into Zethar's eyes with renewed intensity. "There is grave danger in supporting pure evil. I must ask you to pick a side. Dominara Azfet, who manipulates everyone for dark purposes, or the greater good."

"Or what?" Zethar refused to be intimidated.

"Your life could become unbearable." Iaco didn't disguise the threat.

Zethar must be smart about this. "If I agree, what do I get in return?"

The AI inclined his head. "How about redemption for the bad deeds of your past, and a chance at an honest life?"

Zethar scoffed. "I don't care much about the greater good, or redemption, or leading an honest life. I never did."

"What do you care about?" Sarcasm tainted Iaco's tone.

"Since your superb hardware is off the table, I'll take hard credits. Maybe two million..." Zethar smiled at the prospect. He could buy a lot of hardware for that kind of credits.

Iaco the AI nodded. "That's easy to arrange."

"Really? All right, then." Now, Zethar was in his element. "This Dominara Azfet is shamelessly manipulating and taking advantage of me, and I hate not being in control."

"So, do we have a deal?" The AI angel straightened. It looked even taller. "You give us the prisoners, and we will transfer the credits, take care of Azfet, and erase your bad karma."

"I guess so." That was too easy. It made Zethar uncomfortable. "What's the catch?"

"No catch." The AI scanned the office. "A deal is a deal."

"Good." It was unusual for Zethar to take the side of good. But he had no other choice. He couldn't neutralize the AI, since Iaco could read his mind. "What are you going to do with the prisoners once you have them?"

"Do not worry about that. We shall deal with them swiftly and permanently." The unforgiving tone indicated they might get executed. The AI didn't show any empathy.

"That sounds harsh." Zethar shuddered. But he didn't care about what happened to the prisoners. If the angels could eliminate Azfet, that's all he needed. The woman was trouble.

The angel squinted at Zethar. "I also sense a strange energy in the vicinity. You wouldn't happen to know the whereabouts of a violet crystal, a rare gem. We are looking for it."

"Of course, you are." Zethar chuckled. He knew there was something special about that stone. "It's here, but it's very well guarded. Good luck retrieving it."

* * *

Invisible and swift as the wind, Spartacus roamed Pandemonium, unseen. The lady said Panthera was in prison, like a cage, in the maximum-security sector, but he couldn't feel Panthera. He must free her. *"Spartacus save Panthera."*

The large feline slinked on velvet paws toward the detention ward of Pandemonium. It was locked, with special coded doors, but Spartacus did not use doors anymore. He was a champion. His collar made him powerful. He could vanish and take himself to a different place.

Since he'd been to that sector many times with Zethar, Spartacus willed himself to the last security hatch. Then he froze and listened. He smelled the guards behind the bulkhead. He could see the three men in uniform through the metal wall. He could hear them laugh.

Spartacus willed himself inside the security hub, still invisible. He knew the guards could sound the alarm if they saw him. He fixed his attention on the monitors. Here, he could see Panthera and her two friends in a cell. Spartacus couldn't read numbers or letters, but he could read the guards' minds. He knew the way to Panthera's cell. Panthera. He must free and protect Panthera.

"Did you feel that?" A skinny guard scanned the room, eyes wide. "Something brushed against me. I feel watched. There is someone here."

The fat guard next to him laughed. "Not that invisible angel thing again? I don't believe that nonsense."

The skinny guard shook his head. "I also smell something weird. Like an animal smell."

The third guard chuckled. "It's probably that big cat inside the special cell. The smell is coming through the vents."

Spartacus visualized the inside of Panthera's cell like he saw it on the monitors and willed himself there.

Something hit him on the nose and threw him backward. He collided with one of the guards and growled as he rolled and got back on his paws. Why couldn't he get inside that cell?

Then he realized he was the focus of attention. The three guards could see him and rose and aimed their weapons at him.

But no one would prevent Spartacus from rescuing Panthera. If he had to kill and maim like he did in the arena to save her, so be it. The big cat pounced...

The yells, the screams, the smell of sweat and blood reminded him of the arena. It felt good to use his muscles and claws and fangs again. He was still a champion.

Two guards were down. The last one, the skinny one, now disarmed and bleeding from the neck, rushed toward the red button on the main console.

Spartacus pounced in front of him, faced him, and bared his fangs. The man stepped back.

"Open jail with white cat." Spartacus yelled in the man's dense mind. *"And you live."*

The guard blinked several times at hearing the mind voice. Then he nodded nervously, turned around, and walked in the direction of the cells. Spartacus snorted in derision. Guard coward, not brave.

Spartacus recognized the way from reading the guard's mind as they followed a long corridor with thick security doors and hatches, some with keys, some with handprint, some with voice commands, others with code pads.

Half-way through, another guard came toward them, aiming his blaster at

Spartacus. Enraged, Spartacus pounced then ripped the man's throat. Quick and quiet. The way of the cat.

The skinny guard trembled harder, walking on wobbly legs but kept going. He smelled like pee.

Spartacus remained focused on his goal. If the skinny coward tried to sound the alarm, he would die, too.

Chapter Ten

Indra sat up on the white decking and crossed her legs. "I'm mad at myself for having been caught so easily."

"It's not your fault." Kal paced back and forth. "We were not prepared for that kind of technology."

Scanning the bare white cell, very similar to the power-dampening brig on the *Blue Phantom*, Indra shuddered. "How did a thug like Zethar acquire this technology? I can't imagine an angel would ever divulge our secrets. How could this happen?"

Kal's steps grew stiff and angry. "Zethar has many connections in high places, and access to illegal advanced technology and hardware. His entire body is riddled with it. He's two limbs and a brain away from being a robot."

Indra slowed her breathing in an attempt to control her frustration. "I told you going back to Pandemonium was a bad idea."

Kal shrugged. "My crystal is here. I need it. I had no choice."

Panthera head-butted Indra's shoulder and purred.

"Sorry, big girl." Indra scratched the cat's head and turned to Kal. "Panthera doesn't like it when we fight."

"Neither do I." Kal sighed and his shoulders fell. He looked defeated. "I'm sorry, Indra. I shouldn't have brough you here."

"Don't be sorry. I was a stowaway, remember? There is not much we can do now." Indra forced a smile. "At least if we die here, we'll die together."

Kal shook his head. "I'm not ready to die. I have a mission to complete."

"Yeah." Indra snorted. "A mission you don't remember. A mission that could be evil, but still takes precedence." Sadness welled like a cloud in her chest.

At the click of retreating bars inside the cell hatch, Indra glanced at Kal and Panthera. Both heard it at the same time and froze.

"Someone's coming." Kal stepped back as if on a spring. "Friend or foe?"

Indra unfolded her legs. "Most likely foe. I hope they don't use that sonic weapon again."

Kal stepped to the side of the hatch. "Attack plan. Take your places as we rehearsed, and plug your ears."

Indra nodded. Her heart pounded. Fighting without her powers wasn't her forte. She took a wide stance, ready to jump or run, and hopefully escape.

Panthera sniffed the air with interest, maw open, tongue out. She looked more excited than worried. Strange.

The hatch opened slowly with a whoosh of compressed air, revealing a skinny guard with wide eyes. The man trembled, fumbled, and babbled unintelligently. Blood dripped from his throat, staining his gray uniform.

Behind him appeared a large savage beast with cracked fangs, its pelt reddish and scarred, its black harness slick with gore.

Indra almost gagged at the overpowering stench of blood. The obvious marks of carnage on the beast should inspire fear, but angels didn't fear animals. In any case, she had no idea how to fight a big cat... But the beast didn't seem focused on her or Kal... only on Panthera.

Panthera leapt ahead and head-butted the bloody cat. *"Spartacus!"*

Indra realized this might mean freedom. She ran out through the hatch. "Is this your Spartacus?"

The two cats smelled each other and rubbed against each other, huffing and purring.

Indra turned to see Kal frown then come out of the cell, staring at the two felines. "This is Panthera's friend? The Spartacus who has my violet crystal?"

The skinny guard glanced around in panic, then stared at the red button on the main console by the security hatch.

Spartacus growled. *"No alarm."*

Ignoring the warning, the guard sprang for the red button.

Spartacus leapt and pounced on the guard, severing his arm in one bone-crushing bite. The guard screamed. Spartacus silenced him by ripping out his throat.

Indra turned away from the carnage in disgust. Definite confirmation that she was not warrior material.

Then Spartacus faced Indra and Kal, snarling, rivulets of blood dripping from his mouth. Indra could feel her powers returning somewhat and stood ready to protect Kal.

Panthera stepped in front of them. *"Angel Kal, friend. Angel Indra, friend. Escape together."*

Kal's gaze fixed on the violet gem on the beast's collar. "Indra. Look. Here it is. This is my crystal. I can feel its power."

The violet gem flared, as if to confirm his claim. Kal walked toward Spartacus and reached for the stone.

The big cat roared and twisted his head, jaw snapping on empty air. *"No touch trophy. Spartacus champion."*

Kal jumped back, shaking his hand. "Holy Mandala! He almost had me."

When he stared at the violet crystal with open greed in his blue eyes, Indra shuddered at the strength of his bond with the stone. This couldn't be good.

She touched his shoulder. "Right now, thanks to Spartacus, we are free. Maybe we should just get out of here. I remember where our raptor is kept. Let's go."

Panthera huffed. *"Spartacus come with us."*

Kal still stared at the crystal as if in a trance. "Of course, he's coming with us."

"Okay." Indra inclined her head and considered the bloody cat. "I can transport the four of us to the raptor." That was angel training 101. "Form a circle and hold each other's hand, or paw, or whatever. Let's go."

Indra rested her hand on Panthera's head. Kal took Indra's other hand, and wearily touched the powerful leg of Spartacus, while Panthera stroked the male cat's bloody paw.

Indra visualized the inside of the angel raptor and dematerialized the four of them. They rematerialized on the command deck of the *Prism*. No trace of the vibrations that earlier impeded angel abilities. Good. A single guard inside the angel raptor yelled and aimed his blaster at Indra. She punched the air, and a bolt of light immobilized the guard before he dematerialized.

Kal stared at her, puzzlement in his eyes. "Where did you send him?"

Indra felt mischievous. "To an animal cage in the arena's menagerie."

"Nice." Kal chuckled. "Can you tell if anyone else is onboard?"

Indra closed her eyes and mentally scanned the raptor. "I feel no other presence. It's just us."

Spartacus and Panthera lay down, side by side on the decking.

Indra smiled at the two of them cuddling like love bugs. "Let's get out of here."

Kal took the pilot seat. "Prism, are you back online?"

"Aye, aye, Captain." A female android materialized and sat copilot, next to Kal.

Kal's blue eyes rounded in surprise. "Are you Prism, the ship computer?"

"Obviously." The female android managed a derisive tone. "But I'm more than a computer. I'm an AI with all the powers of an angel."

"Holy Mandala!" Kal stared in obvious awe.

Indra smiled in realization. "So, that's how you disconnected from the ship before we were attacked. I was wondering about that."

"Yes." The AI sat very straight. "I migrated into my android body and remained hidden inside the bulkhead."

Indra nodded. "I'm glad you did."

That feature could become handy, but Indra still had a lot to learn about angel technology.

* * *

As he applied his hand on the security door scanner, Zethar recognized the faint hint of copper in the air. Blood. Anger rose in his chest. As the heavy metal hatch slid open, the smell thickened and turned overpowering. The blood on the security monitors and the carnage of badly mangled and decapitated bodies indicated a particularly violent rage. Not unlike his rage right now.

He clenched his jaw and turned to Iaco, the android angel beside him. "Did you keep me occupied in my office, so your friends could slaughter my guards and steal my prisoners?"

"Insults do not affect us." Iaco cast a haughty glance on the carnage. "And this kind of slaughter is not exactly our style."

"Style?" Zethar took a second look and realized the AI was right. "This reminds me of the games in the arena. But only the most powerful beast could have done this." And Zethar could easily guess what beast... but how? And why?

Iaco remained calm and neutral as his head slowly turned to scan the entire scene.

"Let's check the security monitors." Zethar stepped up to the consoles and pushed a few keys. The monitors of the special cell showed it empty, with the hatch wide open. He didn't need to go there to know his prisoners were gone.

"How did that happen?" Iaco's tone remained flat.

Zethar replayed the security feed. The proof was right there before his eyes. Spartacus had somehow found his way inside the high security vault and butchered the guards.

More feeds from the space adjacent to the cell showed Spartacus dematerializing with the angel woman, the albino cat, and Azfet's prized convict. The Dominara would be peeved and Zethar dreaded their next holographic chat.

"Beasts cannot operate security doors or any kind of technology." Iaco sounded suspicious and his luminous blue eyes flared. "Are you trying to trick me into believing your prisoners escaped?"

"I swear I have no idea how or why this happened, but I will find out." Zethar hoped the AI wouldn't decide to end him. Right now, he looked capable of cold murder.

Iaco proceeded through the open hatch toward the cells. "Maybe this is a trick of your technology to fool us, and they are still here, hidden."

"I doubt it." Zethar followed the AI into the safety corridor, knowing quite well they wouldn't find the prisoners at the end of it.

After a few silent steps, the AI paused, as if for dramatic effect. "The violet gem on the beast's collar... it looks like the crystal I'm interested in. How did it come into your possession?"

"None of your business." Zethar fumed. How humiliating to be accused of wrongdoing and questioned about his most sensitive dealings... and by this magnificent android of all people. "I don't understand how Spartacus could do what he did. At one point, it almost looks like he was invisible..."

"I understand it perfectly." The AI chuckled, a strange, mechanical sound. "The cat used the power of the crystal on his collar. And now, our chances to recover it and thwart impending evil are seriously diminished."

Zethar cursed the AI, Spartacus, and the prisoners in his head. How could he have been so stupid? Azfet must have known the power of the stone. She made sure it ended up on the big cat's collar. Zethar hated the manipulating bitch. To think that the stone was within his reach. What he could have done with such powers...

As they walked side by side, Iaco gazed upon him sideways, with almost pity. "I can read your thoughts, Zethar. It would behoove you to turn your life around and choose to do good and serve humanity, for a change."

Did that arrogant bucket of bolts dare tell him how to live his life? "Mind your own business, Iaco. I don't take advice from angels."

"But you might want to take advice from an AI." The metallic bastard managed a deprecating tone. "After all, you understand the superiority of technology since you are part cyborg... by choice."

How dare he? "I don't take advice from anyone. AI or otherwise."

Iaco flashed a cold smile and kept walking.

They reached the special cell. The guards had been mauled, the hatch lay open, and the cell was empty... just as the security feed had shown.

Zethar sighed. "You see? No trick. They are gone."

Iaco raised his head, gazed above Zethar's skull, and spoke, as if to someone far away. "Captain, we have a situation. The fugitives escaped again, this time with the violet crystal. My AI brethren and I believe they are a great danger to this galaxy, and we must initiate the seek-and-destroy protocol."

"Seek and destroy?" Zethar had no idea what was going on, and no control whatsoever. It made him feel small, and the feeling didn't sit well in his stomach. Besides, he would have to answer to Azfet, and that terrified him. "Destroy whom?"

Iaco turned a disdainful gaze to him. "Do not worry, Zethar. Not you. You still have time to rehabilitate yourself and help us in our quest. But if you try to hide anything from us again, we shall retaliate... swiftly and permanently."

Zethar swallowed the lump in his throat. "What do you mean?"

"We shall terminate you, Zethar." No emotion, just cold logic in the AI's tone. "After all, our purpose is to destroy evil."

Hiding his dread at the open threat, Zethar realized he was dealing with a heartless machine... who could read his mind... and had no qualms whatsoever about ending his miserable life. Better to remain helpful and stay alive.

Zethar clenched his jaw, swallowing the humiliation. "What should I do?"

"When this Azfet entity contacts you again..." The AI handed him a small device. "Just press that button, so we can trace her."

Then the AI vanished into thin air.

Zethar stared at the small blue-glowing device. What had become of his power and glory? He felt like a puppet in the hands of an evil sorceress and powerful angels. Despite the acquisition of exceptional technology and his initial recovery of Azfet's fugitive, Zethar's day turned out to be the worst of his entire life.

* * *

Azfet sensed a disturbance in the fabric of the universe and shuddered. Something had gone wrong. She rose and paced along the row of golden Sphynxes.

Caressing her blood stone, she focused on Zethar. The man's hologram manifested in front of her. He looked... scared? Not a good sign.

"Zethar?" She made her voice penetrating. "What bad news do you have for me?"

"How do you know it's bad news?" The tall man with metallic plates on his skull stared at her with rage in his dark eyes. "Or maybe you helped my prisoners escape, so you could gloat and humiliate me even more."

"My important prisoner escaped your angel-proof jail and thwarted you for the third time?" Azfet should have known Zethar couldn't handle such a task. "You are trying my patience, Zethar. When did it happen? How?"

"Spartacus, of all creatures, managed to open the angel-proof cell." Zethar paused, as if realizing she didn't know. "They all vanished, and the angel raptor is missing. And even with your angel tracking technology, we can't locate them."

"Spartacus is with them?" Azfet hated that he saw her surprise.

"That's what I said." Zethar shook his head in frustration. "They all vanished together."

Azfet berated herself for underestimating Spartacus. The big cat had used the power of the gem to free his friend. And now, Kal had an angel, two powerful fighting cats, and the violet crystal in close proximity. That could mean trouble.

She had a cold shiver. How would Nyxor react to this unfortunate hiccup?

She made her voice stern, as if reprimanding a misbehaved child. "I am very disappointed in you, Zethar."

"I don't care. I'm done playing your games." Zethar straightened, full of arrogance. "From now on, keep me out of your little intrigues. I'm nobody's puppet."

"I relieve you of your obligations to me, Zethar." She didn't need to involve him any further.

"Goodbye, Highness." The resolute face was almost comical. He turned away from her.

Azfet touched her blood stone and his hologram vanished.

Admiral Blackthorn's armies were ready to start their conquest, and extinguish the arrogant angels of this universe once and for all... After they were all dead, Azfet could reign as the space tyrant she was born to be. This universe would submit or die.

But Azfet wouldn't take any chances. Angel Guardian Kal might soon recover his memories, and that would make him even more dangerous.

Shivering as she caressed her stone, she emitted a throaty moan. "Nyxor, my love, I need a small favor."

Red mist enveloped her, making her thrill in extasy.

"Anything for you, Beloved." The suave voice reverberated inside her.

"My love..." She sighed. "My nemesis is on an angel raptor named *Prism*, with the violet stone. The local crime lords of this universe are weak and cannot contain him. But he is no match for your army of demons.”

“Anything for you, Beloved. How shall I find him?”

“His violet crystal is tuned to my DNA.” Azfet smiled at the delightful sensations invading her. “Think of me, and the violet crystal will guide you to him.”

“Wonderful.” The mist around her twirled in delicious ways. “Always delighted to be of service, Beloved.”

Azfet sighed with longing as the red mist retreated. Far from being upset, Nyxor would fight at her side. Good.

Time to accelerate her plans. Soon, when she controlled the galaxy, nothing would be able to stop her. And she would have the life she always dreamed of... the life of a goddess, worshipped by all, enjoying all the pleasures this universe could offer, and beloved by the handsome and powerful Nyxor, master of the demonic hordes.

* * *

“The situation is clear, Captain.” Iaco, the AI angel, stood at attention, perfectly still, on the Command Deck of the *Blue Phantom*, bathed in the luminous aura of the surrounding crystal.

“Explain it to me.” Graziella often disagreed with AI logic.

161

Iaco beeped. "Since the foreigner is now reunited with his violet crystal, he may already be stronger than us. And if he is an agent of evil, he poses a danger to us all and to this galaxy. He must be dealt with immediately."

"And by dealt with, you mean killed… no matter the collateral damage." Graziella prided herself on being merciful and refused to sacrifice innocent lives. She didn't feel very forgiving for the self-righteous AI. "Indra, one of our crew, is with him."

"That female angel is obviously compromised, Captain. Biologic angels are vulnerable and unreliable. We cannot afford to take a risk… not with the fate of the galaxy in the balance." Iaco sounded so cold and inflexible.

"I am a biologic angel, and I am the captain in charge for that very reason." Graziella wouldn't let the arrogant machine dictate her decision. "It seems your solution to every perceived threat is to eliminate all the people involved, even our own."

"My solution is logical and efficient, Captain." No emotion whatsoever in the glowing blue eyes.

"Well, I do not see it that way." Graziella took a slow, calming breath. "What about Zethar? Will he help us?"

"For a price. I gave him a locator to activate when Dominara Azfet calls, but she must be shielded by some strong forces. It didn't work."

"Let's focus on finding the *Prism* first, then I'll decide what to do."

No reaction from the AI. "The linked control system we used to track the *Prism* before is now severed. We've been scanning and searching for it, but so far, no luck. It has vanished… and crystal drives do not emit ion trails."

"The foreign crystal must be shielding the *Prism* from us." Graziella wondered about the power of that violet gem. "There has to be a way of locating that raptor. It's one of ours, after all."

"We attempted to make mind contact with Angel Indra, with no success." The AI sounded cold. "Should I consult the Formless One about the location of the *Prism*, Captain?"

"No." Graziella had already tried. "The Formless One refuses to take sides and wants us to solve our own problems. Keep searching."

"Aye, aye, Captain." Iaco saluted and vanished.

Graziella only hoped acting on her instincts wouldn't bring calamity to the galaxy.

Chapter Eleven

As the *Prism* slid into space in invisible mode, Kal fidgeted in his pilot seat. The violet crystal on the beast's collar, just a few feet away, called him. Even as Spartacus was snoring softly on the decking, next to Indra who petted Panthera, Kal could feel the heat of the stone giving him energy. He wanted to flex his muscles and run, not sit quietly inside a raptor.

"Where to, Captain?" Prism, the female AI sitting at his side stared through the forward shield, ignoring the line of monitors scrolling data below it.

"For now, we hide." Kal wished he knew more about his mission. "I need to retrieve my memories. Then I'll know where to go and what to do." He also hoped to get back his powers as an Angel Guardian, since the angels thought he must have been one, but for that, he would need to wear the violet crystal against his skin.

Spartacus growled in his sleep. Could the beast read Kal's mind? He hoped not. Although the crystal on the black harness gave the beast unknown powers.

Next to him, Indra talked soothingly to Panthera, who purred and licked her hand.

Prism narrowed her eyes toward Kal with interest. "You seem different, Captain. Is everything all right? I usually can read minds, but not yours. Some people have difficulty getting used to a ship's artificial brain residing in an autonomous body."

"I admit it's a little jarring, but no." Kal wasn't about to share his personal doubts and preoccupations with a machine.

Indra patted Panthera's neck then rose and stood between them. "Do all the angel raptors have independent AIs like you?"

"Yes." Prism smiled.

"Can you communicate with the AIs of other ships?" Kal realized that could be a problem if they didn't want to be located.

"I certainly can, and I do, periodically." Prism sounded amused. "I have been in communication with the *Blue Phantom*. They were tracking this ship through the link allowing remote piloting."

"What?" Indra paled. "Have they been aware of our whereabouts since we left the *Blue Phantom*?"

"Of course." Prism sounded smug. "AIs always follow procedure."

"Why didn't you tell us?" Kal blanched and turned to Indra. "This oversight could be deadly. The angels want me dead."

Indra's blue eyes widened. "I don't want you to die." She turned to Prism. "Are they still tracking us?"

"Not anymore. I haven't been able to restore contact, not since Pandemonium."

Prism's tone indicated she was enjoying their oversight. "And for your information, I wasn't required to tell you. Any decent captain is familiar with basic rules and angel raptor technology."

Kal felt humiliated. He couldn't believe he didn't think of asking. "Do you know why they stopped tracking us?"

Prism pointed to Spartacus on the deck. "The vibrations of that strange crystal are shielding us from everyone, including the angels of the *Blue Phantom*."

"Well, at least, that's something." Kal felt these vibrations deep inside his bones.

How he yearned to touch that stone. But Spartacus wouldn't let him. Still, the mere proximity of it stirred vague memories and dark emotions that threatened his calm. Was his obsession with it a sign he might be evil? By all the powerful entities in the universe, he hoped he wouldn't lose his mind.

As if sensing his doubts, Indra laid her hand on his arm. Kal shivered at her touch. He didn't shy away but resisted the urge to caress her hand. He must focus.

Spartacus stretched on the deck. *"Good life here. Not cold like Laxxar."*

"What?" Kal gently removed Indra's distracting hand and pivoted his seat to face the beast. "You were on Laxxar?"

"Spartacus with Zethar everywhere." The cat stretched farther and yawned.

Kal glanced at Indra and whistled. "Now it all makes sense."

"What makes sense?" Indra narrowed her eyes at him with a puzzled expression.

Kal patted her hand. "The proximity of the stone on Laxxar might have given me the strength to last as long as I did in the frozen mines."

Indra smiled. "Or, you survived because you are an angel, and we are more resilient than regular people."

Kal pointed to the gem. "This crystal belongs to me. I should be wearing it."

The beast growled. *"Spartacus keep trophy. Spartacus champion. Trophy make Spartacus strong."*

Then the beast vanished into thin air.

Indra gasped. "I didn't know he could do that."

"Holy Mandala!" Kal snorted. "The stone gives Spartacus angelic powers. Great. Am I going to have to kill him to get it back?"

Panthera rose majestically, positioned herself in front of Kal, and growled, baring her fangs. *"Spartacus save Panthera. Panthera protect Spartacus and stone."*

Kal took a deep breath. "Okay. I get it. I won't try to take his stone, I promise."

Indra squeezed his shoulder. "Maybe there is another way for you to get your powers back."

Kal didn't believe that. "What way?"

"I'll explain later." Indra remained mysterious about it.

Spartacus manifested again, rubbing heads with Panthera.

As much as he wanted the crystal and the powers it would give him, Kal couldn't fight the two trained cats for it. Especially since one of them had angel powers. He shuddered at the memory of the carnage in the guards' station on Pandemonium.

Prism chirped. "Captain, I located a planetoid with plant life but no animal life. It has a breathable atmosphere and adequate gravity. We could land and hide there until we have a specific destination."

"Good. We all need to rest our space legs." Kal glanced at Indra, wondering what she wouldn't say in front of Prism, or the big cats, about another way to regain his powers.

"It's been a while since I walked on land." Indra turned away, avoiding his gaze... as if she didn't trust him.

He couldn't blame her, but her lack of trust saddened him.

"How do you plan to get your memories back?" Indra's question hung in the space between them.

Kal sighed. "The mere proximity of the violet crystal might help me remember... but it could take a while. Touching or wearing the stone would be faster and more efficient, but I doubt Spartacus will let me."

The reddish beast growled to confirm the thought. *"No touch stone."*

"Well, maybe you are not supposed to touch it." Indra glared at him. "There is a reason for everything. The Formless One mentioned evil came with you to our universe. What if you and the stone are part of that evil?"

"I cannot be evil. What I feel is duty and obligation to help." Kal refused to consider the possibility. Whatever his mission demanded, he would complete it. "What if I were your only chance to save this universe? The only way to find out is to recover my memories."

"Unfortunately, you are right." Indra's shoulders dropped. "Knowledge is power, and we need to know."

"Good, Then, let's land on that planetoid and try to figure it out." Kal turned to the AI. "Prism, find us a nice spot to land."

"Aye, aye, Captain." Prism's expression froze as she focused on the rapid approach, and the planetoid loomed larger and larger through the forward shield.

Prism guided the raptor in a controlled descent, into the planetoid's atmosphere. The ship shook and flames licked the bay window. Finally, the raptor landed in a sea of tall green grasses.

Kal was impatient to know who he was, but he hoped his memories wouldn't reveal him as an evil monster.

* * *

Kal struggled to run as the battle raged. All around him the world was on fire. His ears rang like gongs. His legs didn't work as they should. He could barely breathe in the smoke. He flapped his wings, but the gravity was so strong on that superheavy world, he only skimmed the surface.

His Angel Guardian brethren running behind him yelled, "Kill her! Kill her! Kill her!"

But Kal couldn't fly any higher in this gravity, not high enough for a clear line of sight. The evil one carried children with her and ducked into a group of other children running alongside her, away from the battle. Azfet headed straight for the shimmering column of golden light, yet Kal couldn't fire.

Azfet knew his weakness, knew he wouldn't fire at the risk of killing innocents. As she reached the open portal, she dropped the children, jumped into the light, and smiled before vanishing.

Kal finally caught up to the shimmering column of light. He landed heavily, flapping, and folding his wings, but he could not enter the light. Not without orders, under penalty of death. Besides, it could be a trap. In any case, he had failed.

The Angel Guardian landing next to him raged, "Why didn't you kill her when you had a chance? You are a disgrace. You are too soft. You have no business being an Angel Guardian."

"I couldn't sacrifice innocent children." Kal's chest constricted at the very thought.

His commander alighted before him, glaring and huffing, large wings stirring a cloud of dust. "What kind of traitor would rather fail than sacrifice innocents to kill his enemy? Azfet didn't care about them. Why would you?"

Kal's cheeks burned with shame. "I believe angels are supposed to protect the innocent, not kill them."

"Angel Guardians protect the universe," his commander bellowed as he folded his wings. "Collateral damage is of no concern. Because of your unwillingness to kill children, Azfet escaped." Each word tolled like a condemnation.

Kal lowered his gaze. "I know. I am truly sorry... but I had no choice."

"There is always a choice, and the mission comes first!" The commander growled like a rumble of thunder. "It's all your fault. Your weakness puts our universe in danger!"

"I'm sorry, Commander, but I do not regret my actions... or lack thereof." There, he said it.

"Commander!" The second in command alighted awkwardly next to the commander and gestured toward the shimmering column. "Fortunately for us, this portal leads to another universe."

The commander relaxed slightly. "Good riddance. Now she is their problem, not ours. Our mission is complete. When we close that portal, our universe will be safe again."

"What about that other universe?" Kal couldn't believe his commander could be so callous. "Azfet will certainly attempt to wreck their worlds. It's her nature. They will need our help to smite her."

"Azfet is no longer our concern." The commander chuckled derisively. "Let them deal with her. Our job is done."

Kal wanted to help. "I'm responsible for their misfortune, Commander. I failed to kill Azfet. Now, I request permission to go after her and stop her."

"That soft streak again. You are hopeless, Kal," the second in command railed. "You are a sorry excuse for an Angel Guardian."

The commander gave Kal a measuring stare. "If you want to follow her, be my guest."

"Great. I will." Kal considered his sword. "At least, this weapon is powerful enough to kill her."

The commander snatched the glowing sword from his hand. "Our weapons cannot leave this universe. All you can take with you is your violet crystal to preserve your powers. It's inert enough to pass through the gates."

"My crystal? That's all?" Kal couldn't believe the callousness. "How will it help? Crystals are not exactly weapons."

The second in command rubbed his chin. "In another universe, it will automatically seek Azfet since you both came from the same place. It will help you find her... and if you get close enough to her, possibly control her by stripping her of the powers Nyxor gave her through his red gem."

"Possibly? But my crystal isn't strong enough to kill her!" That was the real problem.

The commander shrugged. "Here it wouldn't kill her, but in another universe the natural laws might work in different ways."

"So different that my crystal might not work at all?" Kal realized his commander did not care. How callous. "Still. I must go. I must find her and bring her back to face justice."

"No!" The commander shook his head. "Don't bother to bring her back. We don't want her here. We are glad to be rid of her. If you find her, kill her, or send her to the closest hell. Do your best, or your worst... but do not bring her back."

"So, I go through the gate, kill her, then come back?" Kal didn't like his chances of success.

"That won't do either." The commander pursed his lips. "You see... we cannot risk our own worlds. We'll destroy that gate after you go through it, so she can't return. Once you are out of this universe, there is no coming back for you either."

"Even if I succeed, I can't come home?" Kal hadn't considered that possibility. This universe was his home... then again, he never really understood it.

"You don't belong here, Kal. You think with your heart instead of your brain." His commander straightened menacingly. "You broke the code, betrayed your brothers, hesitated to kill to protect them. No Angel Guardian will ever trust you again. I banish you from this universe."

Hot tears rolled down Kal's cheeks. His own brothers had rejected him. But he must protect the life of the innocents, no matter what universe they populated. And he'd failed to stop Azfet, so he must make amends... find her... kill her... or contain her... so she wouldn't bring ruin and devastation upon innocent, unsuspecting worlds.

With a heavy heart, Kal bowed to his commander. "I accept the mission."

Then he stepped into the shimmering column of golden light.

* * *

Indra didn't remember when she'd last walked on land. It felt strange to run free on a green planetoid with an atmosphere and natural gravity. She felt the breeze in her hair, smelled wild flowers and moisture in the air. How she enjoyed the atmospheric blue of the sky, and the gentle heat of a foreign sun. She'd missed it.

That's how she imagined the Land of Many Waters in her mind. That's where the Anvad, including her parents and her siblings, had gone to make a new life. She missed them. She hoped they had made a good home there. One day, maybe, she'd have a family of her own, and maybe she would see them again.

Despite the unity of mind among the angels of the *Blue Phantom*, Indra never felt part of their family. Angels were a lonely sort of people. They didn't socialize, had no relatives onboard. Few took mates, and none had children.

She came upon Panthera and Spartacus, lying in the high grasses and halted. The two cats bumped heads like honeymooners. Kal was there too, sitting legs crossed in a lotus position, so close to the beast, his head only inches from the big cat's collar. The violet crystal hummed and glowed.

Indra watched Kal. Even with his eyes closed, he didn't seem at peace. Tears rolled down his cheeks. His back arched and his body jerked. He emitted a long, distressed moan. Was he having nightmarish visions? She wished she could read his mind... but when she tried, she hit a mental wall.

Indra couldn't stand seeing Kal in such distress, even if it were only a vision. "Kal!"

He opened red eyes full of tears, and they looked through her at something far away. "I was back on my home world."

"It didn't look like a happy vision." That was an understatement.

"It wasn't a vision. It was a memory, and not a good one. Some trial I went through before I ended up here." He didn't seem happy with the knowledge.

"Did you find out what your mission was?" Maybe that would cheer him up.

"Yeah, I did." Kal relaxed his position and shook his head, as if to dissipate the vision.

"So? You don't look happy about it." How she wanted to console him, rub his stiff shoulders, maybe kiss his tears... But she settled for touching his arm.

He shied away from her touch, straightened, and scraped his short black hair. "My self-imposed mission is to get rid of the evil that entered this universe before me, Dominara Azfet."

"Self-imposed?" Among the angels Indra knew, a mission was never an individual decision.

Kal's brow furrowed. "I was rejected by my brethren, kicked out of my home world, sent into exile. They do not care about this universe. They are glad to be rid of Azfet, and of me in one swoop."

"Why get rid of you? I don't understand." Indra couldn't relate to such harsh treatment.

"On my home world, I am a pariah." Kal sighed. "I was held responsible for Azfet's escape from hell. So, when I offered to go after her, they sent me through that portal, with no hope of ever getting back home. They exiled me as a punishment for failing to stop her."

"Exiled for failure? But surely, you did your best." It didn't make sense. "You didn't mean for her to escape!"

"No, I did not. She had help from some demon master. But when I had a shot at killing her, I hesitated." Kal's shoulders slumped.

"Why did you hesitate?" Indra wanted him to be good.

"Azfet used children as a shield. I would have gladly sacrificed my life to kill her, but I refused to kill the innocent." Kal's voice faded to a whisper.

"And the other Guardians exiled you for that?" Indra felt rage building in her chest.

Kal raised his blue eyes full of pain. "Where I come from, I'm considered too soft to be an Angel Guardian."

"And I'm too soft to be a warrior angel here." Indra wondered at the similarities between them. "So, what do we do now?"

"We?" He seemed puzzled.

"Yes, we. You are not alone anymore, Kal. We can work together." Indra thrilled at the idea of working with him, now that she knew he protected the light against the darkness. She could finally trust him.

As if sensing her excitement, Kal had a nervous smile. "Well, we must stop Azfet, or she will enslave this galaxy then move farther out and wreak havoc throughout this entire universe."

The soft breeze curving the high grasses made the threat feel like a dream. "How powerful is Azfet?"

"She is a powerful goddess of chaos and misrule. Your people are not prepared to defend themselves against her twisted mind, her cruelty, or her destructive powers." Kal's jaw tightened. "She is more powerful than any angel in this universe, and her friend, the demon master, is lending her his strength as well."

"Can we stop her?" Indra hoped so.

"I don't know." Kal scraped his face. "When I entered this universe, she had me ambushed at the gate. Then she had my crystal taken from me and promptly ordered my memories erased. Without my crystal I have no powers, while hers have been growing out of bounds."

"How did you end up on Laxxar?" Indra shuddered at the rumors she'd heard about that terrible place. Only the worst convicts went there. "It must have been horrible."

"I realize now that I didn't deserve to go there." Kal sighed. "Azfet paid Zethar to keep me prisoner while she organized her conquest of this galaxy."

"Conquest?" That sounded ominous. "But with what army? The people here are barely bouncing back from their fight for freedom from the GTA and the destruction it left in its wake." Indra still felt sadness at the slaughter of her own people, the Anvad. Only a few thousand had escaped and survived.

"I suspect Azfet's army is not of this world." Kal's shoulders slumped.

"What do you mean?" Indra realized there might be more than one villain.

"The entity that freed Azfet cannot conquer physical worlds on his own, as he has no dominion on the physical realm, so he cannot rule... but he can use her to rule in his place. He can control her, possess her, lend her his armies of supernatural creatures, and experience the physical world through her."

"Supernatural creatures?" Indra hoped her brethren had weapons against that evil. "Do you know who that entity is?"

"His name is Nyxor... the bringer of darkness and suffering." Kal's words seemed to darken the light and bring a cold wind to the overgrown meadow.

"Can he be destroyed?" Indra hoped so.

"I don't know... but the best way to stop him is to kill Azfet." Such determination in Kal's brow.

"Kill her how?" Indra didn't feel ready to fight such evil. "She sounds very powerful."

"Because we came from the same universe, the violet stone can find her and weaken her..." Kal sighed. "It might possibly kill her."

"But you don't know for sure?" This couldn't be good.

"The physical laws of this universe are different from mine. I can only hope..."

"Yet, your crystal now belongs to Spartacus." Indra realized the large cat would never give it up. And neutralizing Spartacus before an important battle would leave them short of a vital warrior.

"Without it, I don't stand a chance." Kal shook his head in dejection. "I lack the angel powers to fight her."

Indra understood the dangers but this was no time to be squeamish. "You are not alone, Kal. This universe has many angels. Together we shall find a way to stop that evil."

Kal smiled as he gazed into her eyes. "I admire your spunk, Indra. Here you are, admittedly not a warrior, weakened away from the *Blue Phantom*, yet you want to go to war against the most dangerous goddess this universe may ever encounter."

Indra smiled. "I may not have all my angel powers right now, but we have the violet crystal on our side. It still hides us from Azfet. She should fear us."

"You are incredible." Kal's eyes shone as he gazed into hers.

Indra felt a delicious frisson. "There are many ways to fight evil. Not all of them include fighting with a sword." Indra chuckled. "But I will gladly fight at your side with nothing but a sword, if need be."

"My people would say the angels of this universe are soft and weak, but you are the most courageous of all." Kal took her hand and squeezed it, then let it go.

Indra shivered with delight at the contact of his fingers. Delicious quivers coursed her entire body and made it tingle. Now that she knew Kal fought for the light, and he couldn't return to his original world, she was more than ever resolute to give him a new home to protect and defend, a new family, a reason to live.

Chapter Twelve

Azfet paced her luxurious temple to curb her frustration, dismissive of the golden Sphynxes on their pedestals, who followed her angry steps with cold eyes. Even the scent of sweet Myrrh couldn't calm her.

She couldn't believe her nemesis had vanished from her far-sight. How could it be? Why couldn't she locate Kal? Why couldn't she sense the violet crystal anymore? She hoped Kal didn't retrieve and wear it. It would restore his powers, and that would be bad for her plans. How she hated the Angel Guardians of her world, especially Kal. Why did the knucklehead have to follow her here?

Born different, from a long line of ancient space tyrants, Azfet was raised as a free thinker. The Angel Guardians of her universe were stern and strict. They had slaughtered her entire family for breaking their stupid rules.

As a youngster, Azfet pretended to conform in order to survive. But once she became an Angel Guardian with strong powers of her own, she showed the other Guardians she could break the rules, again and again, and she wouldn't let their narrow view of ethics dictate how she lived her life.

They arrested her for her repeated infractions and so-called crimes, called her an abomination, a disgrace to their kind, and sent her to rot in a hellish prison.

But even as Azfet suffered excruciating torture, Nyxor had noticed her wild and reckless nature. He'd recognized her special bloodline, that of the ancient space tyrants. He liked her so much, he gave her the blood stone that allowed her to fool her jailers and escape.

Azfet caressed the red gem hanging between her bare breasts, enjoying the scent of her lover and the vibrations emanating from it. That stone gave her more supernatural powers than any other being in this universe.

Yet, the violet crystal could track and recognize her. Since they came from the same universe, it was attracted to her. She could never be in its vicinity, or Kal might find her. And if his angelic powers were ever restored, he might present a real danger. Since he came after her, she assumed he must have the tools to send her back to the hell she'd escaped.

Damn the Guardians and their infernal crystal. And now, she could no longer locate the darn gem. How she loathed the cruel Guardians, and she hated Kal most of all.

As she scanned the dark depths of empty space through her red crystal, Azfet could see the *Blue Phantom*, its captain, and its crew. They all seemed to be in a frenzy. They'd also lost contact with Kal's raptor and, despite their best efforts, couldn't locate it either.

Spying on them wouldn't help Azfet find Kal. The angels of this universe were pathetic, encumbered by kindness and high principles of respect for life. What a bunch of sad puppies. Their protective streak and deep empathy for each other would make them easy to crush.

Now, here, Azfet had another chance to make her mark and live free, outside any rules like her ancestors did. With Nyxor at her side, without regard for the puny people of this universe... She would take what she wanted. No one would be strong enough to stop her, except maybe Kal if he ever retrieved his memories, or was reunited with his infernal violet crystal.

All her attempts to have him killed had failed, but she hoped she could keep him contained and away from her. Maybe Nyxor could help her vanquish the pesky Angel Guardian and destroy his infernal stone... if she asked nicely.

She lay on the white chaise and stretched languorously. "Nyxor, my love..."

"Yes, Beloved." The familiar red mist enveloped her, caressing her to the brink of extasy.

The mist solidified into her gorgeous lover, with glistening red skin, ram horns, white teeth, and hands so skilled at making her swoon. He lay next to her and enveloped her in his arms.

Azfet trembled in his embrace. "Have you detected my enemy, yet?"

He kissed the tender skin inside her elbow. "Of course, Beloved. No one in any universe can hide from me."

"Good to know." Azfet hoped she'd never have to hide from him. "Where is he?"

"Do not worry about such details, Beloved. I can take care of him."

Azfet felt uneasy about the secrecy, but she trusted Nyxor's love for her. "So, you will kill my nemesis for me, for us?"

"You know I do not kill, Beloved. But my minions can if I give the order." His many kisses fluttered up the inside of her arm and nestled in the hollow of her shoulder.

"Then, please, get it done... for me..." Azfet struggled to stay focused under the onslaught of delicious sensations. "So we can enjoy our bliss with total abandon."

"Your wish is my command, Beloved." Nyxor grinned, white teeth flashing. "I will send my demons presently." He rose from the couch, took her hand, and softly kissed her fingers, sending frissons cascading through her entire body.

"I will be eternally grateful, my love." Azfet let go of his hand with reluctance.

"I will hold you to these words, for all eternity, Beloved." Nyxor stepped back and blew her a kiss, then vanished into a red cloud.

Maybe all eternity was a little too much, but Azfet needed Nyxor. All her attempts at containing Kal had failed, and his death would be a welcome relief. Without him to wield it, the violet crystal could be contained, destroyed, or cast away.

Azfet hoped Nyxor would succeed... although an eternity of submissive love might be too high a price to pay for a free spirit like her. But, if she had to lie to get the job done, so be it.

She wished she could be there and watch his demons kill the arrogant Guardian, but it would be too dangerous. Her close proximity could endanger her life.

Now that Nyxor was taking care of Kal, Azfet could concentrate on her conquest. She waved a hand over her red crystal and a mature man in a red uniform appeared as a 3D hologram.

"Admiral Blackthorn!" Azfet didn't bother acting the seductress for him. He was too old for that. All he wanted was gold.

"Highness..." The tall, skinny man bowed low, exposing his shaved scalp... or maybe he was bald. "To what do I owe the pleasure? Is there a new development in our plan?"

Azfet thrilled at the very thought. "It's time to launch our conquest, Admiral, starting with a small blue planet and its population of supernatural beings."

"Highness, I'm a soldier. I do not believe in the supernatural." The old man straightened his wiry frame. His voice still held the strength of a bullwhip. "I believe in preparedness, strategy, superior weaponry, and higher technology."

"Right." Azfet realized her magic was eons ahead of what that man could fathom. "For you, magic is just advanced technology you do not yet understand."

"Exactly, Highness." The man's smile resembled a death rictus, his face made paler by the bright red of his coat. "When you first contacted me to gather the available military forces of this galaxy, I was skeptical. But your infinite reserve of gold performed miracles. Mercenaries, soldiers of fortune, and local warlords rushed from all the recesses of the galaxy to serve such a generous leader."

Azfet smiled. "And the better they serve me, the more they will receive."

"Thank you, Highness. Serving you is a true privilege." The admiral bowed even lower. "Anything for your pleasure, Highness."

Azfet chuckled at the man's narrow mindedness, but she appreciated the impressive fleet and the armies he'd managed to assemble. "With my special weapons, you won't have any problems neutralizing that little planet and exterminating its arrogant population. Then you can blow it up to smithereens."

"A planet?" The admiral cleared his throat. "About those incredibly advanced weapons you provided... are you certain they will operate as you claim on an entire planet?"

"My weapons' destructive power is stronger than you can imagine. They will also neutralize your enemy's so-called supernatural shields and special abilities..."

"Good." The man took a deep breath. "We tested them on inert asteroids, and they performed beautifully, but we did not get a chance to use them in battle."

"Fear not. Your enemies do not stand a chance. The last of these weapons should be arriving to your star base as we speak." Azfet smiled at the prospect of total destruction. "Please, make haste."

"I will, Highness. For the agreed price, of course." The older man's eyes gleamed with open greed.

"Don't worry, Blackthorn. Your gold shipment is being delivered with the last weapons." The old weasel wouldn't even accept credits.

"Thank you, Highness." The admiral rubbed his hands together and cleared his throat. "Where is that rebellious planet located?"

"Its name is Azura, it is forbidden and has been erased from the galactic charts long ago, but I am sending you the coordinates." The formidable angel-killing weapons built upon her specifications, and the intel Zethar provided on Azura would finally come handy.

The admiral bowed again. "Your will be done, Highness."

Azfet waved, erasing the hologram, and smiled. Time to get rid of these measly angels who fooled themselves into thinking they were invincible. Once they were crushed into dust, and after Nyxor destroyed Kal, no one would dare stand in her way.

* * *

Graziella sensed the change in the air. She focused on her angels.

"Captain!" An AI angel materialized into the command deck and projected an image in front of her. "The *Blue Phantom's* scanners detected strange activity between our stars."

In the 3D space between them, Graziella recognized a familiar star chart, and floating between the many stars, obscuring them as they flew in front of them, several groups of black beings, like so many giant bats, flew from the four points of the galaxy toward the same coordinates.

Graziella gasped. She recognized this kind of cloud. She'd seen it before, during the final battle. And she'd hoped she'd never see their kind again.

The AI crew still projected the image from one of his eyes. "What are they? Are they a danger to us?"

Iaco, at her side, beeped. "Consult your archives, AI. These are demons."

189

Graziella shivered at the thought. "Since the final battle, we engineered a special cast of AI angels to fight these creatures, the Demon Slayers. Iaco, here, is one of them."

"We were right to plan for their return." Iaco bowed. "I am at your service, Captain."

"These demons..." The AI stopped projecting. "Where are they going? What do they want?"

Graziella reminded herself she shouldn't spread the panic she felt inside. Many of the angels on the Blue Phantom had never faced this kind of enemy. "They are not coming for us, but I want to know where they are going. Project their trajectory."

"Aye, Captain." The AI crew manifested a 3D chart in the empty space between them. Blue lines surged from the fast-moving black clouds to plot their destination. They all converged toward one single spot, not a planet, but the middle of nowhere in space. Graziella wondered why.

"Set a course for that location." But Graziella realized if they had to fight, her angels would be greatly outnumbered.

"Captain?" Iaco chirped. "Should we contact Azura? And maybe Byzantium as well?"

"Absolutely." This time, Graziella didn't hesitate. "Contact the AI angels of Azura and the Byzantium Space Station. Show them the demonic hordes. They will send the caste of Demon-Slayer AIs to help us. It's their duty to fight when demons manifest in such numbers. This is an open provocation to overpower the forces of good. As of now, we are all under attack."

"Aye, Captain." Iaco closed its blue luminous eyes and went into far communication mode.

Graziella closed her eyes and made contact with all the individual minds of the crew. "All angels on the *Blue Phantom*. Prepare for battle. Stealth mode and battle stations. This is not a drill."

"Captain?" Iaco's blue eyes opened wide and light seeped out of his metallic frame. "There is a problem with Azura."

"What problem?" Graziella hoped it was only technical.

"See for yourself. This is from a brother on the surface." Iaco projected 3D images from Azura, where menacing ships circled the forbidden planet.

As the images grew closer, Graziella recognized the turquoise oceans and green forests of Azura, but something seemed odd. Large military ships hovered overhead, inside the atmosphere. "Impossible! No regular ship can function inside Azura's atmosphere. They are supposed to fall and crash."

The vivid hologram also recorded screams. A strange weapons array striated the sky and struck (?), and Graziella could see angels falling from the sky in a deadly spiral speeding toward the hard ground.

Graziella shuddered. "What's happening? There was no warning, no threat, no declaration of war."

Iaco beeped. "And yet the enemy penetrated Azura's planetary defenses and is devastating the countryside and killing the angel population."

"Do we have a report from them?"

Iaco beeped again and a different voice narrated the carnage. "The enemy seems to use a technology superior to ours. Not only did they neutralize the planetary shields, but they found a way to neutralize our angelic abilities as well. Without them, our weapons no longer function, while theirs are efficient and deadly. Legions of Avenging Angels are helpless, weaponless. We are being exterminated like bugs."

Graziella could not show the fear eating at her insides. "No help will come from Azura, and given the technology of the invader, going to their help would be suicide. Besides, this seems like a coordinated attack, and we have our own battle to fight here against these demons. Maybe Byzantium can send us reinforcements."

"Aye, aye, Captain." Iaco closed his eyes and went back into communication mode.

Graziella focused her mind on the large crystal of the ship's temple. "May the Formless One protect us all."

But she knew the Formless One never took sides.

Chapter Thirteen

Back on the command deck of the *Prism*, Kal itched to grab his violet stone, but every time he as much as glanced at it, Spartacus growled and bared his fangs. Fortunately, the cat remained close, napping with Panthera on the deck, and his proximity gave Kal strength and sharper senses.

At least, he now remembered his past, and his mission. He must confront Azfet, and for that he should be searching for her in space, not hiding on a planetoid. Trusting the violet stone to guide him, Kal set a course in what he sensed must be Azfet's direction.

Indra rose from her side seat and pointed at a section of space through the ship's forward shield. "What is that?"

Kal saw strange movement in the black vastness and focused his keen sight on that sector. "It looks like a moving cloud... or angry waves on a dark ocean."

"This is not a cloud, nor is it waves, Captain." Prism, the female AI sitting next to him, managed a sarcastic tone.

Indra stared at the smudge in space. "What is it?"

"Magnifying..." Prism stared into nothingness, controlling the ship's monitors directly from her artificial brain, which emitted blue light.

The image on the monitors lining the bulkhead closed up on the phenomenon. There it was, a dark cloud, moving like rolling waves at incredible speed, straight for the angel raptor.

Kal shuddered. "I don't remember ever seeing anything like this. Not even in my old memories."

Indra set her hand upon his on the console, sending goosebumps up his arm. He struggled not to react... he could read her feelings. She was scared.

"I've never seen this either." She pulled back her hand and swallowed noisily. "But the angels on the *Blue Phantom* still talk about such things happening in the past... I hope it's not what I think."

Kal stared at the monitors, where the image magnified and refocused. It wasn't a cloud, or waves, but a flurry of shiny black wings flying fast through space. A closer look revealed the leathery wings were attached to horned furry creatures, with snarling faces, fangs, pointy white teeth, long tails, and red eyes.

Indra gasped. "Demons! These are demons!"

Prism beeped and her luminous blue eyes flashed. "I concur. According to the archives, these fit the description of demons Azuran angels faced in the past."

Kal frowned. He'd fought evil forces in his own universe, but never this particular kind. "What do you know about demons? How do they fight? What can they do? Do we have efficient weapons against them?"

Prism beeped. "Demons are inferior lifeforms who respond to evil thoughts and can easily be controlled by dark forces. They have little tolerance for light. They are voracious and feed on the living. They use no weapons, nor do they wear armor, but their skin is impervious to most weapons."

"How did they find us?" Indra's voice trembled. "They seem to know exactly where we are. Doesn't the violet stone hide us from anyone?"

Prism cleared her synthetic voice. "Maybe they can smell us. Many biological lifeforms have a developed sense of smell."

Kal needed more intel. "What else do you know about them?"

"Their natural thirst for blood guides them to their prey." Prism sounded so cold and analytic. "They have the ability to vanish and reappear at will. They are agile and use their sharp teeth to kill and maim, and even pierce through a ships' hull and metal bulkhead."

"Charming." Kal wondered how he could use that information. "You said, they fear light. If we send a wave of bright light, would that harm them? Or at least blind them?"

"No, Captain, it would only disorient them for a few seconds." Prism's tone turned sarcastic again.

Indra still stared at the ominous cloud, her face frozen in fear. "Can they be killed?"

"They are biological creatures, susceptible to being killed, yes." Prism froze, her luminous eyes flashing as she consulted the archives. "However, their natural armor, their speed, agility, and their vanishing powers make it difficult to strike or catch them."

Kal needed something concrete. "Can they be burnt? Irradiated? What works best?"

Prism beeped. "Azuran angels have been known to kill them will light bolts generated from crystal weapons. But you have to be an angel to wield one."

Indra shook her head. "I don't know how strong my powers are right now. I may not be able to use angel weapons, so far from the *Blue Phantom*."

Prism chuckled. "I can. I am an AI angel with my own crystal core."

"Good to know." Kal would need all the fighters he could get.

Prism stared at Indra. "But of course, my crystal is too small to help you."

Indra dropped her head. "I know that."

"That is unfortunate." Kal would have to protect Indra somehow. He returned his attention to the dark cloud. "How long before they get here?"

Prism beeped. "One standard hour, Captain."

Indra sighed. "I wish I could instantly fly the Prism somewhere faraway, like Captain Graziella does... but it takes special powers to do that."

"Don't beat yourself up." But Kal would never run away from a fight. "What arsenal do we have on the hull of this ship?" Kal's previous inventory might not help much. "Something anyone can wield."

Prism cleared her voice. "The two main cannons on the hull, twenty light guns all around the periphery, and the large belly blaster can only be operated by angels with full powers."

"Prism, can you operate all these guns all at once from your seat?" Kal hoped so.

"Many of them, yes, Captain. But not all. It will not be enough if we are surrounded." Prism's voice trailed. "Also, these demons can withstand our shields and pierce the hull."

"Can we poison the shields?" Kal remembered an instance in his past where the Guardians used that technique. "Can we make the shields deadly to them?"

"Possibly." Prism seemed to reflect. "But it will take time."

"We don't have time." Indra bit her lips. "Maybe we should call for help. The *Blue Phantom* is probably looking for us."

"The AIs of the Blue Phantom want to kill us both." Kal shook his head in frustration. "But we may not have a choice." The mission should come first.

Indra sighed. "If the demons get inside this ship, we'll all be dead anyway. There are too many of them."

Prism beeped. "Not me. I can survive. I can just disappear."

The beast at Kal's feet growled. *"Spartacus disappear."*

"Good for you." Kal hated the idea of calling the *Blue Phantom*, but he had no other choice. "Okay. Let Graziella know where we are and what we are up against."

"Aye, aye, Captain." Prism beeped and initiated a call.

"No." Indra took a deep breath. "Let me do it. I know Captain Graziella. She is just and merciful. She will hear me with kindness and understanding."

"All right." Kal realized how different the angels of this universe were from his. No Angel Guardian in his universe could be called kind or understanding.

* * *

In the observation dome of the *Blue Phantom*, Graziella closed her eyes as she sensed the incoming call. "Indra!"

Indra appeared before her in ethereal form, haggard, scared, eyes wide. "Captain, there is a horde of demons rushing to meet us."

"We've detected the horde and we are tracking them right now." Graziella sighed. "What about Kal? Is he a danger to us?"

"No, Captain." Indra sighed. "Kal is on our side. He recovered his memories, and his mission is to kill an evil entity called Azfet."

Graziella trusted Indra. Angels never lied. But was she blinded by Kal? "We know all about Dominara Azfet, but we haven't been able to locate her."

"She hides from Kal who is hunting her. She cannot be in the same vicinity. He is her archenemy and determined to kill her."

Graziella smiled. She always liked Indra. "Thank you, Indra for that information. The *Blue Phantom* and its crew will come to your help. But you should know there are other demon hordes converging toward you as we speak. We tracked their trajectory, and we shall join you shortly."

"Thank you, Captain." Indra's ethereal form smiled and bowed slightly before vanishing.

Graziella refocused her mind and called "Iaco, I have a mission for you."

The tall AI angel bowed to her. "I am at your service, Captain."

"Iaco, you dealt with the cyborg lord Zethar before. I need you to enroll his help. We must find the whereabouts of the entity called Azfet. He admitted having dealt with her recently."

"Yes, Captain. But the crime lord doesn't like angels. Although, he seems to hate

Dominara Azfet even more, and he has major weaknesses we can exploit."

"What weaknesses?" These crime lords had so many.

"Credits... and advanced technology. Zethar loves both equally."

Graziella shook her head. "Then credits he will get. We do not disseminate our technology."

Graziella closed her eyes and communicated her plan to Iaco, then she waved away the AI. "Now, go."

Iaco bowed. "At your service, Captain."

Then he vanished.

* * *

In his office, on the Pandemonium Space Station, Zethar felt a sudden cold breeze and looked away from the row of monitors lining the bulkhead.

His valet stepped in. "My lord, you have a visitor."

"Who is it? Didn't you get a name?" Good servants were difficult to find these days.

Zethar straightened as he recognized the tall silhouette of the AI Iaco, who now folded impressive metal wings. What was with the dramatic effects? As if he would respond to such simple intimidation. As if the hardware wasn't enough to impress him.

Zethar braced himself and rose to his fullest height. "Iaco! To what do I owe the pleasure? Have you come to tempt me with your superior technology?"

Iaco bowed politely. "I come on behalf of the *Blue Phantom*. We are fighting a great evil and we need your help."

"My help?" Zethar smiled at the prospect of profit. "I can contribute ships and my private army to your cause, but it will cost you."

"We are prepared to pay you handsomely." Iaco straightened. "But we do not need your army... we have a better one."

Zethar contained his humiliation, but the AI was right. "Then, by all means, what can I do for you?"

He had already computed in his head how much he should charge for his help.

"Help us locate the entity known as Dominara Azfet." The AI raised his brow.

"Her Highness Herself? That's all?" Zethar whistled. "I turned on the gadget you gave me last time she called. Didn't you track her then?"

"We did. But she instantly vanished." Iaco lowered his head in a good imitation of human shame. "We want to use the technology she gave you to locate and trap angels. We'll use it to trap her. Then we'll use an angel-proof jail to contain her."

"I see..." So, Zethar was right. That technology could be used against her. Good to know. Maybe he should switch camps. He couldn't spend his credits if Azfet had him killed.

Iaco blinked. "Do you happen to know where Azfet is?"

"No. I suspect she is on a ship and moves all the time…" Zethar smelled a fortune coming his way. "But I know how to contact her."

"Would you be willing to do it?" The AI's stare didn't seem to give him a choice.

But Zethar felt a little reckless, giddy at the idea of sticking it to Azfet. "I may be able to help you… for a price, of course."

"That sounds fair." Iaco almost smiled. "But you must set the trap. Call her and lie to her, so we know where to wait for her."

Zethar didn't like the idea of incurring the psycho lady's wrath. "I'm not sure it will work. She can read my mind. She will know it's a trap."

"No worries." Iaco's tone wasn't reassuring at all. "I will be here during the call and shield your thoughts from her."

"You can do that?" Zethar realized he'd made the smart choice. He could charge a king's ransom and get the dangerous psychopath out of his life. "I don't care for that plan, but for the right price, I agree."

Fortune favored the brave. No sniveling coward ever became a powerful crime lord.

Chapter Fourteen

The temple chimes hit a strange note. The cloud of incense smoke floated above Azfet's head. She startled at a familiar vibration of her blood stone.

She rose from her lounge chair and adjusted the slit of her gown. It wasn't Nyxor. Still... "Zethar?"

She waved away her guards, who were not privy to her personal dealings. The four armored Sphynxes leapt down from their pedestals, folded their great wings, then took human shape and filed out in orderly fashion.

The holographic silhouette of the infamous crime lord materialized before Azfet. His skull plates gleamed, his lips curled up, and he seemed to have a new spring in his step... but he didn't bow. "Greetings, Highness. I have good news."

Azfet scanned the man's thoughts for the news and gasped in surprise, but she hid her deeper concerns. "Why can I no longer read your mind?"

Zethar flashed a mysterious smile. "I paid a billion credits to update the hardware in my head, Highness. It does more than make me look handsome and irresistibly charming."

How bold of him to tease her. Could she still trust him? She couldn't imagine Zethar betraying her. He wasn't the hero type and wouldn't want her as his enemy. Besides, he worshipped credits, and she had plenty to offer. Still... "So, what's your good news, Zethar? Did you recapture my prisoner?"

"Not exactly, Highness, but I know where he is." Zethar seemed very sure of himself.

Azfet raised her brow. How could a simple human have done what she couldn't? Nyxor said he could find Kal but wouldn't give her the coordinates. She still resented him for it. "And how, exactly, did you locate my escapee?"

"I have connections in high places, Highness." Zethar's smug smile could mean trouble. "Your archenemy, Kal, is presently alone and vulnerable on the *Prism*."

"Kal?" Azfet's hackles went up. This didn't augur well. The man was digging into forbidden territory. "How do you know his name?"

"I know lots of things, Highness." Zethar's arrogance wouldn't work in his favor. "I intercepted a message from the *Blue Phantom*, saying Kal has his memories back, but not the violet crystal... whatever that means."

"How did you learn so much about Kal and the violet crystal?"

"I spy on angels, Highness. I have moles everywhere. Of course, I know what's happening in this galaxy." Zethar smirked. "I also have many connections to procure highly illegal goods and commodities, like high-tech weapons. I'm a powerful crime lord, with his own military force, not a clueless idiot."

Was this a trick? Perhaps Azfet shouldn't trust Zethar, but what if he told the truth? If Kal was located, and he didn't possess his crystal, this could be her chance. "Where is Spartacus now?"

Zethar straightened and locked his hands behind his back. "Spartacus is on the *Blue Phantom*, with the female angel and the albino cat."

"And where is the *Blue Phantom*?" For some reason, Azfet couldn't locate it either.

"They abandoned Kal to his fate and vanished, Highness. The *Blue Phantom* went so far away that it can't be tracked." Zethar's face remained unreadable.

Azfet was tempted to believe him. The cowardice of the angels of this universe had no bounds. Even on Azura, they were surrendering rather than face extermination. Admiral Blackthorn, however, followed her orders. No prisoners.

"So, Kal is truly alone on the *Prism*?" And with his crystal so far away, he would be vulnerable, with no angel abilities to fight her. How she would enjoy killing Kal herself, rather than leave the job to Nyxor's demons. She could show her handsome devil she didn't need a protector.

"Isn't that good news, Highness?" Zethar seemed delighted.

"Good news indeed." But no one should know about the properties of the violet crystal, Angel Guardian Kal, or the circumstances of their arrival into this universe.

Zethar sat in a desk chair, crossed his legs, and casually glanced at his fingernails. "This information is easily worth half a million credits. Don't you think?"

"Just the information?" The audacity of the man. "You didn't finish the job and capture him for me."

"Of course, I could have Kal picked up." He raised his piercing stare. "But even if I use your superior technology, he might still be too much for my mercenaries to handle. I don't want him to escape yet again, so... I was hoping you could help."

Azfet wanted to smash Zethar's metal-plated skull for meddling, but she calmed herself. Although she didn't quite trust him, he'd served her well so far, and he liked credits above all. Lavish payments would secure his loyalty. "I'm seriously considering your proposition."

"Thank you, Highness." The arrogant tin man bowed, but not low enough for her taste.

"And if your information pans out, you'll be exceptionally well rewarded..." Azfet scanned the man's thoughts for a reaction, but again came up empty. "Enough credits to triple the size of your personal army."

"Excellent." Zethar reached to his desk and turned a screen in her direction for her perusal. On it, series of numbers and symbols. "These are the present coordinates of the *Prism*... check away."

"I will." Azfet stared and memorized the coordinates. "Thank you, Zethar. Credits are on their way."

She waved and the hologram of Zethar vanished.

This could be the chance she'd hoped for, while Kal was weak and alone, her only opportunity to silence him forever. She straightened, closed her eyes, and focused on the navigation controls. "Turn this ship around and recalibrate to the coordinates I'm sending you now."

The ship turned smoothly and purred on its way to its new destination.

If Kal was still there when she arrived, and she could get rid of him for good, Zethar would have proven himself very useful indeed... but he knew too much, and she couldn't trust such a prying associate. He might eventually try to extort or blackmail her.

Azfet would have to terminate him as soon as she got rid of Kal.

* * *

"Coming up on the *Prism*, Captain," a female voice chimed, filling the observation dome of the *Blue Phantom*.

"Thanks." Graziella gazed into space through the clear dome and gasped.

At her side, Iaco the AI emissary, pointed to a dark cloud. "The demons are coming fast, Captain."

Graziella couldn't help the revulsion at the sight of the unholy creatures. "Remain in stealth mode."

"Aye, aye, Captain. Maintaining stealth mode," the disembodied feminine voice pervaded the entire dome.

Iaco stared at the cloud. "I hope they don't have the weapons used on the Azurans. What if we lose angel power?"

"It's unlikely. Demons do not carry weapons of any kind. They are the weapons." Graziella scanned the demonic horde and slowed her breathing to calm herself. "But even if we were attacked with such weapons, the *Blue Phantom* used to be a GTA warship and most of the old weaponry is still operational."

"Good to know." Iaco nodded. "Still. There are so many of them, and Azura cannot help."

Graziella bit her lips. "How far are the AI reinforcements from Byzantium?"

Iaco's luminous blue eyes dimmed slightly. "Very close, Captain... but it's only a few hundred AIs. Their main force went to assist Azura."

"Understood." Graziella would have to fight smart. At least, she and her angels still had their full powers, unlike the Azurans, who were losing their planetary battle. A console rose from the deck and she swiped the ship-wide alert key. "All angels on alert. Everyone, battle stations. Open the armory and prepare to fight in close quarters if necessary."

Graziella hoped the nasty beasts wouldn't breach the hull.

Sirens rang throughout the *Blue Phantom* and heavy AIs stomped along the corridors. Other angels flew to their assigned positions. Graziella focused her mind on her ship. She felt its pulse, sensed the power of its engines. Could it overcome hordes of metal-piercing creatures, bent on killing and destruction?

On days like this, however, Graziella took comfort in the fact that the *Blue Phantom* was under the protection of the forces of good... and was once a sturdy destroyer from an ancient war. This warship had vanquished worse enemies in the past, but would it survive today's battle?

* * *

Kal set his jaw in determination as he selected a bow and explosive arrows, from the weapons Indra had gathered for him. Time to remember his training. He glanced at the violet crystal with longing. So close, yet unreachable. If only he could touch it… wear it. Then he would have a real chance to kill Azfet.

Through the clear flexglaz forward shield, Kal stared at the billowing sea of black wings with growing dread.

Prism beeped. "Here they come. Still too far to fire the ship's weapons."

Kal had never met this kind of enemy and wished he had Guardian weapons.

Indra, at his side, trembled. Her eyes widened. "Prism, can they see us in stealth mode?"

Prism beeped. "I cannot tell, but they are rushing toward us as if we activated a homing beacon."

Kal glanced back at the violet gem on the big cat's collar. It flared. "Maybe the crystal serves as a beacon for these abominations."

Spartacus sat straight and growled, lips raised, fangs protruding, all senses in alert. *"Spartacus ready. Spartacus fight."*

The white feline next to him coughed and rose. *"Panthera hungry."*

Indra glanced at the white cat. "How can you be so hungry all the time? You are getting fat. Soon your tummy will drag on the deck."

The white cat shook her head. *"Panthera eat. Panthera strong. Protect family."*

"Not the worst idea." Kal nodded. "The cats might fight better if well fed."

"Okay." Indra went to the bulkhead where they kept the protein rations. She dropped them on the deck for the two cats. "Eat to get your strength."

Panthera rushed to eat. Spartacus followed her but only nibbled. Panthera gulped his leftovers as well.

Indra petted the white cat. "I'm glad you consider us your family, big girl."

When Indra rose to her feet, she seemed to glow, then her wings sprang out. "My angel abilities are returning. The *Blue Phantom* must be close!" She checked the monitors. "No sign of a ship on the screens."

Prism beeped. "I feel stronger, too. They must be in stealth mode. I can't contact them, but it's standard procedure to remain incommunicado when expecting an attack."

"That makes sense." But Kal still felt helpless about that advancing demon horde. "At least, we are not alone. Does the *Blue Phantom* have effective weapons against these black monsters?"

"Yes. And now, so do we." Indra sat at a big gun station and assumed a meditative pose. "Since my powers have returned, I can fire our angel weapons with Prism."

"We are going to need all the fire power we can muster." Kal would be the only one without angel powers... in a fight against dark forces. It didn't feel right. The violet crystal called to him. How he wished he could grab it.

Angel powers or not, he must complete his mission and save this universe... for those who cared about him, like Indra, and

Panthera. He cared about them, too, and wanted them to live. And yes, this could become his new home… but first, he must save it from Azfet and her fiendish minions.

Indra, staring into nothingness, took a slow breath. "Let's see if our cannons can stop these hellish creatures."

Kal watched Indra as she closed her eyes and focused. Her expression turned fierce. A salvo of bright blue light surged in front of the *Prism* and hit the black cloud like an explosive wave. Demons flew off, blasting in every direction. Their horrified expressions on the magnified monitors failed to melt Kal's heart. He felt no pity for the horrible creatures.

Then more salvos hit the demonic hordes, but they seemed to be coming from above the *Prism*.

Kal stared at Indra then Prism. "Was that us?"

"No." Indra opened her eyes and smiled. "The *Blue Phantom* is hovering above us and protecting us."

Kal adjusted the bow across his shoulder as he stared through the clear flexglaz shield. He felt only dread. "What's happening? The demons are not dying. They recover too quickly. They are reforming their cloud."

Prism stared into nothingness. So did Indra. Many more salvos of blue exploding waves hit the demonic cloud. But like before, only a few demons scattered while thousands reformed ranks. Strange…

"Are you sure these creatures can be killed?" Kal started to doubt it. "Are they physical or just magical?"

"They are physical, Captain." Mockery seeped into Prism's tone. "They simply vanish as the blast hits, then quickly reappear. That's how they dodge the salvos."

"Great!" Kal didn't see a good end to this fight. "Keep firing." But he should be out there, looking for Azfet, hunting her with the crystal. She was the key to victory. Where was she? Probably laughing as she watched the attack from a safe distance.

"Spartacus kill monster." The beast looked wild, pacing the deck, clearly agitated.

Panthera bumped heads with him, trying to calm down the big, rugged cat.

"You may get your chance, big boy." But Kal hoped it wouldn't come to close quarter fighting.

Indra and Prism focused, eyes closed and many more blue waves from the raptor and the *Blue Phantom* hit the black throng of wings, but none caused real damage.

Kal focused on a dim light in space, coming from his left. "What's that?"

Indra opened her eyes and laughed. "A legion of AI angels!"

"Reinforcements?" Kal breathed easier as he watched the phalanx flying in formation, straight for the evil cloud. "It's about time."

But as the phalanx drew closer, Kal realized there weren't enough AIs in it. Still, they charged the cloud and detonated blue light weapons that seemed to disturb the creatures more than the long-range waves.

"Magnify!" Kal stared at the monitors where the spectacle warmed his heart.

He could see the demons' faces as they screamed, their expression horribly distorted, awkward bodies tumbling and gyrating in space with broken wings at odd angles. He could see sizzling wings, broken horns, loose guts and large blood bubbles suspended and freezing in space.

But there were too many demons, the AI angels couldn't kill them all. Another phalanx of AIs came from behind the Prism... probably from the *Blue Phantom*. They added their forces to cause more damage in demonic ranks... but still their efforts seemed futile.

Soon, a group of demons separated from the main horde and rushed toward the *Prism*. They threw themselves on the shields that burned their wings, but they kept coming. They screamed, but the pain didn't stop them from hurling themselves at the burning shields.

Kal swiped the console to change the chemical content and increase the slicing strength of the shields. "See if you like this, demons."

Their distorted faces through the clear flexglaz told of their hunger for flesh. They drooled, and their red eyes rolled in their sockets, as the heads decapitated by the shields hit the flexglaz. Acid saliva dripped from their fangs and sizzled on the metallic glass.

Spartacus leapt onto the console and roared at the devils behind the shields.

They didn't seem scared of him... nor him of them.

Kal remembered the demons had certain abilities. "Can they dematerialize and rematerialize through the hull?"

"Yes, but not through the shield, especially since you spiked it." Prism didn't sound worried.

"May the Formless One protect us." Indra whispered, a haggard look on her lovely face.

"You know the Formless One never takes sides," Prism railed.

Kal considered the surrounding bulkhead. "If these abominations break that flexglaz, or melt it with acid, we are going to lose oxygen."

Indra rushed to the side compartments and opened one. "There are oxygen masks in here. We should all have one, just in case."

"Not for me." Prism chuckled. "I don't need to breathe."

One particularly hard knock caused the ship to rock, then reel uncontrollably. Kal scrambled for balance. Indra gripped her console. So did Prism. Spartacus leapt down to the deck. The two felines planted their claws into the soft decking.

The flexglaz cracked. Air whistled as it seeped out.

Indra passed an oxygen mask to Kal, then she fitted a mask on Panthera and one on Spartacus.

"Hang on to something!" Kal felt the blood leaving his extremities. "Prepare to be boarded!" Then he realized if the flexglaz broke, they would all be sucked out into space. "Let's put a few bulkheads between us and these creatures."

He led the others down the spiral stairs to the middle deck. The sound of breaking metal glass exploded in his ears. The ship shook then flipped.

Kal closed the hatch behind them, watched the seal light go green, then took off his mask. He took a deep breath. "It's okay. We can breathe."

Indra imitated him. But a dozen demons materialized in front of them. Drat!

Kal fired his bow. The arrow exploded harmlessly into the air as the target vanished.

Indra raised her hand and fired a bolt of lightning out of her fingers frying one demon. The others dematerialized. Then they rematerialized together, advancing on Kal and his friends.

Spartacus ripped off his mask with his claws, roared and vanished. He must have pounced in invisible mode, as he reappeared slaughtering a demon in a spray of blood, then he pounced again. Strident screams escaped the demon's throat.

Taking a wide fighting stance, Kal, Indra, and Prism unsheathed their glowing swords. Kal could smell blood and carnage. He remembered the slaughter near the angel cell on Pandemonium and remembered many other battles. The memories sparked his energy.

Panthera shook off her mask, snatched a black furry creature coming at her and ripped off his throat. Then she buried her fangs into its entrails in a feeding frenzy, making loud slurping sounds. *"Panthera hungry. Good hamburger."*

Kal shuddered at her savagery.

Prism sent lightning strikes through her sword, repelling many. Kal chopped a few wings, stabbed at what might be a heart. But the creatures spat acid drops that ate through his white clothes. Holy Mandala! He shook his burned sleeve and swore under his breath.

The acid spit also ate through bulkhead and metal... and through the decking.

Indra seemed to remember her training and fought like an Avenging Angel, leaping high, flying, vanishing, and coming down with a vengeance. But the more demons they killed, even more appeared to fight them. This wouldn't end well.

"Indra?" Kal sliced and stabbed, but his breath grew ragged. "Can you take us someplace more manageable?"

"Seems like a good idea." Indra fought two demons at a time. "But where?"

"I know where." Prism dimmed her luminous eyes as she kept fighting. "There are many secret rooms and passages on this ship, and I know them all. How about here?"

Indra's face seemed to register the information from Prism. "Got it. Let's all hold hands."

Indra emitted a blue wave that pushed back the demons, who scrambled wings over heads then vanished, but not for long.

The two bloody felines rallied toward the three humanoids. They all linked hands and paws. Kal felt the tingling of dematerialization throughout his body.

Fighting with angels had its advantages. But wherever Indra would transport them, the demons would soon follow.

Chapter Fifteen

Graziella gazed outside the clear dome of the *Blue Phantom*, where the space battle raged between AI angels and demons. The horde of black creatures with red eyes attacked the luminous AIs without fear, vanishing and reappearing behind them, biting, and melting their metal, dismembering and killing.

As more demons attacked the *Blue Phantom's* shields, burning their wings on the force field and screaming in pain, Graziella realized fleeing was not an option. This evil must be stopped, right here, right now, and she was all that stood to stop it.

But her strategy was a gamble. If the demons infiltrated the *Blue Phantom*, all might be lost. "How are our shields holding?"

"Shields holding so far, Captain." The feminine voice spreading through the clear dome sounded worried.

So was Graziella, but she must control her fear, or panic could spread through the entire crew.

Iaco, at her side, beeped and turned to face her. "It seems Lord Zethar came through, Captain. He tells me Azfet is on her way. And I can sense her ship approaching. She is heading straight for our angel net.”

“Can we trust Zethar?” Graziella still had doubts about the crime lord. “He isn’t above playing both sides.”

“Maybe, but he got her to come to us, Captain. So far, so good.” Iaco sounded confident.

Finally, a break. “Is the trap ready?”

“Configurating the device now, Captain.” Iaco blinked and the light in his eyes dimmed. “But we have demons on our shields, and the Demon Slayers need to disappear from the battlefield. Any sign of angels in the vicinity, and Azfet might vanish before we can catch her.”

“Right.” Graziella touched her temple and closed her eyes. “All Demon Slayers in space, rally inside the *Blue Phantom* immediately. Leave no trace of our presence, no out of commission AIs or floating parts. Not even a screw or a bolt. We are setting the trap for Azfet, and the *Prism* is the bait. It should look marooned, alone and abandoned.”

Through the clear dome, Graziella could see the AIs disengaging the hordes, sweeping the battlefield, and dematerializing, taking with them body parts and dismantled AIs. Graziella focused on the cargo hold, where all of them rematerialized.

Perfect. “Take the downed AIs and the recovered parts to the body shop.”

Good thing the demons hadn't penetrated the *Phantom's* shields. Graziella mentally flared the shields, sending the demons attacking it flying into space. Then she dematerialized the *Blue Phantom* and rematerialized it a few clicks away from the battle in invisible mode.

No longer able to locate it, the demons turned their attacks to the *Prism*.

Graziella focused on Indra, still on the raptor. "Indra, the *Prism* is the bait. Make sure Dominara Azfet can detect it. Pretend to be dead in space. Only use conventional weapons. Any angel weapon at work might expose our ruse."

"But we are fighting demons, Captain. We can't defend ourselves with conventional weapons." Indra sighed. "Permission to find safety on the *Blue Phantom*."

"You and the cats are welcome onboard, Indra." Graziella felt responsible for Indra's safety. "But Prism and Kal must remain on the raptor for the plan to work."

Indra snorted. "I'm not leaving Kal defenseless, Captain. Even with Prism. He has no powers of his own. The demons would find and kill him easily. Besides, he also needs Spartacus to stay close. The violet stone gives him strength."

Graziella realized how many things could go wrong, and how much Kal meant to Indra. "Then use evasive tactics. Vanish with him from place to place inside the raptor, as fast and as long as you can. Azfet will be here any moment. Once her ship is trapped, you may use angel weapons again, and we will rejoin the battle. We hope her capture will weaken the demons."

"Aye, Captain. Understood." But Indra sounded worried.

As Indra disconnected, Graziella hoped Zethar was really on her side and not playing the field. Azfet had angel net technology, and the trap set for her ship could easily be turned against the *Blue Phantom*. Surprise was Graziella's only advantage.

Iaco beeped. "Captain, I can see Azfet's ship."

"Show me." Graziella focused better with images.

Iaco's eyes dimmed and he projected a 3D image of the Dominara's ship.

Graziella gasped. It was enormous, shiny, and black, in the shape of an inverted pyramid. A shudder of dread shook her at the very sight. That vessel dripped with dark energy and malice.

* * *

Azfet willed the hull of her pyramid ship to clear. As it turned transparent, she walked down the majestic stairs, in front of the rows of Sphynxes, then between the mighty white pillars, decorated with Nile Blue and Blood Red hieroglyphics. The bas-reliefs, depicted animated scenes of her glorious battles to come. The action and the landscape kept changing, but always ended in victory.

As she spotted Kal's raptor, she still had doubts about Zethar's loyalty. How did he manage to hide his thoughts from her?

Now, Azfet could observe the vicinity with her own eyes. Scanning the black expanse, she saw no sign of angel presence. Only Nyxor's demons surrounding the *Prism*. The raptor looked dead in space, shields down, and the hordes had already pierced the hull and were roaming inside.

There would be no need to trap the *Prism* in a net, as Zethar suggested. It was already defeated.

Azfet could not detect the violet crystal, nor sense any other ship in the vicinity. She could, however, perceive some feeble humanoid life on the *Prism*. It had to be Kal, no longer a Guardian, he was alive but weak without his crystal. He must feel so alone and abandoned. Perfect.

Azfet would enjoy killing him. But she didn't wish to fight demons for the privilege.

She sat on her long, curved chaise and caressed the blood stone encased in the heavy gold necklace, hanging over her bare breasts. She folded one knee through the side slit of her red gown, baring a long, smooth leg. "Nyxor, my love, I have a request."

The delicious red mist enveloped her and whispered. "Anything you wish, Beloved."

Azfet tingled all over and reveled in his bewitching scent. "I found Kal. He is weak, and I would love to kill him myself... but your demons are in the way, my love. Could you please call them back, so I can enjoy the kill of my nemesis?"

The mist around her condensed and retreated. Nyxor now stood in front of her, magnificent in his gleaming red skin. "I told you to stay away!"

"I am not accustomed to taking orders, my love." She smiled to soften the words.

"You should not be there, Beloved. It's too dangerous." His strong baritone voice permeated her temple and echoed on the decorated pillars.

Azfet was getting tired of her lover's so-called protective attitude. "I can take care of myself, my love. I did for millennia."

"And yet you let the Angel Guardians catch you not so long ago." The anger in his voice seemed disproportionate. "You would still be in hell if I hadn't rescued you."

"What a terrible thing to say, my love." Azfet hated being reminded of her mistakes.

Nyxor huffed. "Sometimes, you can be irresponsible and reckless. I sense angels and demon-slayers in the vicinity. The *Blue Phantom* may be close by."

"I am right here, looking at Kal's raptor, and I detect nothing of the sort." Azfet was tired of not being trusted. "You only try to control me, my love. You seem to enjoy telling me what to do."

"And for good reason." Nyxor glared at her as if she were a rebellious child. "You must flee immediately. You are in grave danger. You know I can't protect you physically, only warn you of the dangers and control demons."

"I know." But Azfet didn't care for Nyxor's manipulations and yearned for the satisfaction of killing her nemesis.

Nyxor growled deep in his throat. "Then, heed my warning or suffer the consequences."

He vanished suddenly, leaving a void in the temple. But he didn't take the demons with him as she asked.

Azfet started to regret making promises to Nyxor. He was too controlling for her taste. Being bossed around went against her very nature. She was a goddess after all, and should reign supreme.

Alarms sounded and red pulsing lights intruded inside her white temple. "What's happening now?"

"Highness! It seems our ship is trapped in some kind of net." The masculine voice of her security chief on the com system sounded unsure, even frightened.

Azfet felt rage building inside her. She didn't want Nyxor to be right. "Are you certain?"

"Yes, Highness. The technology is very similar to ours."

Zethar was the only one who knew where Azfet was going. He gave her the coordinates. How dare the petty crime lord conspire against her? Did he also leak her own technology to be used against her? "Zethar! You, traitorous serpent!"

Then out of black space, a large destroyer, seemingly made of caerulean crystal, manifested in a luminescent glow. The imposing ship emitted heavenly harmonies and bristled with impressive weaponry.

"The *Blue Phantom*!" Azfet summoned her ship's space cannons in her mind. "Fire!"

A strong explosion rocked her pyramid ship, but nothing escaped the net. Instead, it rocked her ship, sending the eternal flames dangerously close to the draperies. Azfet levitated herself to keep her balance, but tall statues tumbled down many steps, breaking into pieces.

Using her weapons only hurt her own ship. May Zethar die a slow and painful death!

Frustrated, Azfet threw lightning strikes across the temple, hitting a pillar and sending her Sphynxes leaping off their pedestals and running for shelter.

Nyxor was right, being here was a mistake. Her ship was trapped, but she could still escape. She visualized a safe place very far away on an idyllic planet, then dematerialized her body to go there... Nothing happened. She remained in the temple. How vexing.

She paced along the columns to help her think. Had she lost her abilities?

She willed herself invisible and couldn't see her hand in front of her face. At least, she hadn't lost her powers and could achieve that simple task. The net that trapped her ship kept her prisoner inside it, but she still had some useful abilities.

Azfet could barely contain her rage. Zethar had tricked her. How could she have been so gullible? How humiliating. She should have killed the arrogant crime lord.

Then, a phalanx of AIs flying in formation emerged from the *Blue Phantom* and launched a deadly attack on the demons, wreaking havoc on the hordes. Azfet thundered and wished this puny galaxy to collapse upon itself... in vain.

Nothing happened outside the net. Her ship, however, shook and quaked like a bird caught in a thunderstorm. Unable to reach outside the pyramid ship, her powers manifested inside. She realized she was trapped. Oh, the humiliation!

But Azfet wasn't beaten yet. These puny angels had no idea who they were up against.

* * *

Graziella had no time to savor the satisfaction of trapping Azfet.

Iaco, the AI emissary, beeped. "Captain, the shields are down. Hull breach is confirmed. We have loose demons onboard, searching for prey."

Graziella's heart beat at an alarming rate as she made contact with the other angels on her ship. Through their minds, she saw everyone was fighting the demons who had found their way through the shields, and now materialized inside the Blue Phantom. Fortunately, they were few, and her angels had adequate weapons to repel them.

The images assailing her from the crew reminded her of other battles, with the sound of lightning strikes, the slashes of glowing sword, and luminous explosions. So far, the angels were keeping the demons in check, but for how long? Their numbers grew by the second.

Two demons materialized in front of Graziella. Iaco pulverized them with one blasting look.

Iaco, beeped. "Latest report from Azura, Captain."

"Show me." Graziella feared more bad news.

Iaco projected from one eye. A distressing 3D scene unfolded between them.

An unknown voice narrated. "Azura is being enslaved. All the angel weapons have been disabled by some kind of wave, and the small angel population is helpless against the invading army's formidable power of destruction."

In the 3D images, black clad humanoid soldiers, armed with strange weapons emitting red waves, ran the ground, rounding up the population. Blasts of red light killed, maimed, and herded wingless and powerless angels toward enormous mass killing machines.

Graziella's heart bled at the horrible sight of cold-blooded slaughter. Having known Azura in all its glory, beautiful and invincible, and seeing now this spectacle of cruelty and defeat was almost too much for her. How could the Formless One allow such iniquity?

But the balance of good and evil implied that both should have equal sway. The powerful always fell, the oppressed always rose from the dirt. The universe lived in a permanent state of imbalance and balance. Right now, it seemed all was lost... unless Dominara Azfet could be killed. She was trapped, but that wasn't enough to stop the war she had started, and the formidable weapons she'd unleashed.

What could Graziella do? Azfet must be killed, or the entire galaxy would suffer Azura's grizzly fate.

Closing her eyes, Graziella contacted Indra.

*　*　*

Aboard the *Prism*, as Indra was running, she caught her captain's mental call. She motioned to Kal and Prism to stop. They did, and waited for her, the two cats halting as well.

Indra closed her eyes. "Captain. We are barely evading the demons, fleeing from hiding spot to hiding spot. How is it with you?"

"The ruse worked, Indra. Azfet's ship is caught in our nets. You may now use angel weapons to defend yourselves. We also redeployed the AI Demon Slayers."

"Good." Indra saw a glimmer of hope. She gave a thumbs up to Kal. "The *Prism* is falling apart. It won't retain its structural integrity for long with all these demons spuing acid and gnawing at it. Requesting permission to rejoin the *Blue Phantom* now."

Kal, Spartacus, and Panthera listened to her mental call, as Prism broadcast both sides of the conversation.

The captain's voice sounded in Indra's head. *"You may join us whenever you wish, Indra, but we have also been breached and are fighting demons in our corridors."*

"No." Kal stared at Indra, shaking his head. "I can't go back to the *Blue Phantom*. I need to confront Azfet."

Indra's heart beat like a drum. She didn't want to lose Kal. Refocusing on Graziella, she said, "We'll join you as soon as we are done here, Captain."

Kal seemed relieved.

Four demons materialized in front of them.

Indra firmed her resolve to fight. "Sorry Captain, demons are here."

She ended the call, extended her hand, and sent a wave of blinding blue light. Prism did the same. The demons were repelled and vanished but quickly rematerialized and kept advancing.

Spartacus and Panthera leapt. Three demons vanished, but Panthera caught one and ripped its throat. Good cat.

When the demons charged again, Indra held her sword above her head and the blue energy emanating from it formed a shimmering dome to protect them. The demons who attempted to cross the blue shimmer sizzled and screamed. More demons arrived and hurled pieces of bulkhead and decking at the protective dome. The shimmering shield flickered.

Indra was weakening. "I can't hold this very long. What do we do now?"

Kal glanced around. "This ship is falling apart. Time to bail."

"We would be safer on the *Blue Phantom*." Indra hoped Kal would agree.

"No can do." Kal's brow furrowed in a stubborn expression. "I need to fulfill my mission. I must get the crystal in close proximity to Azfet. It's the only way to defeat her and save everyone."

"That's suicide. I couldn't bear to lose you now." Her throat constricted at the thought.

Kal's blue eyes implored her. "It's the only way, Indra. I must do it. Can you take me there? I need your help. What do you say?"

Prism beeped. "It is not the only way. I can take you there. I am an angel, too."

Indra couldn't let him go alone with Prism. She had to protect him or he might die. She sighed. "I don't even know if it's possible."

Prism beeped. "It is if we can rematerialize through the angel net. Can we?"

"Possibly." Indra closed her eyes. "Captain? Kal needs to confront Azfet face to face. He may be our only hope to stop all this. Can you give me the codes to get through the angel net?"

"Certainly." Graziella sounded hesitant. *"But it's dangerous, Indra. Azfet cannot escape, but she is still powerful. Elite warriors are defending her ship, and they have angel powers as well."*

Indra sighed. "Can I and Prism use angel powers inside the trapped ship?"

"Yes, you can... but so can she and her soldiers. Be careful..."

"Thank you, Captain. Just give me the codes." Indra froze for a few seconds as she memorized the codes, then she turned to Kal, who also heard the conversation broadcast by Prism. "We can transport to the pyramid ship now."

"Thanks." Kal nodded. "It's the only way. I have to do it."

Spartacus growled. *"Spartacus go with Kal."*

Panthera hissed. *"Panthera go with Spartacus."*

Prism beeped. "This ship is not salvageable. Without a ship, I'm a simple AI angel, and I will follow my captain into battle whenever and wherever ordered."

Outside their small shimmering protective dome, many grimacing demons clawed at the small dome shield and sneered.

"Watch out!" Prism pointed to the collapsing dome. "Your shield is failing."

"Hold on to each other!" Indra felt her friends hanging on to her arms and legs.

Then she closed her eyes and focused on the codes. She dematerialized Kal, Prism, Spartacus and Panthera, along with herself, enjoying the familiar tingle. Then she let her mind enter the trapped pyramid ship, and the tingle turned to a cold shiver of dread. The energy on that ship dripped with evil and malevolence.

She hoped that decision wouldn't prove lethal for any of her companions.

Chapter Sixteen

Kal rematerialized with his friends in the upper level of the inverted pyramid ship. He glanced right and left. No one in sight. He gawked at the imposing hall and whistled at the sight of monumental white pillars, with gold and blue hieroglyphic writing. It reminded him of ancient places of worship he'd seen in his own universe. The cloying smell of incense pervaded the space.

Majestic steps led to platforms holding burning pits of eternal flames... and above them, suspended in levitation, a large sun disc shone like gold.

Indra looked up and her eyes widened. "Wow!"

Kal scanned the vast temple. "No one in sight. But since our enemies can make themselves invisible, they could be anywhere."

Panthera and Spartacus growled, sniffing the air. They smelled something they didn't like. Kal noticed it, too, deceptive and shifty... the cold scent of pure evil.

Prism remained unimpressed by their surroundings. "Where to, Captain?"

All around the vast hall, bas-reliefs depicted epic battles of arrogant gods against familiar Angel Guardians from his universe. But the moving images seemed to be in constant flux. As if time were fluid and changing, and the outcome might go either way.

The images brought forth many memories. According to the history he knew, the gods had lost, so long ago. Was this a simple trick, or could Azfet manipulate reality? Could she change the past?

Kal recognized some of Azfet's people represented on the frescoes along the platform base. Haughty gods, some with animal heads, who lived lavishly and oppressed the populations. In his universe, the Angel Guardians had slaughtered them all... except Azfet, who survived by hiding among his brethren until discovered and condemned to hell.

But Azfet had escaped, and she must be stopped.

The Angel Guardian tattoo on Kal's left upper arm burned, as if in recognition. He scratched his arm through the white sleeve, to no avail. Maybe it was a sign... of what? Azfet's proximity?

The violet gem on the fighting cat's harness flared. *"Spartacus find Highness."*

Although he still yearned for the stone, Kal started to understand its function. It would guide them to their quarry. He checked his bow, arrows, and sword then smiled, ready for a hunt. "Spartacus, show us the way."

The big cat stretched his neck, sniffed around, then loped resolutely toward a row of bare pedestals. The eternal flames cast moving shadows all around.

Kal sensed something was missing from these pedestals, but what? He shuddered as he felt the tingle of being watched.

Prism scanned all around, all senses on alert, but showed no sign of emotional turmoil.

Kal envied her cool. He motioned to Prism. "Let's get going."

"Aye, aye, Captain." Prism fell into step.

Indra caught up to Kal, Panthera on her heels. "Why are we following Spartacus?"

"The violet gem senses Azfet's presence." So did Kal... and his tattoo for some reason. "It's attracted to her and is guiding Spartacus."

"Do you think Azfet knows we are here?" Indra whispered.

"Hard to say. I hope the gem is hiding us from her." It would make sense.

Panthera moved low to the ground, in full defensive mode.

"We haven't been attacked by her guards, yet." Prism's cool remained unshakeable. "She may not know we are inside her ship."

Indra glanced furtively around. "I hope so."

At the end of the row of empty pedestals, a narrow opening in the floor showed a passage, lit only by torches, with steps leading down below.

Spartacus slowed his walk. Panthera hissed.

Prism beeped and drew her sword. "This could be a trap, Captain. Narrow spaces do not allow room for fighting or escape."

"This is the way to Azfet." Kal's arm itched, a sign they were on the right track. "We must keep going."

Invigorated by the hunt and the imminent danger, Kal found a new resolve in his step. His arms gathered strength from the air around him. He itched for a fight. With or without his powers, his body remembered who he was... a fully trained Angel Guardian.

Spartacus led the way down the narrow stairs, and Kal followed, all senses in alert. Indra, Panthera, and Prism stepped down in a file behind him.

At the bottom of the steps, Spartacus halted, teetering on the edge of a six-foot drop, claws gripping the fake stone. Down below, spread a very long and narrow channel with a low ceiling, dimly lit by torches. At the far end of the channel, the passage seemed to continue further. But the channel floor below, in shadows, emitted a strange sound... like a whistle of wind through thin cracks.

Spartacus bared his fangs, sniffing and growling. *"Not like lizard."*

"Lizard?" Kal's heart beat faster. He strained his eyes to see what was coming, half expecting a dragon. Nothing in sight. Then he noticed the dark channel floor, hissing and slithering with a swarm of writhing reptiles flicking forked tongues between sharp fangs. He willed his heartbeat to slow, to control his fear. "We found the snake pit!"

"Snakes?" Indra's voice strangled. She leaned at the edge of the drop to see better, holding on to Panthera.

"Yes." Kal grabbed her arm and pulled her away from the ledge. "Azfet's family of so-called gods used to revere asps. They kept them on hand to extract their deadly venom."

Indra shook her head. "Venom is a cowardly way to kill."

Prism extended her hand in the direction of the slithering pit. "Should I destroy them, Captain?"

"No!" Indra interposed herself. "These animals are innocent and do not deserve death."

Surprised, Kal stared at Indra. "How do you propose we cross the pit?"

"Prism and I can rematerialize you and Panthera on the other side, silly." Pride tinted Indra's voice.

"No." Kal shook his head. "We don't want to attract attention by using angel power. Now that we are inside her ship, Azfet might sense the energy surge and send her guards to kill us. Right now, stealth is our friend."

"Well..." Indra offered a mischievous smile. "Last time I checked, snakes couldn't fly... we can."

Spartacus growled. *"Spartacus fly."*

"You can?" Kal realized the crystal gave Spartacus more powers than he thought.

"That's great." Indra smiled. "It makes things easier."

"I can't fly, nor can Panthera." Kal hated being reminded of his shortcomings.

Prism beeped. "It's all right, Captain. We can carry you and Panthera across."

The albino cat snorted. *"Panthera heavy."*

Indra chuckled. "Yes, you are, big girl. You have been eating like a pig. But Prism is very strong." Indra turned to Kal and smiled. "Why the frown, Angel Kal? Can't a girl save the day once in a while?"

Kal realized his pride didn't matter. Only the mission did. Besides, Indra was right... and so lovely, even in these trying circumstances. "I'll do whatever is necessary, and right now, this looks like our best option."

"Then let's do this." Indra opened her arms to Kal. "You are going to have to hang on to me tight."

Being in her embrace would constitute a challenge. With his memories back, Kal remembered he was a monk and took vows of chastity in his own universe. Angel

Guardians did not indulge in romantic dealings.

He hid his embarrassment under a timid smile. "Whatever it takes."

As he laced his arms around Indra's lithe body, inhaling her floral scent, he met her gaze, so close... so intense. Feeling her heartbeat against his, he remembered what she said about eloping. In that moment, he understood what she meant, and there was nothing he wanted more... but it could never be... and duty came first.

Prism held Panthera in her extended arms and deployed her metallic wings.

Spartacus stretched magnificent, feathered wings, ready to fly. There was a new light in his eyes. He glowed like an angel.

Kal couldn't help but envy Spartacus as he admired the feline's new powers and nodded in appreciation. But as he held tight to Indra, he realized he wouldn't change places for anything.

"Let's go." Indra flapped her magnificent wings. They flew together, up and down below the low ceiling, to the rhythm of the air displacement, skimming dangerously close to the asps.

Spartacus roared and twisted in midair. What now?

"The asps are jumping!" Prism freed one arm, still holding Panthera on the other, and blasted a jumping snake.

After a few more close calls, Kal was glad to land on the other side of the long pit. "Everyone okay?"

Indra nodded, and he let go of her reluctantly. Panthera bumped heads with Spartacus.

"I'm all right, Captain." Not that Prism would be affected by asps.

"Spartacus okay." The big cat retracted his wings and sniffed the air.

"Good. Then, lead the way, big boy." This was an enormous ship, and Kal suspected there would be more surprises.

* * *

Aboard the *Blue Phantom*, Graziella struggled to remain calm.

"Captain, demons have invaded the temple." The disembodied female voice strangled in panic.

"I'm coming." That was it. Graziella could take no more of this nuisance. "Time to show these nasty things who we are."

She dematerialized then gasped as she reappeared inside the Temple of the Formless One, the heart of her ship. Dozens of demons stared at the large crystal floating near the cathedral ceiling. Blue energy radiated like rays all around the crystal.

Angels flew in and dove upon the dark creatures, who scattered, vanished, and screamed when the lightning from crystal

241

swords hit them. But they simply reappeared in a different place.

"Enough!" Graziella focused on the floating crystal. "All angels, concentrate on the crystal with me!"

Graziella felt the powerful wave of energy rushing through her. Then she let out a loud cry, and a blue wave exploded around her, sweeping the entire temple, so fast, the demons, taken by surprise, couldn't avoid it.

The wave ignored the angels, biologic or AIs, as they were filled with the same energy. But the demons fell down and now writhed on the deck and lamented, with melted wings, slashed faces, broken legs, and fear in their red beady eyes.

"Let's repeat this process, using everyone's energy at once, deck by deck. Let's clear the *Blue Phantom* of this vermin."

"Aye, Captain." AIs and other angels stopped everything to focus.

Graziella gathered their energy, and the energy of all the angels onboard, AI or biologic, and focused on one deck at a time, with sweeping waves of energy that killed demons mercilessly. Angels never sought conflict, but when attacked by evil, they retaliated with deadly force.

Soon, the *Blue Phantom* was clear of the demonic vermin.

Then the angels returned to their assigned stations.

Graziella dematerialized and rematerialized inside the observation dome, where Iaco stared at the space battlefield. Out there, on one side, the inverted pyramid ship trembled as it struggled to escape the angel net. A few clicks to the right, the angel raptor exploded in a shower of sparks.

Graziella closed her eyes. "Indra, can you hear me? Are you safe? Where are you?"

An image of Indra manifested before Graziella in the vast observation dome. "A little busy right now, Captain, inside the pyramid ship, avoiding the guards. I don't think they are aware of our presence on board. Kal tells us the violet crystal is guiding us to Azfet. It may be the only way to find and defeat her."

"Good. But be careful." Graziella breathed a sigh of relief. She liked Indra. "The minute Azfet detects your presence, she will send lethal warriors to kill you. Or worse, she'll use her dark powers to confuse your mind. Keep me posted."

"Aye, Captain." Indra flashed a small smile. "You be careful, too."

"I will." Graziella severed the contact. She hoped Indra would be okay. The girl was brave, but ill-suited for combat.

"Captain?" Iaco beeped. "New reports from Azura. They are dire, Captain." The AI's eyes dimmed. He projected images in the empty space inside the dome.

Graziella shuddered at the terrible sight. The surface of the planet seemed devastated. The jungle was on fire. The oceans boiled with unnatural heat. Dead fish, sharks, dolphins, and whales floated on the waves. Tsunamis devastated the coastal regions.

Enormous enemy ships with looming shadows spewed black soldiers who shot and killed angels on sight. The carnage was too much to bear. Graziella felt the grief of all the angels on the ship as she shared the images in the collective angel mind.

Iaco beeped. "Should we go help Azura?"

"Not yet." Graziella wished she could help, but she had her hands full here. Besides, whatever neutralized Azura's defenses might render her ship defenseless as well. "Killing Azfet might be the best and fastest way to stop the carnage."

"Should we send AI angels to the pyramid ship, then?" Iaco's face didn't show any emotion.

"Not yet." Graziella sighed. The Formless one said Kal wasn't evil. She believed he was sent to help them, and she wanted to help him. "Sending a detachment of angels to the pyramid ship now would trigger the alarms and set Azfet on the defensive." Graziella hoped Indra would be okay. "Stealth may be our best tactic for now."

Iaco nodded. "Aye, Captain."

She prayed the Formless One would help Indra and Kal in their daring quest.

But the Formless One never took sides.

* * *

244

Azfet berated herself for falling into an angel trap. She also sensed something else was amiss. Her ship felt numb. Something escaped her. What was it? She could feel it but not pinpoint it. A while ago, she'd detected a flaring of power on the upper level... then nothing.

Holding her blood crystal, she scanned the many parts of her pyramid ship, temple after temple. Everything looked normal. Any intruder at a top level would have to pass through the asps in order to gain access to the deeper levels. The snake pit seemed undisturbed.

She found solace in that fact. Besides, she had a squad of elite warriors to protect her. Her ship may be caught in an angel net, but she still had powers and her personal guard of shapeshifting Sphynxes in the next room. She wasn't defeated yet. Far from it.

She scanned the guard room and showed herself as a hologram among them.

All the guards in gold armor stood and straightened at attention, locking arm braces, and knocking them twice in salute. The bulkhead bristled with Khopesh blades and spears.

Azfet liked discipline and decorum. It showed she ran a tight ship. "I want a complete sweep of this ship. Check every inch of this vessel with your very eyes. Keep in mind the enemy might be invisible. Go to every temple in person. The angels might attempt an intrusion, and I do not like surprises."

"Aye, Highness," all the guards shouted in unison.

The formidable warriors checked their weapons, spikes, swords shaped like question marks, claws, gold wings, bows, poisoned arrows, melted metal... Then they scattered in all directions. They had done this kind of security sweep many times before, usually as an exercise.

Now Azfet would find out if they were worth the credits she'd spent to engineer them to be so lethal.

Chapter Seventeen

Kal couldn't help but yearn for the violet gem as he followed Spartacus along the brightly decorated columns. Earlier, he'd found peace with the situation, but right now, as he remembered who he used to be, he would give anything to have his angel powers back. It would certainly come handy in the coming fight.

Was it sinful to want power? Was it greed on his part? Or did the sinister vibrations of the pyramid ship influence his judgement? The stink of evil energy brought back more memories of ships like this one, and the so-called gods who wielded absolute power.

Thick clouds of burning incense and cloying perfume pervaded this new level. Another temple... the third so far. It seemed each level of the pyramid as they progressed further down, housed a temple dedicated to a different god. The first was dedicated to Ra the creator god, and the second to Apophis the destroyer, but this one seemed different.

Spartacus stalked around a wide pillar, then halted and growled. The big cat faced the far end of the space and bent a front knee, head down in submission.

"Holy Mandala, what's happening?" Kal stopped short and stared at the big cat, confused about his behavior.

Panthera came to the front and imitated Spartacus. Stranger and stranger.

Prism beeped, looking around, scanning the temple.

Indra bumped into Kal, then tapped his shoulder and pointed to the giant statue at the end of the central aisle. "Look!"

There, at the top of the platform stairs, a monumental black panther statue sat on its haunches, wearing gold, jewels, and a gold crown with a disk.

Kal gasped, remembering old stories about Azfet's people. "This must be Bastet. One of the many children of Ra. A shapeshifter cat. She was Azfet's sister."

"Was? What happened to her?" Indra's eyes widened as she stared.

Kal didn't feel awe, but rather disgust at the way these so-called gods had enslaved the populations. "In my universe, the Angel Guardians killed her long ago."

Spartacus roared and twisted to face Kal, baring his cracked fangs. *Kal kill Bastet?*

"Of course, not." Kal realized he shouldn't upset Spartacus. "My brothers did… before my time, a very long time ago."

Spartacus growled and turned back to pay his respects. Panthera bumped heads with him, as if to calm him. Then, the two cats trotted up the central aisle, between two rows of statues on their rectangular pedestals. Sphynxes with lion manes, wearing full metal armor that gleamed like gold.

Kal realized the empty pedestals in the previous temple must have once carried the same kind of Sphynxes. He wondered why they would be missing.

The two felines reached the base of the giant statue, climbed the steps, then licked the enormous paws of Bastet with reverence, purring loudly as they did.

Prism beeped. "Captain, we do not have time for ridiculous worship."

Indra chuckled. "Ridiculous for you maybe, but for these two cats, it's important. A similar civilization once existed in this universe, where cats were worshipped like gods. Maybe subconsciously, Panthera and Spartacus remember those times."

Prism shook her head. "I don't like it."

"Since when do AIs have likes and dislikes?" Kal was uncomfortable, too, but would never admit it.

"It's an expression." Prism managed to sound annoyed. "I mean, nothing good can come from such beliefs. What if the statue is poisoned? Or imbued with evil technology? It could damage or influence the cats and endanger our mission."

Kal realized Prism had a point. "Spartacus, Panthera! We have a job to do."

The purple gem flared on the big cat's leather harness. Spartacus growled in protest but both felines stepped back from the statue, bent a knee to Bastet, then loped back to the group.

Spartacus hissed. *"Bastet talk. Say Azfet dangerous. Hiding in temple bottom of ship."*

"A talking statue?" Kal hesitated. Animals never lied, but they might be duped by clever technology. "It could be a trap."

"Sometimes statues are imbued with the spirit of a deity." Indra smiled. "My people often consult Helsara through her statues and receive useful advice."

"Helsara?" First time Kal heard about her. "Who is she?"

"The mother goddess of love and harmony for the Anvad people... my people. Helsara often speaks through her statue in the temple." The blissful smile on Indra's face revealed much about her beliefs. "Like the Formless One, who speaks through the Blue Crystal."

Kal had never seen this side of Indra and found it unsettling. "How can an angel believe in goddesses when they serve the Formless One?"

Prism chirped. "People with a hint of supernatural powers often like to pass themselves as deities... to exploit others."

"Maybe." Indra sighed. "But I worshiped Helsara long before I became an angel. Some deities are a vessel expressing the will of the Formless One."

"Panthera agree." The white cat licked Indra's hand. *"Panthera hear Bastet, too."*

"I guess anything is possible." Kal still had so much to learn about this universe. He frowned. "But why would Bastet betray her sister?"

"Bastet not like sister." Spartacus shook his head, as if for good measure. *"Sister bad. Kill temple cats."*

Kal still wasn't convinced. "What if it's a trick to get us trapped at the bottom of this ship?"

"No, Captain. I agree with the cats." Prism's hand seemed stuck on one of the pillars and she dimmed her eyes. Then she projected a 3D hologram of the inverted pyramid. "I just accessed the ship's engineering designs. We are here." A blue dot pulsed on the third level down. "And Azfet resides in her temple, which occupies the entire lower tip of the pyramid."

The bottom section of the inverted pyramid came alive with an ominous red pulse. It reminded Kal of blood pumping through a heart.

Indra smiled. "Then let's manifest directly inside her temple."

Kal cleared his throat. "It may not be the best idea. We don't know what kind of boobytrap or shield or army she set up to protect that part of the ship. We better proceed carefully, with stealth, under the protection of the violet gem."

"Guys!" Indra's voice choked. "Is this supposed to happen?"

Kal glanced at a hint of movement in the main aisle. The Sphynxes came alive, at least two dozen. Leaping down from their pedestals, they charged the small group.

Spartacus roared and faced the attackers, baring his fangs. So did Panthera.

Prism levitated, extended her palm, and fired blue lightning along the aisle. Indra drew her sword and took flight. A bolt of energy surged through her blue blade and hit the Sphynxes like a wave. But the hybrid animals with human faces were able to duck it or vanish then reappear. It didn't stop them.

Spartacus roared and charged. Panthera followed his charge.

As the Sphynxes kept advancing, Kal drew his bow and let an arrow fly. It bounced off the metal armor of a hybrid, causing no damage at all. He felt so inadequate. Finally, he drew his sword and charged, joining Spartacus and Panthera in the melee of growling beasts, dodging powerful claws, leaping, stabbing, as best he could.

But the Sphynxes changed into humanoids and shot energy weapons. Kal realized his team was outnumbered and overwhelmed. They were doomed.

Then Kal felt a tingling and rematerialized in a different part of the ship.

Indra smiled at him. "Now that we are discovered, there is no need to hide our angel power."

Prism beeped. "And with the blueprints in my brain, we know exactly where to go. We are now much closer to Azfet's temple... and she can't detect us."

Still, as his memories of similar raids returned, Kal suspected it wouldn't be easy.

* * *

Azfet let her crimson gem rest between her breasts. Why couldn't she see what was happening on her ship?

A Sphynx materialized in front of her, morphed into a tall, armored guard, locked his arm braces in front of his heart and knocked them twice. Then he bowed, eyes to the deck. "Highness, we found the intruders."

Azfet breathed easier. "Congratulations, Commander. How many were there?"

"Two humanoids, an AI, and two large felines, as big as Sphynxes, Highness."

"Tell me they are all dead." Azfet hoped they were. She couldn't sense their presence on her ship, not that she did before. She hated being blind.

"Sorry, Highness." The commander's voice strangled. "The intruders killed several of us, with their savage beasts, blue swords, and lightning strikes. Then they simply vanished."

"They killed my Sphynxes?" Azfet fumed. So much for her invincible guard. First call to duty, and they underperformed.

She narrowed her eyes at the commander. "How could you let these puny intruders get the best of you? You are supposed to be the elite in security, protection, and enclosed warfare."

"Sorry, Highness." The man expanded back into a large, armored Sphynx, claws gripping the deck, ready to pounce on her... or flee. "The savagery of the beasts, their formidable weapons and abilities took us by surprise."

"They are not formidable! And you have abilities, too." Azfet huffed. "Where are they now?"

"Unknown, Highness. They do not show on scanners, so we can't track them." The Sphynx commander lowered his human head, exposing his lion mane, but his muscles bulged and his sharp claws didn't retract.

"Scramble the entire guard, find these intruders, and kill them on sight. It's an order." Azfet was tired of their incompetence. "Before I decide to kill you instead."

"Understood, Highness." Fear flashed in the Sphynx commander's eyes, then he tapped the gem on his chest and vanished.

Azfet would have to be creative, think of deadly ways to stop the intruders. She didn't know where they were, but she knew her ship well. All the entrances, strategic bottlenecks, and passages. And all the special shields prevented re-materialization.

In any case, she was safe in her personal temple. The technological boobytraps protecting it would prevent them from entering, or manifesting directly inside.

If only she could locate the violet gem... How she hated the uncertainty and the insidious fear gnawing at her insides.

* * *

"That was a close call." Winded by the battle with the Sphynxes, Indra leaned against a black pillar decorated with gold. She wasn't cut out for that kind of work and missed the serenity of a peaceful life... in harmony with nature and the universe.

Kal wiped blood from a scratch on his face and adjusted his bow across his shoulders. "There were still a dozen alive when we vanished, which means they are looking for us. And when they find us, they will return in greater numbers."

"Good hamburger." Panthera licked her bloody lips and head-bumped Spartacus.

Kal shook his head at the felines then raised his blue gaze to Indra. "Now that the enemy knows we are inside, maybe the angels of the *Blue Phantom* could come and distract the guards for us."

"Good idea." Indra motioned Prism to broadcast the exchange for Kal.

Prism's eyes dimmed.

Then Indra visualized Graziella in her mind. "Captain, we are all right, but Azfet

255

knows we are here. We had our first skirmish. We could use some help to keep the guards occupied."

"Understood." Graziella always sounded so calm and grounded. "I can send a phalanx of AI angels."

"Great." Indra hesitated. "But be careful. We just fought some Sphynxes. They are shapeshifters, can phase in and out, and they use energy weapons."

"Where do you want me to send the AIs?"

Indra nodded to Prism, who projected the blueprints of the pyramid ship.

"I'm not the best strategist." Indra turned to Kal. "Maybe, you should explain."

Kal walked to the 3D schematic and pointed. "This is where we are, in the temple of Horus... close to Azfet's temple, here."

The lower tip of the inverted pyramid glowed red.

"It would confuse them if the AIs appeared here." Kal pointed to a middle level. He looked so strong, so confident. "It would keep them off our back. Although the guards are powerful, I suspect their numbers must be limited."

"Understood. Don't worry. I'll be in contact with the AIs and monitoring their progress from here. Let me know if you need more help." Graziella managed to send comforting vibes. "Good luck to you both. We are counting on you."

"Thanks, Captain." But Indra didn't really want the responsibility. She severed the link.

"Watch out!" Kal grabbed her and pulled her down behind a pillar.

A squadron of shapeshifting falcon warriors, swooped upon them from the ceiling, in a flapping of gold wings.

Spartacus and Panthera leapt high and pounced.

Prism took flight and fired upon the giant falcons from above. A few faltered, only one fell.

Then the giant birds spewed noxious gas and dripped melted metal upon them.

Spartacus roared and generated a protective violet bubble enveloping humans, felines, and Prism like a shield. It also deflected the melted metal and kept out the toxic gas.

Indra's heart beat like a runaway drum. This wasn't the life she dreamed of as a teenager. There had to be a better way to live.

She grabbed hold of everyone and dematerialized them to a different temple on the way down the pyramid. Hopefully that one would be empty.

* * *

Azfet couldn't help but pace her temple in frustration. She'd never felt so blind and helpless, and she hated the feeling.

A warrior materialized in front of her and saluted. "Highness. Still no success in locating the intruders with the cats."

"What about the mechanical abominations who just boarded my ship?" AI angels disgusted her... machines pretending to have a soul.

"These AIs are strong, and carry destructive energy weapons, Highness." The guard's voice shook.

"But you are stronger than them. Why don't you kill them all?" Azfet couldn't tame the anger in her voice.

The guard bowed low. "We are fighting them as best we can, Highness."

"Not very efficiently. You are here, reporting negative results, instead of sacrificing your life in my name." Azfet realized the problem with her troops was that they lacked conviction and resolve.

Azfet couldn't take much more of their incompetence. Hot rage rose inside her. She pointed two fingers at the guard and a ray of red energy surged from them to hit him in the face. The man flinched and shrank under the strain. He screamed as his face glowed red, then his entire body turned incandescent, before melting into a gold puddle on the temple deck.

Azfet felt better. Killing soothed her soul and gave her strength.

But although safe for now, she remained trapped. How long before her shields failed?

She started doubting her ability to get out of this mess unscathed.

As much as she hated to ask for help, she had no choice but hope Nyxor could find a way to make himself useful.

She sat on her lounge chaise, relaxed against the back and rubbed her blood stone with an easy smile. "My love, is there anything you can do to help my situation?"

Red mist formed around her, and Nyxor, the magnificent red-skinned entity, manifested, nude and gleaming, ram horns, eyes, and white teeth bright in contrast with the red devil face. "What now, Beloved? I thought you didn't like being told what to do."

"I apologize for being so stubborn." Azfet managed a semi-humble smile. She could play the submissive female when it served her. "You were right. I shouldn't have come here... but now that I'm trapped, I'm sure you can help me get out of this situation."

Nyxor scoffed. "Are you really so helpless? You haven't even tried to get out yourself."

"I did try." Azfet could play the damsel in distress. "I still have abilities, but I'm trapped inside my ship, and only safe in this protected temple."

"You forget who you are, Azfet." Nyxor stepped closer, exuding pheromones. "Your powers of suggestion are uncanny, Beloved. You can still influence minds inside your ship, can't you?"

"Of course." Azfet fought the wave of desire assailing her. She realized she hadn't played her last hand, yet. But being reminded by him stung. "So can you, my love. And you are not limited to this ship."

Nyxor smiled and caressed her cheek. "You are right, Beloved. I am the lord of temptation, after all. Maybe I shall help you."

"That's all I ask." Azfet rose and caressed his skin, infusing the gesture with promises. He might try to subjugate and control her, but he would not succeed. And she could manipulate him as well. Two could play this game.

After a sensual kiss and a caress, Nyxor stepped back and smiled. "See you soon, Beloved."

Then he vanished, and the temple felt empty. Why did Nyxor always leave her wanting?

Azfet shook herself and gathered her wits about her. Time to show these puny intruders the extent of her real powers. She was curious to see how they'd react when she altered their reality.

* * *

Kal stopped walking, wondering where he was going and why.

Spartacus halted and growled. *"Spartacus lost."*

The albino cat sat and licked her paws. *"Panthera lost, too."*

Confusion fogged Kal's mind. "What happened? Did you lose the scent?" The gem on the feline's collar flared, triggering a hint of understanding. "That violet stone should be showing us the way."

Indra's eyes darted right and left in surprise, as if seeing her surroundings for the first time. "Where are we? Where are we going?"

Prism beeped. "We are in the temple of Osiris. Still five more levels to go to reach the bottom of the pyramid. Why are you all acting so strangely?"

Kal found it difficult to focus, even with his training. "It seems we are influenced by some of Azfet's spells. She is trying to confuse us. We were warned about this."

"Then just follow me." Prism beeped and took the lead. "I have the schematics, and my mind is clear. No magic spell can influence an AI."

"Good." Kal motioned to Indra and fell into step with Prism, glad he could trust her... but could he? He shook his head to erase the doubts.

Then the giant shadow of a black panther hovered over them. Spartacus and Panthera halted and bowed in submission. Kal drew his sword. Could a sword kill a shadow? Vaguely aware that the shadow wasn't real, he felt compelled to react anyway.

Indra followed his lead and drew her sword as well.

"What are you doing?" Prism sounded frustrated. "Stop fighting ghosts and follow me. It's our only chance."

Kal reluctantly sheathed his sword. "Indra. There is nothing here. We are fighting shadows."

Indra nodded and also sheathed her sword, but still glanced furtively all around.

Kal sighed. "Convincing Spartacus and Panthera might be more difficult."

Indra walked to Panthera and rubbed her head. "The goddess is not really here, big girl. It's an illusion. We must continue our mission. Spartacus, too."

Panthera purred then rose and huffed her understanding.

Spartacus shook his powerful shoulders in a mighty shudder and the gem on his collar flared. *"Spartacus find Azfet."*

"Good. Stay focused." Prism walked ahead toward narrow stairs leading down. "At least these spells will not affect the AI angels keeping the guards occupied. They are effectively engaged three levels above us."

"Good." Kal fell in behind Prism.

When Indra took his hand, he felt guilty about enjoying the warm contact, but did not withdraw. They were probably close to death and deserved this small comfort. She gazed up at him and smiled then they walked, hand in hand.

Would they ever get to the bottom of this malevolent ship… without getting killed?

Chapter Eighteen

Graziella shuddered with dread as she sensed the cold draft sweeping the observation dome of the *Blue Phantom*. Something malevolent had penetrated the shield.

Outside, through the clear dome, she could see the inverted pyramid ship still struggling inside its trap. AI angels fought the demons in space with some efficiency, but it seemed new demons manifested faster than they could be killed, and their numbers kept increasing. The angels were losing this battle.

Iaco stared at her. "I detect something wicked among us, Captain."

"I feel it, too." Graziella feared she might have underestimated Azfet. Could the malicious woman reach her despite the angel net? For good measure, she shielded her mind and focused on the crew. *"Protect your thoughts from being read. Something evil found its way inside our ship."*

A red mist whirled in front of Graziella on the deck, and a surge of inappropriate desires assailed her. Then the mist thickened and took shape. It morphed into a flawless, naked male, tall, with gleaming red skin over defined muscles, and impeccably curled ram horns. Although she preferred women, his seductive gaze compelled her to look at him, then he smiled, revealing perfect white teeth.

This couldn't be good. Graziella checked her mental shield so he couldn't read her mind.

Iaco aimed his palm at the apparition. "Requesting permission to destroy the intruder, Captain."

Graziella doubted it would work, but this man was attractive enough to stir strange feelings inside her, and she didn't like his manipulative wiles. "Permission granted."

Iaco fired a bolt of blue lightning from his palm. It sizzled and hit the red man, but the intruder didn't even flinch, didn't protect himself, nor seemed to suffer any pain or damage.

The apparition laughed at Iaco's failed attempt. "You are wasting your time, puny robot. Your primitive universe doesn't possess a weapon capable of touching me. I cannot be destroyed."

Graziella struggled to keep a calm demeanor. "Who are you? And what do you want?"

"My name is Nyxor and I came to win you to my side. The winning side." The handsome red man walked toward her, smiling seductively. "I can do a lot for you, Captain. It's the deal of a lifetime. Fame, fortune, luck, anything you desire can be yours..."

Graziella had never heard of this entity. She sent a thought to consult the archives. The answer hit her like a boomerang. *"Nyxor is the great corruptor, from another universe, with no physical pull or presence, but he manipulates people through his formidable power of suggestion."*

Nyxor stepped very close and caressed Graziella's cheek.

She ignored the caress and his sweet scent and managed to step back and laugh at him. "You are wasting your time with me, Nyxor."

"So, you recognize me as a worthy challenger..." He kept eye contact.

Graziella struggled to break his spell. "I am a captain, an angel, and an Amazon warrior to boot. Only the weak of mind crave fame and fortune. Get off of my ship, Nyxor. You have nothing I want."

"An Amazon? Oh, I get it." Nyxor immediately morphed into a gorgeous, naked woman with the same gleaming skin and irresistible charm. "Does this shape please you, Captain?"

Graziella felt a surge of hormones rush through her, but she turned away. She started to realize although this entity could not affect the physical world, Nyxor's power of suggestion could be deadly to her universe.

She took a calming breath and faced the beautiful naked woman. "Sorry, Nyxor, I am in a committed relationship. Angels are faithful."

"But you could have it all." The Nyxor female offered a red crystal on her open palm. "Take it, Captain. This will give you great power and can fulfill all your desires."

But Graziella was a warrior angel. "I already have access to crystal... but mine is blue and promotes the good in people. You have nothing I want."

"Think again." Nyxor whispered, too close to her ear. "You could save the lives of your crew... who are certain to die otherwise..."

"Angels do not fear sacrifice." Better die than help evil triumph.

"Do you speak for your entire crew?" Nyxor took a few steps away swaying generous hips, then faced her again. "No one is completely fulfilled, Captain. So many frustrated desires."

Graziella focused her mind on her crew. *"All angels, focus and meditate on the Formless One. The great corruptor is among us."* Then she gazed at the red entity. "Sorry, Nyxor. You will not find anyone to corrupt here. Our AIs are impervious to your charms."

"AIs can be convinced through logic." The suave voice held a hint of threat. "They can be disrupted by static and become glitchy."

"Maybe, but our AIs cannot be turned. Trust me. The crystal at their core is in permanent contact with the Formless One."

"The captain is absolutely right." Iaco nodded and glowed with radiant blue light, confirming her words.

Graziella smiled. "As for our biological angels, they are one with the Formless One, and blind to your wiles."

The Nyxor woman stepped back in surprise. "Surely, you lie, Captain."

"Angels cannot lie." Graziella smiled. "Check for yourself."

The observation dome filled with angels sitting in midair, in deep meditation. Their radiant faces showed contentment. They looked fulfilled, happy with their lives. Their thoughts expressed in words echoed through the dome. "Eternal thanks to the Formless One for the opportunity to serve among the angels to protect the righteous and defend the light against the darkness."

Nyxor changed back into a male and made a disgusted face. "There must be exceptions. Everyone has weaknesses. All the angels of this universe can't be incorruptible."

Graziella had enough of him. "Our angels are strong and loyal, Nyxor, so leave us."

Iaco extended his palm, ready to strike, but it wouldn't do any good.

Nyxor flashed a knowing smile. "How about your precious love interest. Is she ready to be sacrificed? Are you ready to sacrifice her?"

The image of a beautiful amazon angel appeared. She was on her knees, wings flapping, suffocating, struggling to breathe, clutching her chest and throat. Tears rolled down her cheeks. Graziella struggled not to show her distress. Was the image true or fabricated?

Then Graziella remembered Nyxor could only suggest, not kill. She closed her eyes and made contact with her loved one. *"Relax, empty your mind. Whatever you are experiencing is only an illusion."*

The young woman relaxed and could breathe again. She smiled at Graziella with love and adoration in her eyes. Then the image vanished.

Graziella stared at Nyxor. "Now, leave!"

"You cannot win this fight." The red entity stared at Graziella. "I will help Azfet destroy you all." Nyxor slowly swirled back into red mist, laughing. "You outsmarted me this time, but I will find a way to break your resolve."

Graziella shuddered as the red mist disappeared, leaving her shaken. She hoped he wouldn't be back anytime soon.

"Captain!" A panicked angel voice erupted into the dome. "Demons... thousands of them attacking at once, they ate through our shields! Many are inside."

Graziella felt the blood leaving her extremities. "Sweeping protocol, deck by deck, again and again!"

"Aye, aye, Captain."

Iaco blinked. "Should we recall the AIs currently fighting on the pyramid ship, Captain?"

"No." Although it would certainly help. But Graziella considered Kal and Indra's mission even more important than saving the *Blue Phantom*. "Killing Azfet may be our only hope to save this galaxy."

Nyxor's desperate move to seduce the angels to his side confirmed it.

* * *

Indra shuddered as moving red shadows, like red ghosts, or mist entities, followed the small group at a distance. Sometimes they flew, other times they leapt, or walked on the walls or the ceiling, or they jumped from column to column like red monkeys. So weird.

"Should we address these red ghosts following us?" Although, Indra doubted they could be fought.

Prism beeped. "I detect no ghosts."

"Probably some trick of the mind." Kal remained focused.

The small group went down more and more flights of stairs. Who needed elevators when they could dematerialize in one part of the ship to rematerialize in another. But stealth and avoiding the use of angel power was their best hope to catch Azfet by surprise... although the red shadows, if they were real, probably reported their position.

Indra's entire being cringed at the idea of getting closer to Azfet. Anyone intelligent enough to understand the danger would stay as far as possible from the woman's influence.

Besides, a new wave of strange energy now spread around them as they reached the lower levels... like a subtle red mist smudging the lines, diluting and masking everything around them. Indra could feel it chilling her bones. It made her want to retch.

As they emerged into yet another temple, lined with black columns gleaming with gold hieroglyphics, Spartacus roared. The gem on his collar flared. *"Bad man here."*

"What bad man?" Indra sensed something much more powerful than a man.

Panthera sniffed the air. *"Panthera hungry. Panthera kill."*

Kal halted. "I sense it, too."

Then Indra saw it, a red entity, like a horned man, laughing at them.

Prism chirped. "Scanning... scanning..." Her head effected a slow, full turn around her neck. Weird. "I detect an unknown vibration in the air. Scanning to identify the unknown element..." Her head kept spinning. "Scanning... scanning..."

"Who is that red man?" Indra wondered what kind of vibrations could affect an AI?

"What red man?" Kal sounded on edge. "Prism, snap out of it!"

Prism seemed discombobulated. She kept scanning, making no sense, speaking gibberish, her head spinning faster and faster, like a child's twirling toy.

Kal turned to Indra with an accusing stare. "What did you do to Prism?"

"Me? Nothing." Rage mounted inside Indra's chest for being unjustly accused.

She wanted to hit Kal. She wanted to kill... she knew it was wrong, but she couldn't help it. What was happening? The more she resisted the pull of violence, the more it took hold.

Spartacus roared at the tall ceiling then planted himself between the two. *"Stop!"*

Although Indra realized Spartacus was the only sane one in their group, she still wanted to rampage and attack Kal.

Panthera faced her and hissed, baring her fangs, saliva dropping from them as before a scrumptious meal. *"Panthera hungry."*

Indra realized something was making them crazy and only Spartacus was immune. She closed her eyes, invoking the Formless One... in vain. She couldn't establish the connection. She still wanted to fight Kal. Despite her resistance, she couldn't help but draw her sword. She stepped to stab him in the heart... aware that if they started fighting each-other, they were doomed.

* * *

A guard manifested in front of Azfet and saluted. "Highness, the intruders are fighting each-other in the temple of Anubis."

Azfet rose from her chaise and smiled. "The god of the underworld... how fitting." She caressed her red crystal and scanned that temple. "The perfect place for them to die."

Then she sensed the delicious presence of her lover. He had engaged the intruders... lured them into fighting each other. Good.

But then, she realized Nyxor was on her ship, and meddling without her knowledge... again. Making decisions for her, taking control of her life. But she would have none of it. Time for her boy toy to understand his real place in her grand scheme of things. Time to show him who would rule this galaxy.

Azfet snapped her fingers. "Guards! Follow me to the temple of Anubis!"

A hundred guards materialized and saluted, then they tapped the insignia on their chest and vanished. She followed them, but only in ethereal form.

Azfet appeared in the underworld temple of Anubis, the black god with a jackal head. She stood proudly, surrounded by her guards. "Nyxor, what are you doing?"

The AI angel was spinning her head and spewing gibberish.

The angel woman leapt high into the air, wings flapping, then fell down upon the Guardian with a wicked strike. She seemed to be winning, using angel weapons against him. Only Kal's superior training allowed him to survive so far.

The albino cat was watching, and waiting for one to fall so she could finish off and eat the loser. As for Spartacus, the beast seemed to have vanished.

The red mist condensed into Nyxor's perfect form. "I am winning your battle for you, as usual, Beloved." He chuckled. "As you can see, I have them at each-others' throats. They don't care about you anymore... they just want to kill each other."

"I see..." The scene was almost comical, but Azfet raged inside. Nyxor had overstepped his bounds once more.

Spartacus, the red beast from the Pandemonium arena, manifested and roared. He seemed immune to Nyxor's suggestions. Maybe the violet gem protected him. The violet crystal on the cat's collar flared. Then the large feline stepped in her direction.

Glad she wasn't here but safe in her temple, Azfet still stepped back.

Spartacus stopped in his tracks. Could he tell she wasn't really there?

Azfet returned her attention to the gloating Nyxor, who ignored her, checking his impeccable fingernails.

She hated his superior attitude. "I don't need you as much as you want me to believe. I can take care of myself... and I don't like to be constantly ignored and manipulated."

"So, your affection for me is not real? You only use me for convenience?" Nyxor's grin turned cruel. "Do you wish for me to leave?"

"I do." Since the two angels kept attacking each other, Azfet's guards could handle a stupid gladiator cat.

"Have it your way, Beloved." Nyxor stepped back, and red mist swirled around him. "You do not deserve my help. But be warned... without me, you will lose this battle."

"I never needed you to win my battles, Nyxor." She chuckled. "Be gone!"

"You will miss me." Nyxor gave her a haughty glare then vanished into twirling red mist.

"Guards! Kill them all." Azfet would show Nyxor who was the true ruler.

Then she withdrew her ethereal presence. Let the guards deal with the bloody chore.

Chapter Nineteen

The red cloud obscuring Kal's thoughts and vision thinned somewhat. His body fought, in automatic self-defense mode, for his survival. He caught lightning on his sword, countering strike after strike from above. He was tired from battle. The smell of brimstone made it difficult to breathe. He couldn't remember why or what he was fighting.

As the red mist dissipated further, he could make out the face of his enemy. A winged woman... Indra? Why was he fighting her?

As if in slow-motion, Indra, flushed with the heat of battle, struggled to flap her wings. She looked fierce and exhausted as she aimed her glowing sword in his direction once more. But this time, no lightning surged from it as time slowed further.

To Kal's right, human looking guards in gold armor, engaged Spartacus. Red lightning surged from their traditional Khopesh sword, shaped like a question mark. Spartacus pounced and ripped a guard's throat, while keeping the other guards at bay with a violet bubble shield. Several enemies lay on the fake stone deck of the temple, a few moaning and bleeding liquid gold, others dead.

At the end of the wide aisle, a black statue of Anubis, with the head of the jackal, seemed to preside over the carnage. Kal now remembered that particular god in Azfet's family as the one who escorted the dead to the underworld.

Panthera snuck behind a Sphynx and pounced on its back, ripping off his armor and tearing pieces of flesh from his flank. Then she glided toward the shadows to devour her prize with gusto, emitting happy sounds and licking her lips and paws.

To Kal's left, Prism stood like a statue, eyes closed. Judging from the blinking lights on her white uniform, and the soft buzz she emitted, she was rebooting. In the middle of a fight? Not the most appropriate time for that. But she must have her reasons.

As his mind cleared further, Kal realized what must have happened. They were tricked into fighting each other by an insidious red being by the name of Nyxor, but somehow, the foreign influence was dissipating. As he blocked a strike of Indra's sword, he looked into her eyes.

She frowned, then he saw the same understanding flooding her face. She blinked and pulled back her sword.

Then everything returned to normal speed.

Kal nodded to Indra. She nodded back.

Prism chirped. "Reboot complete, ready for action, Captain."

They focused on the guards rushing toward them and fought with a united front. Several guards fell under their angel swords. Spartacus pounced and bit into golden flesh. Although exhausted, Kal kept fighting.

A guard, scanning the scene across the temple of Anubis, gasped as he realized the spell was broken. Then he tapped the insignia on his chest and vanished... to report to Azfet? Did the guards' powers of dematerialization work through sophisticated technology? Was their insignia a transporting device? Could it allow entry to Azfet's chambers?

Kal motioned to Indra and Prism. "Only a few guards left. Let's finish them off."

Then Kal, with Indra and Prism at his side, rushed toward the remaining guards. The enemy rushed toward them, but Indra's lightning strike stopped one guard. Kal dodged a few red bolts, then skewered another guard with his sword. Prism sent an exploding blue ball that killed three instantly.

Spartacus leapt and ripped another's throat. Golden blood seeped into the porous stone deck. The few remaining guards tapped their insignia and vanished.

Since all the guards had left, Kal leaned against a pillar to catch his breath. His throat felt dry. Every muscle in his body screamed with pain. Indra landed, folded her wings, then leaned next to him, her chest heaving with exhaustion.

Prism saluted, fresh as a sparkling new factory unit. "What are your orders, Captain?"

Panthera joined the group, her heavy stomach dragging low to the deck. *"Panthera eat bad people."*

Indra ruffled the white cat's head. "Yes, you did. Good girl."

Spartacus growled but showed no sign of fatigue. It seemed the violet crystal gave him unlimited strength. *"Spartacus champion. Kill many."*

"Yes, you did." Indra smiled at the feline. "Thank you for that."

"I have an idea." Kal walked to one of the fallen guards and knelt, then snatched his insignia... like a gold coin with Azfet's effigy. The very touch of it sent a chill through his body.

Indra joined him. "What is it?"

"I suspect this is our best chance to get to Azfet." Kal motioned to Prism and held up the insignia. "Can you analyze this device?"

Prism beeped and small laser beams surged from her luminous eyes, casting shadows on the gold drawings decorating the wide pillars. Then the laser beams danced all around the small badge, probing it. "It is a sophisticated transportation device, Captain."

"Just as I thought." Kal felt a ray of hope. "Does it contain the security codes to Azfet's personal quarters?"

Prism beeped. "Aye, Captain. I can identify and isolate these codes."

"So, maybe we can use these codes to manifest inside her chambers..." Kal dared to hope. Since the red mist had cleared, his confidence in the mission returned. He could finish the job.

Indra nodded. "Should we each wear a device?"

Prism beeped. "It is not necessary for me as I now contain the codes, but it would be safer for a biologic entity."

Indra ran from fallen guard to fallen guard, plucking their insignias, then gave one to Kal, who applied it to his white angel uniform, where it stuck like a magnet. Indra placed one on Spartacus' collar.

Panthera huffed and approached Indra, nudging her arm.

"I didn't forget you." Indra smiled and set one on the white cat's chest, where it adhered of its own. "There." She lifted her gaze to Kal. "Amazing, this device sticks to anything... even cat fur."

"Let's hurry, before the guards return with reinforcements." Kal realized he was on the verge of completing his mission. His heart beat like a runaway ion drive, tumbling through the universe at interstellar speed.

Prism displayed the ship's schematics and pointed to the lower tip of the inverted pyramid. "This is where we want to manifest. Azfet's temple."

"Upon my signal..." Kal made eye contact with all of them in turn.

They nodded and formed a circle, hand or paw poised over their devices.

"Go." Kal tapped his device, watching his companions do the same, including the cats, tapping with large paws.

* * *

Kal materialized in a dark place, lit only by smoking fire pits, and lined by monumental pillars. The cloying smell of burning incense and myrrh pervaded the temple. He checked his companions. They all stood there, taking in the empty temple.

Then the walls vanished, as the hull of the pyramid ship turned clear, offering an unobstructed view of the space battle raging around the *Blue Phantom*. Thousands of demons devouring the blue shields and tunneling inside... how could the angels possibly survive it?

To the side, the wreck of their exploded raptor floated at an odd angle, shedding parts and pieces of bulkhead that drifted around it.

Indra's eyes widened, but the set of her mouth and the firm grip on her sword showed resolve.

Prism scanned the space with its multiple levels, niches, altars, pedestals, wide columns, and bas-reliefs. "Where to, Captain? This temple seems empty."

"Is this Azfet's residence?" Kal's voice shook. He was so close, yet couldn't see victory. But his angel tattoo smoldered. "Where is she hiding?"

Spartacus growled. The gem on his collar flared brighter than ever before. A sure sign of Azfet's proximity. "*Highness here.*"

Indra walked around, looking in every direction... but the pillars could hide the enemy.

"She can make herself invisible." Kal squinted, to no avail. "But not to the violet crystal." A flash of movement from the corner of his eye made Kal turn. "Sphynxes!"

The hybrids in gold armors leapt down from the top of the high pillars and surrounded them. Kal's friends formed a small circle, each facing out, protecting each other's backs. Spartacus generated a violet bubble shield around them.

Still no sign of Azfet. Kal raged inside. She was here, watching them, mocking them, and laughing inside.

In a flash of bright light, an entire phalanx of AI angels manifested high above them, targeting the guards.

Kal took heart. He might achieve his mission after all. "How did the AIs get here?"

Prism beeped. "I sent them the codes."

"Good call." Even without the stone, or his angel powers Kal felt confident. He now remembered everything about his former universe... and why he came after Azfet. She was his responsibility. He must get her back to hell.

A dozen Sphynxes grew wings and took flight to meet the AI angels. Giant gold falcons swooped down on the AI angels. The gold-armored guards attacked on the deck.

Spartacus released the bubble shield and the companions charged together, while the AI angels on the outer circle wreaked havoc from above. Kal realized guards and Sphynxes were one and the same, changing shape at will. So did the golden falcons.

Feeling a surge of new energy, Kal charged. Despite their abilities, the guards and Sphynxes struggled as more AI angels joined the fight. Soon, the enemy lay bleeding or dead on the stone deck, and none remained standing.

"Is that all?" Kal couldn't believe it.

One AI angel nodded. "We exterminated scores of them on the upper levels. According to our calculations, all the guards are out of commission."

"Good to know." But Kal needed to find Azfet.

Spartacus roared. The gem on his collar flared, and the large feline loped toward a stone altar... or rather, a large sarcophagus with a heavy lid.

Kal followed the cat to the stone coffin then ran his hands along the smooth top. "The stone is flaring brighter. She must be inside."

Prism motioned to the AI angels. "Lift that stone."

Using rays coming out of their eyes, the AI angels lifted the heavy stone and set it aside.

Kal bent over the open sarcophagus to look inside. "It looks empty, but she is here. I can feel it."

Spartacus roared, making the pillars vibrate. The violet gem flew off the cat's collar and hovered above the sarcophagus, revealing Azfet lying inside.

The evil woman rose, rage evident in her perfect, symmetrical face, the snakes on her headdress hissing.

Kal stepped back a few steps.

Azfet's eyes glared at him. She straightened as if to levitate above the sarcophagus but remained bound by gravity and had to step out of it instead. The proximity of the violet crystal made Azfet mortal and vulnerable, as the Guardians thought it might. Good.

"Puny humans, weak angels, and stupid robots! You cannot vanquish me. I am a goddess!" From her frustrated facial expression, Kal realized she no longer had powers.

"And I am an Angel Guardian, sworn to end your reign." Kal saw his chance to strike. He raised his sword. "You kill and enslave people for convenience and pleasure. You do not deserve to live. I'm going to send you to the real hell, and this time, you won't be able to escape!"

Before Kal could strike, Spartacus pounced.

"No!" Azfet dodged out of the cat's path then twisted around with a Khopesh blade in her hand. She stabbed the big cat's flank. Blood spurted. Spartacus collapsed in a bloody heap with a kitten's pitiful cry. Kal remembered with horror that Azfet poisoned her blades with snake venom.

Furious, Kal raised his sword. The violet gem now hovered above Azfet's head. Kal remembered and realized what was happening. "I banish you to the hell from which no one returns."

Kal struck, not Azfet, but the violet crystal.

Holy Mandala! The gem flared and made the entire ship vibrate. Kal could feel it in his very bones. Good.

* * *

Azfet hated the fear that twisted her entrails. The vibrations of the violet gem made her weak. Not only did it neutralize her powers, but now it threatened to tear apart her very molecules.

Could Nyxor help? Did he still have feelings for her? He wouldn't let her be killed. She was his beloved. As she cradled the blood crystal he'd given when they met, the source of her might, she called to him.

"Please, my love. Indulge me one last time. Restore my powers, so I can defeat my enemies."

But as the vibrations of the violet stone intensified, her blood crystal vibrated at the same rate. It glowed like melted lava and burned her hands. She cried and let go of it. But it kept vibrating faster and faster as it hovered in front of her.

Then the gem that had given her so much power shattered and exploded into a million tiny shards. Azfet screamed at the loss. As the smithereens floated around, they twirled and evaporated into a red twirling mist and vanished, just as Nyxor used to do.

Unable to contain her rage, Azfet turned to Spartacus, lying on the stone deck. "You, fiendish beast. You were supposed to keep the violet crystal away from me, not bring it to me."

Spartacus, in his wounded state, found the energy to growl at her.

"I'm not afraid of a lowly beast. You are already dead anyway." She spat on the wounded cat.

Angels and cats kept staring at her with awe in their eyes. Why? Even the Angel Guardian from her universe seemed frozen with his sword in hand. Why didn't he finish the job?

She couldn't help but pour her rage upon Kal. "What are you waiting for, stupid Guardian? Why don't you finish me off? You are a coward, Kal. No guts. This world is perfect for you. It is soft and narrow-minded, like you.”

As the vibrations through her body intensified, Azfet realized the violet crystal was now stuck to her chest. She grabbed it and pulled at it but couldn't get it off. She pleaded for Nyxor's help in her mind... to no avail.

Never had Azfet felt so alone and helpless... how humiliating, especially in front of Angel Kal, his friends and the AI angels. As a goddess, Azfet deserved better.

Then in a flash of movement, Spartacus leapt at her again. Stupid cat. Azfet felt the formidable claws piercing her skin. Unbelievable... the cat clawed at the violet stone on her chest, trying to get it back. But the stone only sank deeper into her chest.

The Angel Guardian pulled Spartacus away from her. The cat collapsed at the foot of the sarcophagus. Then the Angel Guardian thrust his sword into the violet stone itself, pushing it deeper inside her chest... into her heart.

Azfet cried out at the intolerable pain. She touched her wound and looked at her hand, dripping with golden blood. A torrent of it poured out of her wound, and she couldn't heal herself without her powers.

Then the Guardian collapsed. Was he dead?

She realized she was the one dying. “No!”

All the molecules in her body vibrated and separated. She exploded into a zillion drops of golden flesh, but her consciousness was still there. She could see and feel everything. Damn that infernal crystal. Then the violet stone itself disintegrated as she did. This was the end... her body was no more.

"Nyxor, I am sorry. Please help me escape my fate." But it was too late.

The giant statue of Anubis descended from the temple above, through the ceiling, and levitated next to her astral body. "Come with me, Azfet, daughter of Ra, Goddess of Chaos."

So shocked she couldn't speak, Azfet simply nodded. This couldn't be happening. Not to her.

As Anubis escorted her soul deeper into the underworld, Azfet realized her journey wasn't over. At the threshold of the afterlife, stern angels waited for her... and large cats with wings... the guardians of the underworld. She hated these cats.

Even in ethereal form, Azfet shuddered. "Oh Anubis, do not judge me too harshly. I did plenty of good in my long life."

Anubis shook his jackal head. "My judgement is always just, Highness. As I weigh your actions against the weight of a feather, I see that even the little good you did, you did for selfish reasons, or to hurt someone else."

A cold, metallic fear stiffened Azfet's ethereal body. "What is my sentence?"

"I order your soul to be kept in permanent torment with no hope of escape, for all eternity." The god of the underworld lowered his jackal head. He had spoken. There was no recourse.

Azfet emitted a silent shriek and tears rolled down her cheeks. The hell the Angel Guardians had devised for her in the past was a paradise, compared to what Anubis had in store for her.

In that moment, Azfet trembled with dread... but it was too late now. She had no other choice but to suffer her grizzly fate.

Chapter Twenty

Indra rematerialized in the healing bay of the *Blue Phantom,* the limp body of Spartacus sprawled at her feet. The cat's breathing remained shallow and irregular. Black blood oozed from his stabbing wound, and his eyes stared into nothingness.

Indra glanced all around the clean blue space lined with beds. "Please, he needs help!"

Two healing angels in long white robes manifested in front of her. "What happened, Sister?"

"Stabbed by a blade with aspic venom." Indra's voice trembled.

She still shook from the horrible blast that destroyed Azfet's body. Even the red crystal had vaporized. She hoped the evil woman would get a fitting punishment in the afterlife, then regretted wishing ill to the dead.

One healer knelt by Spartacus, seeking a pulse in his paw. "The poor beast is at the threshold of death."

"Can you save him?" Indra hoped they would.

"Hard to say." The angel laid a luminous healing hand on the feline's neck. "He is completely paralyzed and the venom is getting dangerously close to his heart."

The second angel knelt and laid his hands on Spartacus as well. "It will take the full power of the Blue Crystal and the minds of many healers to save him. But I promise we'll do our very best, Sister."

"Thank you. He's a hero and deserves to live." Indra hoped he would. And Panthera would be so sad if he died.

A third healer appeared. "How about the other biologic entities involved in the struggle?"

"Kal and Panthera are exhausted, but not physically wounded." Indra was glad for that. "Prism took them to my quarters to rest."

Then Indra felt the call of other angels, asking for help to clear the decks of infiltrating demons. She closed her eyes and joined her mind to theirs. Against her closed eyelids, she visualized blue flashes from the large crystal in the main temple. Then the blue light exploded, sweeping the many decks, accompanied by the screams of dying demons. Indra shuddered at the violence, but it was necessary.

"All decks are clear," a feminine voice announced overhead.

Indra opened her eyes and took a last glance at Spartacus, being levitated to a comfy bed. He was a warrior and a friend. She wanted him to live.

She sighed and bowed to the healers. "I leave him in your capable hands. I must report to the captain."

* * *

Indra rematerialized inside the observation dome, where Graziella, Iaco, and Prism stared at the marooned pyramid ship. To the right, in space, half-way to the wreckage of the *Prism*, AI angels and demons fought a desperate battle. Demons twisted under lightning strikes, vanished, then reappeared, screaming, with distorted faces.

Indra stepped to Graziella and saluted. "Captain, should we help the AIs?"

Graziella shook her head. "AI angels are designed to fight demons, and better suited for space battle than we are."

A disembodied female voice filled the dome. "Shields are restored, Captain. Now that we are clear of intruding demons, the *Blue Phantom's* hull can be mended. Repairs are underway."

"Good job." Graziella smiled, a rare occurrence lately.

Indra wanted to be useful. "Captain, now that Azfet is no more, what are your orders?"

"We shall go assist Azura in their battle, but first we must destroy this abomination. No trace should remain of Azfet's presence... or her evil technology. It could fall into the wrong hands." Graziella closed her eyes and

292

stood very still. "All AI angels in space, return to the *Blue Phantom*."

Outside, the AI angels vanished.

"All AI angels are onboard, Captain," the female voice sounded confident again.

"Good." Graziella took a deep breath. "Target the pyramid ship and fire at will."

Outside the dome, batteries of surface cannons shot blue lightning on Azfet's ship. Fire flared bright, then a formidable explosion blew the entire ship to tiny pieces. It burst into a billion shards of red and black flexglaz, gold dust, and white stone. Larger pieces disintegrated on the shields of the *Blue Phantom*, as attested by a shower of flaring rainbow lights all around the dome.

As the view cleared, the remaining demons cried and screamed in pain, wounded by the projectiles ejected by the exploding ship. Incandescent demon wings batted aimlessly, exhibiting wide holes in the leathery flesh. The surviving creatures, in full panic mode, rallied away from the carnage and shrieked and grimaced, obviously frightened. They weren't accustomed to tasting defeat.

Among them rose a cloud of red mist, an insidious shadow swirling around them, whispering in their ears, but the demons weren't listening anymore. Instead, they fled or vanished, leaving only the red cloud alone and abandoned in black space.

Then the red cloud rose and grew in size. Its shapeless mist coalesced into the shape of a gigantic humanoid with red skin and ram horns, hanging in black space, facing the *Blue Phantom* in obvious defiance.

"Nyxor..." Indra shuddered at the memory of how the evil entity had tricked her into fighting Kal.

Everyone inside the observation dome held their breath. Except the captain.

Graziella closed her eyes in concentration. "Fire at will."

Blue lightning surged from the surface cannons, hitting the giant Nyxor. Indra hoped it would kill him but suspected it might not.

Nyxor only laughed as the blue lightning struck and pierced his ethereal form creating holes. Then his body reformed around them, filling the holes.

"Our weapons are ineffective, Captain." The feminine voice filling the dome sounded frightened.

"Sorry, Captain." Iaco sounded disappointed. "As he pointed it out earlier, this Nyxor cannot be killed... even by angel weapons."

"I agree." Indra shivered with dread. "He doesn't have a physical body."

Graziella sighed. "Which is also why he cannot simply destroy us. He has no hold on the physical world."

The giant Nyxor in space pointed an accusing finger at the *Blue Phantom*. "This a warning to the puny angels of this galaxy. I shall return, and I will avenge Azfet's death...

and destroy you all for this insult to my greatness."

Then Nyxor swirled back into red mist and vanished.

Everyone in the observation dome let out a sigh of relief... including Indra.

Graziella straightened her tall frame. "I have no doubt he will return after he seduces another evil soul to act on his behalf. But it won't be anytime soon."

"Repairs are complete, Captain. The ship is ready to fly." The feminine overhead voice sounded relieved as well.

Graziella took a deep breath. "Crew of the *Blue Phantom*, prepare for battle. We are headed for Azura. May the Formless One be on our side today."

But Indra knew the Formless One never took sides.

* * *

When Indra visited sick bay, Spartacus was asleep on a mattress on the floor, but she couldn't tell if it was a good sign or not. She wasn't surprised to see Panthera lying and napping by his side. These two cared for each other very much.

A healing angel manifested inside the bay, folded her wings, and alighted on the deck.

"How is our hero doing?" Indra hoped for good news.

"Out of danger and recovering nicely." The healing angel smiled.

Indra glanced back, as she sensed a familiar presence entering the bay. "Kal. Are you back to normal?"

He looked a little pale, but the intense blue in his eyes reflected happiness. "Just a little shaken but fine otherwise."

"I'm glad." Indra couldn't help stepping up to him and touching his arm. "Look at those two."

Kal didn't shrink from her touch but glanced at the sleeping felines and smiled. "They get along well."

The healing angel nodded. "Spartacus has a very strong constitution. As resilient as one of our angels."

"The violet crystal gave him the strength of an angel." Kal looked a little sad. "Now that the stone is gone, however, his strength will not last."

Although Indra had never tested the blue crystal on felines, she was hopeful. "He could get the strength he needs from our blue crystal."

"Maybe. But it's not the same kind of energy." Kal knelt and caressed the big cat's flanks. "The blue crystal makes all beings gentle and kind. The violet stone's energy was more aggressive, more suited to his fighting temperament."

"Do you still miss the violet crystal?" Indra hoped he didn't. "I know you craved it at some point."

"Yes, I did." Kal shook his head. "But I now understand it was never meant to remain in this universe."

Still, Indra detected a longing. Would Kal ever recover from its loss?

The healer broke the uncomfortable silence. "Spartacus also has the best medicine of all... the love of his mate."

"His mate?" Indra blushed and wondered if she could help Kal heal. Then she took a second look at Panthera, purring against Spartacus and realized they were a bonded pair.

"You didn't know?" The angel chuckled. "She carries his brood and is close to giving birth."

Indra gasped at the realization. "No wonder she's always hungry, and her belly is so round."

Kal rose, gazing at the two felines. He chuckled. "Even cats have secrets."

Indra hoped Kal would never keep any secrets from her. "What about us. What do we do now?"

"The battle is not over yet." Kal's face softened. His blue eyes gazed upon Indra.

Indra squeezed his shoulder. "But when it is, what we do next is for both of us to decide... together."

"What do you mean?" Light filled his face.

Indra had a delicious frisson. "You know what I mean. You fulfilled your mission. Azfet is no more, and you are now free of your Guardian duties. You are not a Guardian nor a monk anymore."

He gently pushed back a strand of black hair that had escaped her bun. "Whatever happens next, we'll face it together."

"I'd like that." Indra couldn't believe Kal would choose her over any other kind of future. She was swimming in a sea of happiness... although, she wasn't exactly free from her duty to the *Blue Phantom*. The captain would have to grant her permission.

She raised her face to his for a kiss, with a gentle touch on his shoulder. As he encircled her waist, Indra relaxed in his embrace and closed her eyes to enjoy the softness of his lips, savor the sweet taste of his tongue.

The overhead alarm whistled. "All angels, battle stations, we reached Azura's orbit. Space debris from an intense battle. Enemy ships in the atmosphere, crashed angel and enemy ships, and the planet surface is a full-blown battlefield."

Indra reluctantly let go of Kal and gazed into his deep blue stare.

He flashed a hesitant smile and cleared his voice. "We should make ourselves useful."

Indra shook herself from a dreamy daze. "I know where the weapons are."

"Good." Kal followed her out of the healing bay, along the blue corridors, following the emergency strip of blinking lights. "I hope some of those weapons can be wielded by non-angels."

"Some can." When they reached the armory, Indra pointed out the blue energy blasters that Kal could use.

Kal grabbed two of them, and a dozen explosive grenades. He smiled. "I feel better now."

"You still remember how to pilot an angel raptor?" Indra took his hand.

He squeezed her hand. "Better than ever. I have all my memories back."

"Then let's go to raptor bay One." Indra visualized the raptor bay and dematerialized them both.

* * *

Kal banked the angel raptor, getting a good view of Azura from orbit through the forward shield. "Is the planet supposed to look like this? All gray and smoky? The oceans are festooned with crimson, the jungle is burning... I thought it was a blue planet."

"According to the archives of the *Blue Phantom*, it was bluer and more luminous than any other planet in this galaxy... but not anymore." Indra's voice cracked. She looked so sad at the sight of the devastation.

Prism beeped. "Careful. The enemy is still here. Their weapons neutralized the blue crystal at the planet's core and disabled all angel technology. We don't want to fall from the sky."

Kal flew at lower altitude, keeping an eye on his instruments. "I detect only one enemy ship in the air, but many more on the surface. It looks like their small fighters crashed, but the troop transports simply landed.

Prism beeped. "They deployed an army on the ground."

Kal had nightmarish visions of black soldiers exterminating peaceful populations. He'd seen this kind of warfare before. "We have to stop them."

He spotted the large ship hovering above an agglomeration of blue domes. The black behemoth seemed to have difficulties remaining in the air. As if something was interfering with its instruments.

"Our cannons are operational." Indra sounded determined. "Targeting the enemy ship."

Salvos of blue lighting surged from the raptor. Other raptors from the *Blue Phantom* also targeted the black ship. Multiple strikes tossed it like a floating toy on a pond. Its shields sparked, then petered out. Then its engine exploded, and it fell from the sky toward the fields below, like a deflated black balloon, away from the domes.

Kal breathed easier as he followed the falling behemoth at low altitude. All around, he could now see dead people and animals littering the ground. On the beaches, red crabs the size of military tanks lay on their sides, dead. The ocean's edge had turned red from weapons fire, and freakishly large sharks and whales floated belly up on the surface.

In the populated areas, many destroyed domes exposed their insides, some with blackened hydroponic farms, others flanked by broken angel statues, looking like official buildings, temples, or residences.

"I don't see any AI or Avenging Angels." Kal's voice choked at the thought of so much carnage among the angel population.

Prism beeped. "By neutralizing the blue crystal, the enemy weapons made AIs and angels vulnerable. They lost their battle and likely their lives."

Indra's voice perked up with hope. "The death of Azfet and the destruction of her red crystal must have weakened the enemy's tech. I bet that blood stone was powering their weapons."

Prism beeped. "Azura is in ruins, and the blue crystal at its core is inert."

"Can the blue crystal be reignited?" Indra sighed. "I wonder what it would take to spark it back to life?"

Kal remembered a long-ago instance, in another universe. "Our raptor's weapons are emitting blue crystal power, are they not?"

"Yes." Indra squinted at him.

"What if we fired them at the inert core? Might it reignite its energy?"

Prism beeped. "Possibly. Definitely worth a try."

Indra nodded. "Maybe we should tell the *Blue Phantom* and all its raptors to fire at the nearest concentration of blue crystal."

Kal swiped his console. "*Blue Phantom*, we think a concentrated strike of blue crystal energy weapons could reignite the planet core."

"Agreed." Captain Graziella's voice came on loud and clear. "All angel ships in the air, target the base of the hill between the domes and the sea. Its crystal cave is directly connected to the planet core. Upon my signal, concentrate all your firepower on that hill."

"Ready, Captain." Indra set her hand on one cannon's trigger. Prism took the other one. Indra closed her eyes.

"Fire at will!"

Salvos of blue energy streaked through the air from the *Blue Phantom* and all its raptors. The hill by the sea seemed to absorb all that firepower. The slopes turned blue and glowed like a pulsing beacon.

"Chain reaction detected. It seems to be working. Keep firing!" Graziella's voice regained strength.

More blue strikes hit the hillside. Kal could only watch as the entire hill seemed to be made of glowing crystal. Then the many domes started to glow as well. Around the agglomeration, energy barriers came alive, like vibrating defensive walls.

"Yes!" Indra exulted. "The crystal is coming back to life and vibrates higher than ever. I can feel the vibration of the planet core energizing me."

Prism nodded. "I can detect it, too. The planetary defensive weapons are coming back online as well, and the natural shields are reactivating."

Indra's face radiated bliss. "Any surviving angels, AI or otherwise, will now be able to recover, and finish the fight with their full powers."

"It worked. Now, cease firing on the hill!" Graziella's strong voice. "Let's focus on winning the fight on the surface."

Kal flew the raptor very low, skimming the ground toward the lines of black soldiers rushing out of the downed behemoth. "Fire at will!"

Indra and Prism peppered the lines of black soldiers with blue flashes of fire.

Then Kal hovered his raptor over the wreck of the large enemy ship.

A small phalanx of winged angels flew from a group of nearby domes and entered the broken hull of the black behemoth. When they came out, they pushed in front of them many black clad soldiers, restrained by invisible chains. Among them, an admiral in bright red uniform.

Indra closed her eyes as if to communicate with other angels. "Is the fight over?"

Prism projected the images from the ground and voiced the exchange. "We have the admiral in charge. We are taking him to be held in a prison dome."

"What about his soldiers?" It seemed Indra wanted them to pay.

"We took many prisoners, but others escaped, hoping to survive in the jungle." The surface angel scoffed. "No intruder can survive Azura's wilderness."

Strange comment. Kal was intrigued. "Why is that?"

"Azura is not just a planet, it is alive, self-aware, and conscious. Now that we revived the crystal core, it will fight with us." Prism projected images of the surface.

Torrential rains doused the jungle fires. Large saber-tooth felines chased isolated soldiers like prey and devoured them. Giant birds dove upon the invaders, shredding armor with their hooked beaks. Then, as the sun lowered on the horizon, and soft lights appeared around the remaining domes, enormous wingless dragons emerged from the ground and joined the hunt against the invaders.

As Kal landed the raptor inside the energy barrier enclosing the largest group of domes, he was confident Azura would recover. The planet had lost many lives, but it survived the destruction. Kal also hoped the admiral would receive his just punishment for betraying the entire galaxy to an unspeakable evil.

* * *

The next morning, as Kal stood on the terrace overlooking the temple esplanade, the night rains had washed away the smoke, and the vibrant blue sky carried a soft breeze bringing the scent of tropical blooms. After the night's cleanup, with the hilly landscape on one side, and the ocean on the other, the place looked like a true paradise.

Kal was acutely aware of Indra, standing at his side. He no longer felt guilty about his feeling for her. That guilt had been a remnant of his former monastic life.

A few feet away, Panthera and Spartacus lay in the morning sun. Both cats looked well and happy, rolling on the cool stone, exposing their bellies. Panthera's looked rounder than the day before.

The ruler of Azura, a tall woman wearing blue veils, and a long sword hanging from her hip, walked toward them with a graceful stride and smiled. "We owe you a great debt. Thank you for all you have done. You may ask anything of us, and it will be granted."

Captain Graziella walked toward them as well. "Does this also go for the *Blue Phantom*, my lady?"

The great lady nodded. "Your dedication to the well-being of this galaxy is commendable, Captain. I know you and your crew are not Azuran citizens, but you are welcome to join us anytime."

Graziella smiled. "We are wanderers, our ship belongs in space, not in a planet's orbit. We like the freedom to go wherever we can do the most good."

"I respect that." The tall lady gazed far away over the calm sea. "Your wanderings saved us all when we were taken by surprise. We were not prepared for a weapon that could neutralize our crystal core."

"What will happen to the prisoners?" Kal asked.

The lady inhaled a slow breath. "As you may not know, with our numbers greatly diminished, we need to recruit more angels."

"Recruit?" The ordinary term didn't seem to fit angels.

"Since the crystal makes us barren, we cannot reproduce." The lady sighed. "We shall keep the prisoners contained. In time, the planet will transform them into angels like us."

Kal remembered how he became an Angel Guardian, long ago, in proximity of a large violet crystal floating above the main altar, in the temple of the monastery where he'd lived an ascetic life since childhood. "So, anyone who stays here long enough becomes an angel?"

"Yes." The lady smiled. "This planet's crystal core is so powerful, it makes angels of all who live here in a matter of weeks or months, depending on the individual."

"Really?" It seemed a little too easy to Kal.

The lady smiled. "Our crystal is abundant and powerful."

Kal nodded. "In my universe, it took me decades of monastic life to achieve angelhood."

"You are welcome to stay if you wish and be an angel again." The lady inclined her head. "It will take time to restore Azura to its former glory and train and educate new angels to carry on the work of the Formless One."

Kal shook his head. "I don't think so." He gazed upon Indra. "We were hoping..."

Indra squeezed his arm. "Captain Graziella, if I may..."

"Speak, Indra."

"I know it's sudden, but I was hoping to be freed of my commitment to the *Blue Phantom*."

Graziella smiled. "Our full-fledged angels are free to leave anytime, Indra. You know that."

Kal laced his arm around Indra's shoulders. "We were thinking of starting a family, and neither the *Blue Phantom* nor Azura would be the best place for that."

"Where will you go?" Azura's leader seemed amused.

Indra exulted. "I was hoping we could borrow a craft and go to the planet of the Anvad people... my people. My clan and my family live there."

The great lady nodded and gazed upon the couple with empathy. "It's important to know where you belong."

Graziella nodded. "It sounds like a wonderful idea."

The great lady smiled. "Take any of our vessels. We owe you so much. You saved our planet. You saved the galaxy, and possibly the entire universe, by coming to our world, and defeating an evil we couldn't."

"Thank you, My Lady." Kal cleared his voice. "But I was just doing my job as a Guardian."

"Don't be so modest, Kal. We should throw you a parade. Unfortunately, today is a day of mourning. We must lay to rest our defunct brothers and sisters." The great lady turned to the two cats. "What about you, Spartacus, and you, Panthera? Where do you want to live?"

Both felines stopped their cuddles and stared at the lady. *"With Kal and Indra."*

"Wise choice." Graziella nodded. "The *Blue Phantom* lacks the natural wilderness for you to run free."

"Exactly." The great lady smiled. "You could live here, but most cats in our jungles are much larger than you are and could mistake you for prey."

Spartacus emitted a growl of protest. *"Spartacus champion, not prey."*

"Of course not." Graziella chuckled then turned to Azura's leader. "My Lady, my crew and I will be happy to stay a while and help rebuild Azura.”

“Thank you, Captain. Your help is greatly appreciated.”

“Then what will you do after that?” Kal couldn’t help but ask. “I have no doubt Nyxor will return. He promised to do so and avenge Azfet.”

The tall Azuran lady gazed in the distance over the sea. “We must prepare for his return, figure out a way to affect his reality, develop weapons that can reach his own dimension, his own plane of existence. So, when this Nyxor shows up in our universe again, we can avenge our dead brothers and sisters, and all the others killed in his name.”

Panthera rubbed against Kal’s hip, and he automatically scratched her head.

Indra laced one arm around his waist. “It seems we have preparations to make. We are going on a long voyage.”

Kal kissed her forehead. “I can’t wait to meet your family. See, I never had one. It must be nice.”

Chapter Twenty-One

A month later, on the Anvad planet, the Land of Many Waters...

Indra inhaled the fragrant breeze blowing between the columns of the circular temple on the cliff. It felt strange to stand in heavy gravity again. The gentle air whispers ruffled her yellow silk wedding dress. The birds outside sang hymns to celebrate the end of summer.

She stood with Kal, holding his arm, in the central circle, at the foot of the majestic statue of Helsara the Bountiful, the Anvad goddess. A dense crowd in colorful garb surrounded them on all sides, filling the outer circle. Gazing into Kal's blue eyes, Indra couldn't help grinning like a silly girl. He looked so handsome in red silk pants and jacket.

Kal caressed her hand clutching his forearm. "Are you okay?"

"More than okay." She exhaled slowly and relaxed her grip. "How about you? This is not your religion."

"Religion is man made." He chuckled. "Over centuries as a monk, and a warrior angel in another universe, I learned that our connection with the divine lies inside us and doesn't require organized religions. This said, I do like Helsara. She is an embodiment of compassion, nurturing, and fairness... an excellent vessel for divinity."

"Glad to hear it." Indra took a slow, calming breath. "I can't believe we survived so many dangers, and I am back among my people."

Indra considered the two rulers of her people. Queen Kefira, direct descendent of the goddess, no longer looked the fierce warrior princess Indra remembered. She had morphed into a lady, wise and stately.

Her consort, King Blake, former captain of the *Blue Phantom*, stood next to her at the foot of the statue. Like Indra he'd renounced angelhood for love and family life. He looked regal and content, and anyone could tell he had no regrets.

Since they'd left the *Blue Phantom*, Indra's angel abilities had gradually faded and vanished, but she didn't miss them... nor did she miss quasi-immortality. She delighted in the idea that soon, she would be fertile again.

Queen Kefira, approached the couple and addressed the crowd. "We rejoice at Indra's return and welcome Kal with open arms. Today, they formally join to start a new family among the Anvad."

Indra detected a distinct belly bump under the queen's purple silk robes. A very auspicious sign.

"Indra..." The queen smiled at her with infinite kindness. "Three cycles ago, you gave up your dream of a family and joined the crew of the *Blue Phantom,* to insure the salvation of your people. The Anvad will always be grateful for your sacrifice."

Indra choked at the memory. It had been a difficult decision, but she had made the right choice... in the end, it had led her to Kal.

"But somehow, fate brought you back home, and we are glad for it." The queen gestured encompassing the crowd. "The five thousand souls you helped in those hard times are here today with their new children to celebrate your return, welcome Kal, and share in your newfound happiness. They all join me to bless your union."

Indra's throat constricted. Tears of gratitude blurred her vision. She squeezed Kal's arm and he pressed her hand with his. She reveled in his sturdy strength, feeling truly blessed.

The queen straightened solemnly. "In the name of Helsara the Bountiful, I officially declare you, Indra and Kal, bonded in the eyes of the goddess. May your love keep you together, happy, and whole, in peace and harmony, for as long as you live."

Indra raised her gaze to the looming statue behind the queen. Helsara seemed to be smiling upon them, protecting the Anvad, as she had done for millennia. For the first time since she escaped her destroyed home planet, Indra was truly home.

She faced Kal, and he enveloped her in his strong arms for a kiss. Indra rose on her toes, closed her eyes, and savored the sweet contact of his lips. She never wanted this moment to end.

Like a blessing of the goddess, a gust of wind swayed the temple chimes, creating a delightful tintinnabulum that filled the dome. The Anvad cheered and applauded and threw flowers in the couple's direction. Somewhere outside, flutes and tambourines started a joyful tune.

Reluctantly, Indra turned from Kal's embrace to face the crowd. Together she and Kal stepped into the wide aisle leading to the main temple exit. As the couple walked by, the Anvad showered them with flowers and blessings, some blowing kisses from afar. Many reaching hands patted their shoulders or brushed them with light fingers to wish them happiness.

Outside, on the green lawns atop the cliff, children ran around the statues and the flower beds. They squealed with glee as they splashed each other with the water of the central fountain.

In the shade of a tall tree, Panthera was feeding her litter of cubs, two white females like her, and one reddish male like Spartacus. The proud father lounged nearby, observing, protecting. Next to him lay another large cat with beige markings.

Kal frowned. "I thought there were no large predators on this planet."

Indra remembered the cat. "His name is Karak. He was with us on the Anvad refugee transport. He is the queen's faithful protector, her only bodyguard."

Kal nodded. "I guess, now that the queen is safe, he must be enjoying the freedom of retirement."

The crowd from the temple spilled on the lawn and in the flower gardens.

Indra's family caught up with them. Two dozen smiling faces, aunts, uncles, and cousins, surrounded them and hugged them both profusely. Indra enjoyed the effusions, but Kal looked a little overwhelmed and stepped back.

"Everything is ready for the feast!" someone announced on a megaphone.

Indra rushed to rescue Kal from her family and took his hand, then started toward the path to the lovely town below, with white stone buildings. "I hope you are hungry."

Kal chuckled. "I am starved."

"Good." From the path, Indra could see the recently harvested fields, with bales of hay at regular intervals. Groves of fruit trees alternated with fields and pastures, where livestock grazed. A wide stone bridge spanned the lazy river estuary at the bottom of the valley. "You better be prepared to dance the night away."

"Dance?" Kal's eyebrows rose. "All my life I was a monk and a warrior, not a ballerina. I do not dance."

"Don't worry, old man, I'll teach you." Indra laughed. "You still have a lot to learn."

* * *

"Indra!" Kal scanned the sandy beach in the direction where he'd seen Indra walk away a few moments ago. His heart beat faster when he couldn't see her.

The setting sun touched the wavelets and festooned them with gold. The air smelled of roasted meat and late summer blooms, as he walked along the bottom of the cliff. Behind him, in the distance, the crackling of bonfires, happy cheers, as well as flutes and tambourines, punctuated the festivities with joyful rhythms.

Most of the Anvad had already drunk too much wine in his estimation, but they had a lot to celebrate, besides the return of one of their heroes. They were flourishing on their new world.

Kal realized how much Indra had blossomed in the few days since they arrived. She was opening up to happiness. She'd found the perfect place where she belonged. But for him, it would take time. He'd never known loving family life, or even abundance... only austerity, deprivation, duty, and sacrifice. This new kind of life would take some getting used to.

"Are you not enjoying the festivities?" The strong male voice carried over the breeze.

"Your Highness." Kal bowed to the king. "Centuries of ascetism are not easily cast aside.

"I understand more than you know." The king smiled. "I also was a warrior angel before ending up here."

"I know." Indra had told him the story. "How did you make the transition? How did you switch from captain of the *Blue Phantom* to queen's husband and family man?"

"I found my purpose." The king glanced at him and smiled. "I think I know how you can find yours."

"Really?" Kal still wasn't sure he could fit in this society, but he wanted to be useful.

"I'm going to need help training our new military." King Blake locked his hands behind his back and started walking along the beach, away from the festivities.

Kal walked alongside him, his feet sinking in the soft sand. "Why would you need a military? You are the only people on this planet, and so far away from the trade lanes, no one knows you exist."

"True... for now." The king pursed his lips and sighed. "Yet, we should be prepared."

"Against whom?" Kal knew a society should always be ready to defend itself, but he could see no imminent threat.

"As the central planets of this galaxy are re-organizing and training their own military forces, the many gangs of marauders and pirates ravaging their territorial space will be pushed farther and farther away from the center and the trade lanes." The king sighed. "It's only a matter of time."

Kal felt a spark of his warrior nature returning and nodded. "I see what you mean."

"If or when they discover our hidden paradise, they will covet our resources. We must be ready to defend ourselves and our way of life." The king pursed his lips. "Prosperity has its drawbacks."

Kal remembered his schooling long ago. "You are right. The planets who take peace for granted are always the first ones to be crushed."

"We have the know-how and the natural resources to build ships and planetary weapons."

Kal gasped. "You brought that kind of technology with you?"

"Yes, of course." The king straightened. "The Anvad had an advanced civilization on their home planet. We brought Anvad technology and angel technology... clean, invisible from afar."

"Impressive." Kal realized he knew little of the Anvad and started appreciating their sophistication.

The king sighed. "But with such a limited population, it will take time to reconstruct and expand it here. We'll also need warriors and military experts to train the future soldiers who will operate our fleet."

Kal shuddered as he remembered something else. "Nyxor, the enemy we just sent back to his own dimension, also swore he would return and destroy us all."

"So, you understand peace is an illusion. Sooner or later, we'll have to fight to defend it, and we must be ready." The king extended his hand. "Do you accept my job offer? Do we have a deal?"

"I cannot think of a better way to use my expertise." Kal shook the king's hand. "Thank you for this opportunity to serve, Highness."

"You are welcome. See you in my office in about a week... I don't want to cut short your honeymoon." The king winked at him then turned around, walking back toward the festivities.

Service was something Kal could understand. With this new purpose in mind, he could build a meaningful life here with Indra. The though of his former block mates on Laxxar flashed in his mind. It seemed like so long ago... He hoped they, too, had found their place in this universe.

Shading his eyes from the red, sinking sun, he recognized familiar silhouettes splashing in the wavelets lining the beach. Indra, her long black hair flowing in the breeze, was playing tag with Panthera, Spartacus, and Karak, the queen's feline. Nearby on the beach, the three cubs lay asleep on her yellow silk scarf, to protect them from the sand.

Kal approached the lovely tableau stealthily and stood next to the sleeping cubs. To think that Azfet and Nyxor could have destroyed all that beauty in order to rule!

Panthera was the first to spot him, then Indra ran up to him and threw herself into his arms.

Kal caught her and held her tight. How he had missed this wonderful feeling all his life without knowing it. "This is the best feeling of all... being loved."

"Isn't it?" She chuckled. "So, what do you think of life in the Land of Many Waters, so far?"

Kal nuzzled her hair and inhaled the heady coconut scent. "I can definitely get used to this..."

Panthera and Spartacus rubbed against both of them.

Indra laughed and pulled him down to the sand. "Sit. I want you to meet the new additions to our extended family." She held the cubs in her lap with such tenderness... caressing their heads and rubbing their bellies. "This is Luna, and this one is Bianca... and the boy is already strong and feisty. I named him Brutus. He will hunt blue rabbits and deer when he grows up."

Kal raised his brow. "What? No reconstituted proteins?"

"Life on a planet with abundant wild life is different. Predators keep the gene pool clean as they prey on the weak, the lame, and the diseased. Besides, children should be allowed to make their own choices when they grow up."

Kal's throat went dry. "You are going to make such a wonderful mother."

As Indra gazed up at him, with eyes no longer blue, but dark, liquid, and full of love, Kal realized he'd found his home... not this planet, not his home world, but Indra. She was his home from now on.

The End

Also published by BWL Publishing Inc.
from author Vijaya Schartz

Blue Phantom series:
Book 1 - Angel Ship
Book 2 - Angel Guardian

Byzantium series:
Book 1 - Black Dragon
Book 2 – Akira's Choice
Book 3 – Malaika's Secret

Azura Chronicles series:
Book 1 - Angel Mine
Book 2 - Angel Fierce
Book 3 - Angel Brave

Chronicles of Kassouk series:
Prequel: Noah's Ark
Book One: White Tiger
Book Two: Red Leopard
Book Three: Black Jaguar
Book Four: Blue Lioness
Book Five: Snow Cheetah

Ancient Enemy series:
Book 1 - Anaz-Voohri
Book 2 - Relics
Book 3 - Kicking Bots

Single title sci-fi romance:
Alien Lockdown
Snatched

Archangel twin books:
Archangel Book 1 – Crusader
Archangel Book 2 – Checkmate

Also check out Vijaya Schartz's medieval
fantasy series
based on Celtic legends: CURSE OF THE
LOST ISLE

Book One – Princess of Bretagne
Book Two – Pagan Queen
Book Three – Seducing Sigefroi
Book Four – Lady of Luxembourg
Book Five – Chatelaine of Forez
Book Six – Beloved Crusader
Book Seven – Damsel of the Hawk
Book Eight – Angel of Lusignan

Vijaya Schartz also published
contemporary romance

Ashes for the Elephant God
Asleep in Scottsdale

Award-winning author Vijaya Schartz never conformed to anything and could never refuse a challenge. She likes action and exotic settings, in life and on the page. She traveled the world and claims she comes from the future. Her books collected many five-star reviews and literary awards. She makes you believe you lived these extraordinary adventures among her characters. So, go ahead, dare to experience the magic, and she will keep you entranced, turning the pages until the last line. Find more about Vijaya and her books at http://www.vijayaschartz.com